GRAVE MISTAKES

A NECROMANTIC ADVENTURE

J M SAMLAND

Book Cover Art by Martin Grasso

Illustrations by Ryan Allen

Ben,
Your tireless efforts and insights as an editor have helped transform the core of my writing process, bringing new levels of frustration and joy to my life.
Thank you.

INTRODUCTION

B efore writing *Realms of Terswood*, I had plans for a trilogy following a young noble girl that falls for a boy, and then their relationship continues after his untimely death. That's actually how my previous novel, *Arcanym*, started until I realized I wanted to write about a shy gay boy instead. I tried going back to the "girl meets boy, boy dies" trope again for *Grave Mistakes* and at least got that far this time. That's not a spoiler, it happens pretty early.

Before this book, I would have identified as a pantser—a writer who only works from the barest outline, allowing the story to flow as it happens. Pantsing is nice and all. It's creative and fun, but also results in a lot of wasted content. Whole scenes must be gutted or scraped once I work myself into a corner. It worked out okay for the *Chronicler's Awakening* trilogy, as I was able to repurpose some of those scenes later. So, in the interest of efficiency, I actually figured out what I wanted to happen in this book before I started writing it. Imagine that. I can't guess in advance everything that will happen, so there's still a lot of fun pantsing. Especially when Lord Sebastian is present.

This is my sixth novel, my sixth time writing one of these introductions. Does anyone read them? If you've read this far, you'll probably not skip the first chapter, which is labeled the prologue. So many people skip them. I don't know why.

They're usually a scene that takes place outside of the book's timeline or from a unique perspective. They give a hook and brief view of the world you're about to enter. They're important! I can see skipping the author's bio or introduction but not the prologues. They're part of the story. If you're still reading this, don't skip the prologue, please.

One final note to the reader. Notice how the last three paragraphs have nothing to do with each other? That's how my brain works. Enjoy!

PROLOGUE

With a final crack that split the deadened air, the hellfire faded from the abomination's sunken eyes. Ser Mourningsword fell to his knees, gasping for breath in the fetid chamber. Calling for a grace of holy light proved useless in this place that stank of death and profane magic. With a mumbled prayer to Elysara and the Grand Matriarch, he rose, grasping the handle of his war hammer and wrenching it free of the beast's chest. His weapon broke into motes of brilliant yellows and whites as he released it. He absorbed the power into one gauntleted fist and drew the greatsword from his back with the other.

What lay at the top of this accursed tower would take every scrap of his strength to banish.

Hefting the blade in both hands, the paladin stepped around the final fallen guardian, to the iron-banded arched doors beyond. He grunted, channeling his might into the shoulder, pushing against the door, pulling strength from his brothers that would never see their holy mission to an end. Their reward would be eternal, but Ser Mourningsword would not let another mortal suffer under the yoke of the dead. No more of his order would die holding their numbers at bay.

The Dread Lord of the Deadvale's tyranny would end today.

The door gave way on heavy hinges to the macabre throne room. A ceiling of murky stained glass showed hints of the swirling storm with flashes of soundless lightning. Stout iron chandeliers dripped tallow from a hundred candles and ancient, heavy tapestries covered the stone walls.

Mourningsword saw none of it, focusing on the throne set high on a dais and the one seated upon it. None had laid eyes on the Deadvale's ruler before, at least none that lived. He expected a warrior in hulking armor or a skeletal mage in resplendent robes. He did not expect the Dread Lord to be a Dread Lady. The dark gems of her tall crown caught in the candlelight as she drummed long, thin fingers on the armrest of her throne. She stared at him, her eyes glowing ice blue.

"At long last," she said, her voice low and smooth. "I had a worry your Matriarch's finest would never produce one that might reach me."

The paladin blinked away his initial confusion. Calling again to the saints, he took a deep breath, holding his sword's tip pointed firmly at the dead queen.

"You have slain untold numbers, fiend. By your hand, or by the unholy abominations at your command. I, Ser Oswin Mourningsword, First Brother of the Order of Six and Eight, will see your reign end here, today."

Her eyes trailed a fine mist of blue as she stood. Laced with delicate crystal threads, her midnight purple gown clung to her lithe form to pool at her feet. "I commend you, First Brother, and nearly pity that such conviction will come to nothing."

She flexed one hand gracefully, and the room's dark corners glowed with pinpoints of red hellfire. A dozen sets of holy paladin armor, stained and rusted with old blood, shuffled into the light of the tallow candles, unholy light visible through the slits in their helmets. Mourningsword instantly recognized two sets of armor as those worn by comrades he had entered the tower with days ago, while others spanned centuries of designs for the church's holiest warriors.

Mourningsword left the Forge, accepting without a whisper of doubt that he, or someone of his band, would either slay the Dread Lord or all would fall in trying. Yet, seeing his brothers standing in service of the church's greatest foe, the paladin felt doubt creep into his veins for the first time since taking his vows nearly twenty years ago. His sword dipped an inch, unsure he could raise it against his brothers, even to save himself. Even if it meant slaying the lich. What awful and unknown powers were at her command to allow this truly unholy act? Would he fall to their swords and hammers, only to be raised to stand against the next generation of the Grand Matriarch's warriors?

"They each fought admirably," said the dead queen. She glided down from the dais and circled one paladin wearing tarnished golden armor, wielding a morningstar and tower shield. "Each served their goddess to the final blow. Now they serve me." She traced a nail along the armor's pauldron and strode to stand at the base of her dais with the armored paladins flanking her. "As time means little, I would offer you a moment's rest. Collect your thoughts and speak whatever final prayers may bring you comfort."

Mourningsword's weapon dipped lower. His arms ached, his legs ready to give out. A lifetime of service to the goddess and Grand Matriarch led to this moment. Not only his life, but the lives of all those surrounding him, their bodies littered across the tower's lower levels. Hundreds that had fought against the dead and failed. All had led to nothing but empowering the enemy of the goddess.

He would not raise arms against his brothers.

His greatsword clanged to the stone floor.

His armor, always a symbol of his faith and devotion, now hung heavy across his shoulders. He twisted the locking joint of his right gauntlet to let it fall beside his sword. He reached for his left.

"If the goddess and Grand Matriarch will me to fall and join your ranks, I will do so as a man. I will not give another of my order to the dead."

She watched him shake free his right rerebrace. "You must understand, this makes no difference. Your faith means nothing after the final blow. Your corpse can don your armor just as easily as you now strip it." The risen paladins moved one step closer.

"They will kill a man, not a paladin."

The queen cocked her head and stepped forward, putting an icy hand on his, stopping him from removing his helmet. So near, he stared into those frigid eyes and knew immediately and without doubt that his goddess was not all-powerful. Here was a creature untouched by Her grace; devoid of Her touch, yet thriving.

"You are a fascinating specimen, Ser Oswin Mourningsword. Quite fascinating." She stepped back, and the fallen paladins advanced.

CHAPTER 1

A SPOILED APPLE

Gabriela held up the spoiled apple, taking in its sharp scent. Others might cringe and gag, but it reminded her of home. She glanced over her shoulder at the packed market. No one had noticed the little wave of her hand, but she knew she had to undo it. Gabriela called to the powers that responded sluggishly on this side of the Crack and waggled two fingers over the apple.

Before she could enact her will, the fruit seller turned to her, frowning and extending a hand to Gabriela. "I'll get rid of that for you. Take two on me if you don't tell anyone about it." She winked.

"No, thank you." Gabriela held the mushy apple close and smiled at the vendor. "I'll find a bin and toss it for you."

"As you like." The apple vendor moved to her next client, the exchange already forgotten.

Gabriela took a few steps away and lifted the apple again, breathing its fragrance deeply. She glanced up as the crowds parted for a moment, creating a path to the town square and the three riders atop their horses. The lead man, a noble by the shine of his dark, wavy hair, strong jaw, and perfect cut of his wool coat and leather riding gloves, stared directly at her, despite the hundreds of others to stare at.

Why is he staring? Did he see...

Gabriela looked down at the spoiled apple in her hands and quickly hid it behind her back to let it roll to the ground.

One of the other riders, with longer blond hair tied back in a leather strap, said something, momentarily pulling the noble's attention. He looked back to Gabriela once more before nudging his golden palomino into motion, and the crowd shifted to fill the space between them.

Gabriela wrung her hands and glanced across the shoppers, looking for anyone who might have noticed the exchange, but no one paid her any mind. Keeping her basket of dried herbs and fresh greens close in the crook of her elbow, she wove through the crowd, making her way to the town's outskirts. Pulling up the hood of her vermilion riding cloak, she kept her head down, wary that each turn might leave her standing alone in front of the handsome noble with piercing eyes. She exhaled fully when she finally saw her pony and escort at the crossroads. As she approached, she glanced south to the sheer cliffs overlooking the sea and north along the well-worn road leading to every other living town in the world. Beyond her pony and guardian, a fourth path could barely be made out among the weeds and overgrowth.

"You took quite a while, Princess," came the hollow voice from the fine suit of leather armor. "Much longer, and I might have risked coming in for you."

"Sorry, Lord Sebastian," said Gabriela and busied herself with stuffing her purchases into the gelding's saddle bags. "I couldn't find the egelberry. I had to circle the market four times before I saw it at the spice merchant right at the front."

"I needn't remind you that we should already be on our way home. We won't make it to the inn by nightfall if we don't leave now. Or at least very soon to now."

Gabriela turned to him with a smirk. "Whatever would I do without your timely reminders about things you needn't remind me of?"

"Clever as always," Lord Sebastian gave a single, echoing chuckle. "Have you seen Aura?"

"No, but she's always around somewhere. She must have been as overwhelmed as me in the market. It's not like her to miss a chance to knock things over. Just let me make sure…" Gabriela compared her scribbled list beside the contents of the saddle bags. "Oh, fish eyes! Ice ginger! I looked right at it and… I'll just be a minute."

Lord Sebastian creaked and shifted with unease. "Now I really must remind you, Princess. Mum will be furious if I don't return you on schedule."

"Oh pish, we both know you've never seen my mother angry a day in my life. Twenty minutes, in and out, and we'll be on our way."

"I doubt whoever is waiting for that ice ginger back home is so impatient that it can't wait. Mum might not let you come to town again if you annoy her."

"Fifteen minutes, in and out." Gabriela took a single step toward the bustling market but hesitated. "You were one of them. Do nobles ever come to a town like this?"

Lord Sebastian hummed. "I should think not. Mytara may seem a bustling metropolis by local standards, but the nobles from Vinby or the capital would see it as a backwater peasant town. Why do you ask?"

"No reason." Gabriela focused back on the little city. "Be right back."

Her soft boots sounded thunderous on the worn cobbles, only drowned out by the clomp of a passing horse and the squeak of a cart.

Gabriela thought of the noble on the horse and his piercing, deliberate stare. She shivered but still smiled as she pulled her hood a little closer.

Maybe something was going on behind me. I never looked around until after he was gone. That's probably it.

The merchant selling ice ginger must have been lonely. Gabriela grinned and made noncommittal noises while the vendor prattled on about harvests and what underground bugs worked best with which fertilizers before flowing into talking about a nephew with foot fungus, seeming in no rush to make change or hand over the roots. Lord Sebastian's warnings buzzed in Gabriela's mind, and she finally snatched the ice ginger from the merchant's hand with a mumbled "thanks" and "keep the change." She turned quickly and ran into a solid wall of soft brown wool.

Gabriela gasped and hopped back, but a hand clad in supple leather touched her shoulder.

"Didn't mean to startle you," said the deep voice with a twang like her mother would use when telling a story from the capital. Gabriela looked up at the noble's strong jaw and piercing pale gray eyes, no longer on horseback. He half smiled at her, exposing whiter and straighter teeth than she had imagined possible.

It's like his teeth have no personality.

She realized his hand was still on her shoulder and debated how best to remove it.

Mama always says to use your words first.

"You didn't startle me," Gabriela said, losing herself in those eyes like moon-light across the— "Can I help you?"

An unseasonably chill wind blew across Gabriela's cheek and through the man's hair. He pulled his hand back to brush it back into place.

"Actually," his smile broadened the slightest. "I think you could. Care to take a walk?"

Gabriela breathed in, calling the sluggish powers to come a little nearer should she need them. "I'm in a bit of a hurry, no."

He looked genuinely hurt, and Gabriela wanted to change her answer, but Lord Sebastian would be upset, and that would be worse than harming the feelings of a random, very attractive noble. He could be the romantic lead from any of the books in her mother's library that made her blush.

His grin returned, and though her experience in reading people was woefully lacking, Gabriela thought his look was genuine. "Five minutes," he requested with a wink.

Twenty years of her mother ingraining warnings about the people from town, and much more the nobles from the wider world, went out the proverbial window with that wink. They could still make it to the inn tonight with another quick delay.

"Five minutes."

"Glorious. Let's step just around the corner, where it's quieter," he said, sliding his hand around her elbow, gently directing her. She instantly decided she hated the gesture. Two men standing behind him, the blond man that spoke to him on the horse and perhaps that man's brother, shifted to let the pair pass.

Gabriela pulled the powers a little nearer still.

They stepped around an apothecary's shop, and the ambient noise of the market was cut in half. His hand dropped from her elbow as they continued at a stroll moving south. "As I am sure you know," the man started, "I am Brynmor Highgate, Marquess of Melodis."

Gabriela did not know that but assumed all nobles introduced themselves with the assumption you should already know their story and that giving their name was a mere formality.

"Gabriela," she said, leaving off any exciting titles. "Gabriela Marwol."

"Beautiful name. Unusual name. Were you named for your mother? Grandmother?"

"No."

"A woman of few words. I can respect that," he chuckled. "Mysterious."

Gabriela stopped and turned to Brynmor. "I do have somewhere to be. How can I help you, Marquess Highgate?"

"Please, call me Brynmor. Jon, Job," he waved at the two men trailing them. "I'll meet you at the tavern this evening."

The men clearly disapproved of their dismissal but nodded and turned back toward the market. Brynmor gestured down the narrow alley of damp cobblestone shaded by the apartments leaning inward from two or three stories high on either side, and they continued their walk.

"I'll be quick," said Brynmor. "My uncle, Duke Rhys Highgate, wishes to include this area in his duchy. Mytara and the surrounding region stand alone, isolated between Melodis, the sea, and the Crack. He sent me to open a dialog about such a prospect."

The alley opened to steep stairs leading to a lower section of Mytara. Gabriela could see over the roofs below and a sparkling view of the sea beyond. Lord Sebastian was right. By the sun's position, they would have difficulty making it to the inn before the full moonrise. Though they didn't really have to make it that far.

Gabriela paused at the first step. "Why me? You should go to the local queen or..." She stopped to remember titles from her books. "The mayor or city council."

"I thought you might help me with exactly that." Brynmor took his eyes from her to focus on smoothing the front of his wool coat. "You see, I'm a complete outsider here. I don't know the customs of Mytara. If I come to them with talk of annexation with implied assimilation, they'd toss me out. I'd return to my uncle a failure."

"Why would you think I could help?" Gabriela kept an eye on the sun, hoping her barely restrained annoyance would help to expedite the conversation.

"I feel a kinship to you, Gabriela." Brynmor's eyes drifted back to meet hers. "Not *kinship*. An attraction. You're an outsider, too."

"What? How did—"

"I wouldn't ask that you help with any of the negotiations; just tell me some of what you first did when you came to Mytara."

"Why do you assume I'm not from here?"

"Your clothes are a century outdated, though they fit you quite nicely. Up close, I see your eyes twinkle with intense mystery. But I first noticed your hair. Everyone in the region has straight, dark hair. Your soft curls are as pale as fresh snow." He reached a gloved hand to touch a stray lock that lay across her cheek.

Gabriela felt her initial interest in the marquess shrivel up with the inane comparison.

A brick smashed into the cobblestone, missing them by a few feet.

Brynmor looked down at the brick, then up at the building roofs with more confusion than worry.

Not now, Aura!

"That only got my initial attention, making you stand out in the crowd, as it were. Then I saw you perform dark magic," he finished.

Her heart leaped to her throat. "What? No, that's absurd."

Brynmor let out another slow chuckle, waggling his fingers over his palm, miming what she must have looked like with the apple. "Your secret is safe with me."

Gabriela let out a puff of breath. Her mother had been clear about her remaining unnoticed in town. She had to steer the conversation away from that. "Why do you want to blend in? You're a noble. You can go and do what you want."

"Maybe so, but my uncle has put much into securing his borders. I want every advantage here. The duchy overlaps the Crystalwood Gardens, and he's regularly fighting off the dead abominations that rise from there. If his territory included Mytara, he could close his lines right up to the Crack."

Gabriela turned from him, looking down the twenty steps of hard, flat stone quarried from the cliffs just south of town, like most of the city's construction. Her mother saw little need for Gabriela to know the intricacies of politics, but she knew enough that a solid front along the Crack would soon mean a solid front *beyond* it. This man's uncle, this duke, would invade her home in time. "I can't help you, Brynmor."

He stepped in front of her, on the edge of the first step. "I'll admit, there was more. I honestly thought you could help my mission, but also..." He pulled the glove from his right hand and traced his knuckles down her cheek. "You're beautiful, Gabriela."

The power surged, and she slapped his hand away.

Time seemed to catch its breath as Brynmor stumbled backward, flailing his arms in the empty space over the steps. Gabriela's fingertips briefly reached the edge of his pristine woolen overcoat, only to close on air. She watched his horrified face, the piercing grey eyes suddenly vulnerable, fall away from her. Tumbling feet over neck down the steps, each impact punctuated with a crunch, he finished in an awkward pile at the bottom.

The power was no longer sluggish, now flooding through her. Without thinking, she performed the motions she'd seen her mother do a hundred times.

CHAPTER 2

IF THE COAT FITS...

Gabriela slumped against the building on one side of the alleyway, gasping for breath that wouldn't come quickly enough. A black mist pulsed at the edge of her vision, keeping in perfect rhythm with her frantic heartbeat. She stared down at her fingers that shook and twitched, yet she managed to hold onto a slender tendril of power, the work of her reaction.

A voice whispered in Gabriela's ear. "He's slipping. Bind him like me."

The thin filament of magic trailed to the marquess glowing faintly beside her. Her vision strobed with every heartbeat, but Gabriela saw a place in her chest with another such string and hastily tied Brynmor's around it.

When her breath finally caught up, and her hands were shaking less, she crept to the stairs' edge and peered down at the heap of brown wool at the bottom.

"I'm sorry."

She saw herself slapping away his hand, pushing him back with a nudge of uncontrolled power. His pale gray eyes went through a host of emotions and accusations before he toppled backward.

"That was a surprise," said a deep, twanging voice beside her. Gabriela looked up, and through, Brynmor beside her. He delicately prodded his neck with his one ungloved hand.

She ignored him and carefully stumbled down the steps, looking in every direction for a witness or passerby. Luckily it seemed most were still at the market or already home for dinner.

"Gods and saints, what in all the hells happened here?" Brynmor exclaimed when they neared this body. "Who..." He trailed off when Gabriela rolled him over, tapping three fingers to his chest. She cringed at the unnatural angle of his neck.

Gabriela jumped to her feet between Brynmor and his body... Brynmor and his ghost? "I can fix this. We have to get you to Mama."

"He's dead. He's me. I'm..." Brynmor stepped back, clapping his hands over his mouth, and Gabriela felt the slight tug of the tether holding him in place.

"And Mama can fix it." She looked around for fabric or anything to make a stretcher. The list of new tasks flooded her mind, everything that would have to be done, and quickly. She took Brynmor's body from under his arms and dragged him a few feet before dropping him again.

"Hey! Careful with that!" shouted his ghost.

"Keep your voice down!" No one else could hear him, but he didn't have to know that. "What do you weigh, like sixteen stone?"

Brynmor scoffed. "Less than thirteen, I'll thank you. I maintain a careful diet and exercise regime."

"I can barely drag you ten feet. I can't drag you all the way out of town."

He stamped his foot, crossing his arms. "Stop this immediately! I demand to know what is happening here. Why is this man wearing my coat?"

Gabriela rubbed her hands over her face, noticing the blue sky fading to pink. Time was running out.

"It's confusing, I know. I've talked with dozens in your situation, though none as fresh as you. Try to stay calm and trust me."

"Trust you? *Trust you?* We're standing over a well-dressed gentleman that looks very much dead and—"

Gabriela squatted beside his body, and, other than his neck and a few scrapes on his cheek, Brynmor's wavy hair and strong jaw looked as vibrant as they had only a few minutes before at the top of the steps.

Before she pushed him.

Before he tripped.

"I... I don't understand what's happening here," he said.

"I p— you fell down the stairs, Brynmor. You're dead."

"But... no that doesn't make sense. I'm right here. How can I be looking at myself?"

"You're a ghost now."

"No. You are mistaken." Brynmor raised his gloved hand, turning it over, confusion never fleeing from his brow. "What then?" he asked. "You can't leave this man here. Not wearing a coat that fine."

The thought passed through Gabriela. *Who would know?*

"My men saw me leave with you. They would find you and question you. My uncle would come."

Gabriela waved for him to be quiet. "I need help." She picked him up again and hefted Brynmor to lean against a wall, posing him like a passed-out drunk. A passed-out drunk with a very expensive coat. She started pulling it over his shoulders and down his arms.

"You kill me, and then you rob me?"

"No!" she spat. "It's for Lord Sebastian. I'll go get him and disguise him with your coat. Then he can help me carry the bo... you out of the city." The body slid to its side as she tugged. Gabriela made to pull it upright again, but the new pose looked natural enough and didn't draw any attention to the neck.

She tossed the coat over her shoulder, and only then did she realize her hands were empty. "Fish eyes, again! Where did the ice ginger go? I must have dropped it when you... at the top of the steps. Help me look."

"I'm not leaving my body," said Brynmor and crossed his spectral arms.

"You already did. Come on." Gabriela carefully scanned each step for the handful of roots. At the third, she felt the tug in her chest forcing Brynmor to remain near her.

"What devilry is this?" he exclaimed.

15

"Mama can explain it better, but I've bound your ghost to me." Gabriela found the ice ginger root at a step near the top and shoved it into the inner pocket of her traveling cloak. She picked a westerly route to avoid the bulk of the market and started briskly through the narrow streets. After a few strides, the pull at Brynmor's tether lessened as he made an effort to keep up with her rather than be dragged.

"What then?" he asked.

"After I get you to Mama? She'll have some way of fixing you up. I know she will."

"Before that. Jon and Job will search for me if I never show up at the tavern tonight. They'll assume foul play if I'm gone, but Harvey is still in the stables."

"Fish eyes," Gabriela cursed, but the solution came to her just as quickly. "Then you'll ride out on your horse. We'll get him from the stable. Lord Sebastian hefts you up, we ride home, and Mama fixes you up."

The alleys opened to a clear view of the crossroads and the leather armor pacing beside the pony. He rushed to meet her.

"Princess! You had me worried to death. Well... I was worried! You were gone..." His leather helmet shifted to consider Brynmor. "Oh, good job, you found another. And he's fresh." Lord Sebastian made an echoing sound like clearing his throat. "Good sir, this may be very confusing to you, but we are here to usher you to—"

"It's not that," Gabriela said and added the ice ginger to her gelding's saddlebag. "He's a noble, and there was an accident and—"

"She pushed me down the stairs!" Brynmor nearly yelled and ran his hands through his ethereal, wavy hair.

Lord Sebastian looked back at Gabriela. "We know better than to do that."

"It was an accident! Help me get his body on his horse, and we'll take him back to Mama." She shook out Brynmor's wool coat and flourished it over the knight's shoulders.

"How stylish." Lord Sebastian held out his arms to consider the coat's fine stitching. He looked up at Brynmor's ghost, back at the coat, and back at Brynmor wearing the same thing. "You had an excellent tailor, good sir. We're quite nearly the same measurements."

"Absurd. That coat is worth a townhouse around here, and you toss it on over your armor." Brynmor grumbled and crossed his arms.

"We'll never make it to the inn in time with all this, Princess."

Gabriela glanced out to the sea and sun. He was right.

"They'll let us in after dark," she said. "I'm sure they will. Besides, we only have to make it partway before we have issues."

"Why does he keep calling you princess?" Brynmor asked.

"Cute nickname, don't worry about it," she said quickly. "Where are the stables, and how far is that from your body?"

"The stables are by the north entrance, and my..." Brynmor paused to take a deep breath, "body is halfway across town."

"Divide and conquer," said Lord Sebastian. "I will retrieve the corpse and meet you at the stables. He took a tumble down some stairs, you say? The ones leading from the market level, perhaps?"

"That's the one," said Gabriela. "I propped his corpse against the wall at the bottom."

"Don't call it a corpse," said Brynmor. "This is my body we're talking about."

"I'll save the lecturing about how this is a terrible plan for later, Princess." Lord Sebastian considered Brynmor again, looking him up and down. "Carmel will be safe here with the others." Lord Sebastian patted the pony and turned to head into town.

"Be careful," Gabriela called after him.

"What did he mean, *others*?"

"You'll see soon enough." Gabriela pulled up the hood of her traveling cloak yet again. She patted her gelding on the flank and set a path directly toward the market.

"I can't be seen in town like this," said Brynmor, tugging at her back.

"No one will see you."

"How's that? I'm glowing blue and white."

"Did you see many ghosts before?"

"Before what?"

"Before you started being one."

Brynmor didn't respond for a long moment.

"But you can see me," he finally said.

"I'm special. No more questions. People will look if they see me talking to myself."

Gabriela passed through the market again, the far thinner crowd as the day dwindled to evening. She turned north at the town square where she'd first seen the marquess, high upon his noble steed, and the buildings shifted from rough stalls to well-crafted, permanent shops. Jaunty piano music drifted from a bustling tavern, and Gabriela felt Brynmor's tug toward it. She turned to him, struggling against an unseen force as he tried to pull away.

"My men are in there," he grunted. "They can send for my uncle, the duke, who will settle all of this."

"Settle what? They'll bury you and go to war or something to avenge you. Mama's told me how people handle things on this side of the Crack," said Gabriela and continued toward the stables, dragging the ghost with her.

"This side of the Crack? What do you mean *this* side of the Crack?"

"Shush! People will look at me if they see me yelling at ghosts they can't see."

"Abduction! Kidnapping!"

Brynmor kept yelling, unheard by all except Gabriela, until they reached the stables. A young hand was shoveling hay for one of the dozen workhorses in their stalls while the three palominos of obvious fine breeding sniffed at the trough in front of them.

"Harvey!" Brynmor rushed forward, nearly yanking Gabriela toward the center horse. His eyes widened with a snort.

"Stop that. Horses can sense you just enough for you to scare them," said Gabriela.

"Need something?" asked the stable boy. He approached and leaned on his pitchfork, chewing something. His posture was one of a man in his forties, but he couldn't be older than fourteen.

Gabriela adjusted her hood, hoping it hid her pale hair. "The marquess sent me for his horse. Could you take it out for me?"

"I don't know. He paid me decent money to keep his horse in all night."

"I paid him far more than the value of his slovenly care," Brynmor grumbled.

"He wouldn't be asking for a refund if that's what you're worried about," said Gabriela. "Consider the extra pay a tip for your fine service."

"I don't know," said the boy. "I shouldn't be giving out the nobles' horses without some note or something." He spat a dark glob on the ground and swept hay over it.

"That's quite alright, my boy," came a hollow voice behind them. "I come for my horse."

Brynmor shrieked, and Gabriela turned to see Lord Sebastian wearing the fine wool coat. His leather helmet was tucked under one arm, and his other gauntleted hand rested at the side of Marquess Highgate's head at the collar of his armor. With the sun growing low behind him, the dead expression on Brynmor's face wasn't immediately apparent.

"I had too much to drink, as we nobles do, and asked this wench to fetch my horse for a ride," said Lord Sebastian.

"I don't sound anything like that," said Brynmor.

The boy squinted, blinked hard, and nodded. "Sorry, sir. Right away." He moved to the front of Harvey's stall, glancing back. "Nice armor you got there."

"Thank you," said Lord Sebastian. "It was crafted by the finest smiths using techniques long lost—"

"We'll be just around back," said Gabriela, pushing the armored man out of the stables.

"Where's the rest of my body?" Brynmor asked with growing panic.

Lord Sebastian patted his chest. "I told you, we're nearly the same measurements." Brynmor's head lolled to the side, and Lord Sebastian grabbed it by the wavy hair to stay upright before pulling his helmet back on. "It wasn't the easiest feat to put myself on around you, especially when I got about halfway through it, but here we are."

"By all the gods and saints, what have I gotten myself mixed up with?" Brynmor rubbed his hands over his ghostly face. "A death mage and, what, living armor?"

"I'm not exactly *living*."

"Where was your money?" Gabriela asked. "We need to tip this boy to keep him quiet."

"Use your own guld," said Brynmor without looking up.

"His coat was jangling," said Lord Sebastian, shaking a pocket of the wool coat with a muted tinkling of metal.

Gabriela reached over and pulled out a leather purse just as the stable boy led the majestic golden horse around the corner. She pressed it into Lord Sebastian's glove and pulled her hood a bit lower over her eyes.

"Ah, thank you, my boy," beamed Lord Sebastian. "I'll go for my ride now, totally alone, while this wench returns to... wenching. A tip for your quiet troubles." He offered the pouch of guld to the boy, who accepted it and was gone without another word.

"That was more money than that little urchin would see in his life!" said Brynmor.

"Wenching?" Gabriela asked.

"Apologies, Princess, I was deep in the character," said Lord Sebastian.

"I've never used those words in my life," said Brynmor.

"Well, that time is in the past now," Lord Sebastian said and put a foot in the stirrup. Harvey snorted and shied away. "Help me up, would you, dear?" he said to Gabriela. "This man weighs more than he looks he should."

Brynmor grumbled.

"I got so caught up in the moment, I didn't ask the plan behind all this," said Lord Sebastian from horseback. "We're just taking him back with us? Yet I see him tethered to you, implying you had some hand in keeping him a ghost. You said Mum will do something for him?"

"He needs to be resurrected."

"Oh, I see," said Lord Sebastian, sounding hollower than usual, then chuckled dryly. "Don't we all, now and then. Well, no sense in waiting around longer. He's not getting any fresher, as they say."

"This feels deeply disrespectful," said Brynmor.

They kept to the outer edges of the town until Gabriela saw Carmel standing at the crossroads, though no longer alone. In the last dying evening light, a half-dozen softly glowing spirits milled aimlessly around the old pony. They drifted like smoke, waning in and out of vision, more the suggestion of a person. Most gave the impression of being older, but at least two were closer to Gabriela's age.

"Ghosts!" said Brynmor. "They do exist!"

Lord Sebastian chuckled down from the horse. "I have some terrible news for you, good sir."

"They're the real reason I came to town, not just for some herbs," said Gabriela. "Mama sent me to gather up the stray ghosts and spirits and usher them across the Crack, where they can reside until they're... ready."

"I'm definitely not ready," said Brynmor. "Whatever that might mean."

"No one is right away," said Lord Sebastian. "If you don't mind, Princess, I should like to stay on the horse a while longer. Getting our new friend out of me will take a bit more time than I'd like to spend out here in the crossroads. We can strap the good marquess' corpse over his horse in the morning."

"Of course, Lord Sebastian."

Gabriela took Carmel's reins and led him along the overgrown trail west, followed by the noble steed, a half dozen tired ghosts, and a very confused one.

CHAPTER 3

CHEAP WHISKEY

When Eleanor told her parents that she'd accepted a job working directly for Duke Highgate, they had been ecstatic. Being the daughter of a sheriff's deputy and a children's toy maker from a nothing town on the east coast, she had a steep hill to climb through society. Quitting the Aetheria mage academy in her final semester as she was being kicked out didn't help her reputation, but she was back on track now. She would make her mark in service to the nobility. Her parents would be less proud if they knew what she actually spent most of her day doing.

Eleanor drummed the fingers of one hand on the stout wooden table, muted by the thick leather gloves she wore. The other rolled a glass tumbler of amber whiskey between her thumb and forefinger. With a deep breath, taking in the sour ale and questionable food of the pub, she dug in the leather pouch before her and took out two guld pieces. She set each down with a clanking thud and slid them to the center of the table.

"More than fair compensation for the marquess' costs," Eleanor said, knocking back the whiskey and breathing in the sharp bite.

Cheap. Overpriced, but cheap. They tried to age it but failed miserably.

The innkeeper sitting across the table, a wiry woman with dark eyes that darted everywhere but at Eleanor, swiped the guld into her hand and crossed her arms again. That was more money than the establishment made in a week, maybe a month.

"I didn't mention the cask of wine he took, did I?" she said.

Of course you didn't.

"Is there anything else?" Eleanor asked.

The innkeeper scratched her chin and shook her head. "Not that I remember off hand, but if I think of something else, I know where to find you."

Eleanor took another guld piece from her bag and slid it across the table. It was enough to buy a dozen casks of wine finer than anything this establishment might offer, but it was all she had. The duke didn't seem aware of smaller denominations of currency.

"Thank you for your hospitality, and on behalf of Duke Highgate, I appreciate your confidentiality and discretion." Eleanor pushed back from the table and turned to the door, taking her wide-brimmed leather hat and jacket from the hook as she passed them. Both were several sizes too large but worn and comfortable, having belonged to her father.

On the dusty streets of whatever this town's name was—the most recent stop for the marquess—Eleanor took the notebook from her breast pocket. Flipping it open, she scanned the list and scratched off the last item, "Clean Hill Inn." She glanced back at the flaking sign over the door and across the flat street. *Maybe something was lost in translation.*

Finally ready to move on, she crossed to her horse. Well, the duke's horse, but after riding the midnight stallion for almost a year, she hoped the horse masters back in Friholm forgot.

"That took entirely too long, Treasure," she said, pulling a canvas map from the left saddlebag. The bag jingled, reminding her she carried enough wealth to buy the town.

Stupid nobles.

Eleanor pressed the map flat against Treasure's flank and traced a gloved finger to the tiny pulsing red dot over Solia and a few small drawn house shapes.

"The man at the brothel said he went south," she said to the horse and followed the faint roads on her map to Mytara, with far more house shapes. A bigger town meant more places for the marquess to get into trouble. More places she'd have to stop. But the only thing farther south and east was the sea and only the Crack to the west. There was nowhere else for him to go. She'd be able to catch up and maybe get a day to herself.

She folded and replaced the map before pulling herself onto the behemoth creature.

"Come on, Treasure," she said, tapping the reins once. "Let's go clean up Brynmor's mess in Mytara."

CHAPTER 4

MIDNIGHT RIDE

"**N**ow wait! Stop right now! I demand to know what's going on here before I take one more step!"

Gabriela turned to Brynmor, standing on the overgrown path with his arms crossed. Even as a semi-translucent ghost, she couldn't fault his beauty and regal stature. From how he stood shifted to the left hip, to the effortless tilt of his head, he exuded an air of nobility and careful breeding. He matched so many of the descriptions of princes and noble knights from her books.

"No time for dallying, my good sir," called Lord Sebastian from the front of the procession. Any issues that Harvey the horse might have had at first at being mounted by his recently deceased master seemed to have quickly waned. Lord Sebastian expertly guided the palomino back through the group of ghosts.

"He's right, Brynmor," said Gabriela. "We have to get to the inn."

"There were a half dozen perfectly decent inns back in Mytara," Brynmor said, gesturing the way they'd come. "There's nothing this way but the Crack."

Gabriela glanced up at Lord Sebastian beside her.

"I know this is terribly confusing, Brynmor, but you have to go along with things. The inn is beyond," said Gabriela. "We have to get there before the moon reaches its highest."

"Or else what?" said Brynmor.

"Or else all these ghosties go away forever!" Aura said with a giggle, fading into view, casting her uneven green light across the grass.

"Aura, that is most unkind to say out loud," said Lord Sebastian.

"Who is this now?" Brynmor shouted.

"Great time to show up, Aura," Gabriela grumbled. "Brynmor, meet Aura. She's the one that tried to drop a brick on you in the alley."

"She... she what?"

"Brynmor, please, we have to get to the inn. You can ask all your questions there."

He uncrossed his arms and started moving toward her. She felt the tension between them lessening as the tether binding them slackened. "What... what does that mean, that the ghosts will go away? Will I?"

"Ghosts are tied to a rhythm of magic synchronized with the moon," said Gabriela. "I untethered these in Mytara and have to get them to the inn to tether them there. Then in the morning, we can continue to the village."

"This sounds... tiresome," Brynmor groaned but was moving forward again and they all continued toward the Crack. "What about me? And her?" He gestured at the wave of green light that was Aura flickering through the tall grass.

Gabriela watched the poltergeist for a moment before turning back to Brynmor. "You'll both be fine. You're bound with greater intention. The rest of this lot need to get to the inn." She moved between a young boy and a slowly pulsing amorphous cerulean cloud to Lord Sebastian. The caravan continued.

"Well said, Princess."

"I think calling me that is confusing the marquess."

"Is that so?" Lord Sebastian sat a little straighter, causing Brynmor's head to flop to the other side. "It doesn't seem to take much to confuse the chap."

"Weren't you just chiding Aura for being unkind?"

"Ah, but I'm a noble, Princess. The rules apply differently to me."

"I dare say few outside the Deadvale will honor your titles since you died a century ago."

"What?" Lord Sebastian raised a gauntlet to his chest, seeming genuinely hurt. "I dare say I'm twice the noble right now as any other, living or dead."

Gabriela stared up and rolled her eyes. "What will we tell my mother?"

"You mean, what will *you* tell her. I'm going straight to the cleaners. This body is leaking something terrible."

"She'll do it, though, right? Resurrect him? She has to."

"There is little to nothing your mother *must* do."

"But Brynmor's uncle, if he finds out—"

"You needn't convince me of the reasons and dangers, Princess. Focus your energy on your wards. We're almost to the Crack, and you know how restless the ghosts will get as the moon comes up."

In the growing gloom of night, the ravine would be easy to miss and fall to one's death. Lit by three-quarters of the moon low over the horizon, the Crack weaved a meandering trail around the Deadvale.

Lord Sebastian pulled Harvey to a stop, and Gabriela continued a few paces to the edge, where a rotted, rickety bridge spanned the sixty feet over utter darkness.

"Where are the guards?" asked Brynmor.

"Guards?" asked Lord Sebastian.

"Why isn't this bridge guarded? What keeps the dead from crossing?"

Lord Sebastian snickered. "Why would they want to? You forget how long the Crack is; how impossible it would be for any force to patrol it."

Gabriela had a hand on the bridge's railing. "Aura, where are you?"

The ghost's giggle echoed across the empty chasm, but she remained hidden.

"Aura, promise me you won't do anything like what we've talked about, and I'll read you a story when we get home."

"What does that mean?" asked Brynmor.

Lord Sebastian patted Harvey's neck and swung out a leg to dismount. "She's worried Aura will cause the bridge to collapse under your horse."

"She wouldn't!"

With a flicker of light like moonlight rippling over a pond, Aura appeared. "Why wouldn't I?"

Gabriela snapped her fingers to get the poltergeist's attention. "Because I'm asking you not to. We still have over an hour to the inn and not much longer to get these fellows to their safety for the night. I'm tired and don't want to deal with your foolishness, Aura."

"Fine! Maybe you won't have to deal with me ever again!"

With a quick flash, Aura disappeared.

"I would weep, were I able," said Lord Sebastian with a dull sigh, tugging the horse toward the bridge. "I do wish you two would get along better."

"That thing won't support Harvey!" said Brynmor. "We must find another way to cross. Or better still, return to town and a warm fire."

"Stop it!" Gabriela shouted and stomped up to Brynmor, glowering up at him. "You don't get it. In an hour, these other ghosts will cease to exist. Without something tethering them here, they'll drift to nothing and just be... gone."

"Is there any harm to that? Ghosts don't belong here. They should move on."

"Quoth the ghost," said Lord Sebastian.

"Where's your empathy?" asked Gabriela. "I guide them to a place where they are safe until they are ready to move on, however each might come to that decision."

"I am a viscount, a marquess. That is hardly any way to speak to me."

Gabriela jammed a finger into his chest, pushing him back a step. "No. Until I can manage otherwise, you're a ghost."

Brynmor raised his ungloved hand to his chest. "I felt that. I thought ghosts didn't feel anything. I haven't felt anything else since... since..."

Gabriela turned from him to start across the bridge.

Lord Sebastian followed, leading the horse fearlessly across the ancient wood. "I suggest you take all you think you know about what it is to be dead and pretend you never learned it, good sir. Now is the time to begin your true education."

Walking single file allowed Gabriela a moment alone to think. Not that Brynmor or the other ghosts couldn't float over the gorge beside her, but she wasn't about to tell them that.

"I could have left him and run," she muttered to the empty chasm. "I'd be at the inn by now with only Aura teasing me about accidentally murdering a man. She'd forget it within two days, anyway. A bit of teasing would be nothing compared to how upset Mama will be if I drop these ghosts on my first time from home without her."

She looked down at her hands, remembering that numbing surge of power that overwhelmed her as she watched Brynmor slip backward. It felt foreign to be filled with power enough to ensnare his spirit as it fled his body. *That must be how Mama feels all the time.*

The rocky fields and scrubby bushes on the far side of the Crack looked no different in the glow of moonlight, but there was a distinct change to the air. The subtle charge tickled her nose until she adjusted to it within a few breaths.

"It'll be tight, Princess," said Lord Sebastian. "Perhaps you should ride ahead on this horse. I'll catch up with Carmel and the corpse."

Gabriela bit her thumb, considering the option. The ghosts from town would move as she willed them to and otherwise remain in place. As long as she moved no faster than a horse's trot, they wouldn't fall out of her range. Any faster would risk stranding the ghosts in the middle of the Deadvale, to disperse with the high moon.

She looked across the beautiful palomino. "I've never ridden a horse so large."

"He seems well-mannered enough." Lord Sebastian pulled to a stop.

"It'll be difficult, what with Brynmor and Aura tugging at me the whole time."

"Keep your lean forward and maintain a firm grip on the saddle horn."

Gabriela nodded.

"What's this now?" asked Brynmor as Lord Sebastian helped her onto Harvey.

"Time's against us." Gabriela glanced at the moon still low over the horizon, knowing it would rise quickly once it had its momentum. The horse tensed beneath her, sensing her anxiety. "Try to keep up, but at least don't resist my pull."

CHAPTER 5

GUARDIAN ARMS

Willows wept over the old road, blocking the view of the moon as it rose. Gabriela couldn't decide if that was better or worse. Nothing could be done about its pace, even if she could follow the moon's progress. She would make it to the inn in time, or she wouldn't. Gripping the saddle's horn tight, she glanced over her shoulder, quickly counting the ghosts from town and Brynmor jogging with a look of confused panic plastered over his luminescent face. The others dragged along, not noticing their movement.

What does that feel like?

If Aura was any indication, Brynmor could clearly move as quickly as he wished, but he clung to his mortal limits set by legs and lungs, neither of which mattered any longer. Not when those were miles back down the road, secure within Lord Sebastian. Aura, meanwhile, zipped through the trees, casting phantom shadows and disturbing owls.

On this side of the Crack, Gabriela sensed magic waning quickly as the moon rose. As her worry surged that she'd taken a wrong turn, she glimpsed the inn through the trees and was at its front gate a moment later. Brynmor huffed beside her as she tied Harvey to the hitching station.

"This place looks... wholly inappropriate for... one of my rank."

Gabriela glanced across the wide windows of the three-story inn, some broken and most with threadbare and ripped lace curtains. Paint flaked from the siding, and the roof sagged below where "Guardian Arms" had been emblazoned a few generations ago. Beside the main door, a single candle flickered from a table on the wide, wrapping porch. She realized she was smiling and looked up at the moon again. She'd made it. Barely.

"What's so special about this place?" Brynmor asked.

"Mama explained it as a crossroads of magic."

"Meaning what?"

"Magic flows around the world in things like rivers. A few of them cross here, making it safe to release the ghosts to go on their merry ways."

"That simply isn't true. Magic is a gift bestowed by the goddess."

"If you say. Come, Viscount Brynmor. Time to meet some new friends and play some cards." She waved him toward the front door.

"You can't leave my horse out here."

"Lord Sebastian can't be more than fifteen minutes behind us. He'll take care of Harvey."

Gabriela walked to the front door with the other ghosts shambling behind. Brynmor slowed to tap three fingers to his chest before stepping onto the porch. Her mother had brought her by the inn a few times, but the last had been at least a year ago. While she wanted to stay up for hours hearing travelers' tales of the ghosts and others wandering the Deadvale, she was also dead tired.

Picking up the candle, Gabriela pushed the door open with an echoing creak to enter the reception room with wide steps leading to the upper levels. Lit by only the feeble candle and moonlight filtering through the gauzy drapes, she crossed to the reception counter as uncertainty crept into her gut.

"Weird," she mumbled.

"So much for cards." Brynmor examined the nails on his gloveless hand.

The other ghosts shuffled past, some going up the stairs, others moving to the rooms on either side of the entryway, fading from sight.

"Well, that's done. Mama will be happy," said Gabriela. "Oddly quiet in here."

"Why would anyone be caught dead in such a condemned pile of... do you hear that?"

A single faint piano note rang.

Gabriela frowned. Waving, she led Brynmor to the parlor. Four rickety round tables with worse-looking chairs took up most of the room, but beside the cold hearth, a man sat slumped in front of the upright piano. Gabriela recognized the inn's owner as he hit another somber key.

"Mister Tanner?"

She wove around the tables as he turned, glowing a little brighter when he saw her.

"Ah! Princess! You're a sight, for sure."

The hearth flared with a shadowless green flame.

"Where is everyone, Mr. Tanner?" Gabriela looked across the dusty tables with dusty cards and dusty mugs.

"Wishin' I knew. Couple of weeks ago, the regulars just up and left, then no one else has come by. Who's your friend?"

Brynmor stood a little straighter beside her. "Viscount Brynmor Highgate, Marquess of Melodis."

"That whole thing's your name, huh?"

"He's new to being a ghost, sorry." A wave of dizziness hit Gabriela. She steadied herself with a palm on the hearth's mantle. "It's been a long day. Would you mind if I went to my usual room?"

The ghost innkeeper nodded. "Course. Sleep well."

"I don't suppose you have a royal suite here," said Brynmor.

"You don't need to sleep in your... condition," said Gabriela. "You and Mister Tanner should talk; he could give you tips on what to expect as a ghost. I'd say he's an expert on the topic, having run this inn for over a century."

"You're too kind, Princess," beamed the innkeeper.

"Good night, gentlemen."

Gabriela weaved through the tables again to lean against the doorframe to the reception room.

"Wait a moment," called Brynmor.

She turned, and the room moved a little quicker than she expected, forcing her to grab at the wall.

"How can you leave?" he asked. "I thought we were bound to a set distance from each other."

"The inn's magic is specific to attract and nurture ghosts. It'll grant some leeway with our tether, and I'm only going up one flight. Still, I wouldn't recommend you go wander the grounds or you might find yourself not existing. Now, if you'll excuse me, I must lie down."

Brynmor nodded and turned his attention back to Mister Tanner.

Jerk. He looks like a prince from my books but certainly doesn't act like one.

The single candle's light danced across the walls, throwing shadows around the stair's wooden banisters. Gabriela kept a hand on the railing as she ascended, paying little attention to the cobweb-shrouded portraits along the wall as she passed them. Halfway to the top, the wallpaper glowed a brilliant green before Aura burst through. The ghost hovered in front of her with hair floating as if she were under water.

"Gone, all gone, Gabs."

Gabriela gasped. "Not the ones we just brought?"

"No, no, just all the others that should be here."

Gabriela let out a sigh of relief but tightened her grip on the railing. "Mister Tanner said as much. Maybe they found a place to settle in for the solstice."

Aura bit her lip, shaking her head with eyes wide. "No, they was called, called away."

"Called? What would call the ghosts?"

"Or who."

"No, don't be silly. If someone had the power to summon ghosts, Mama would know about them. There must be another explanation." Gabriela swayed on her feet. Whether it was the day's excitement or the use of magic for the marquess, she didn't trust herself on the stairs. Pushing past Aura, Gabriela continued up to the bedrooms. "Mister Tanner seems to have resisted the call, and you're still here. It's nothing to worry about, right?"

Aura rushed past her and through the first door on the right. Gabriela pushed the door open a moment later. The bedroom looked precisely as she'd left it a year ago, other than more dust on the shelves and leaves by the window. Setting the candle on the nightstand, she pulled back the sheets and punched the pillows. The green ghost floated by the window, looking up at the moon.

"Aura, would you keep an eye on the friends that came with us? I'm sure they must be nervous, being dragged to a strange place. Maybe you could give them some comforting words." Gabriela sat on the bed to pull off her boots.

Aura snapped around with a wide grin. "Mister Fancy Glove, too, then?"

"Just the others. Leave Brynmor to Mister Tanner."

"I don't like him, the fancy man."

Gabriela slid into the bed. Lumpy mattress or not, the soreness in her legs from so much walking and riding instantly melted away. "I get that you don't like him from how you tried to drop a brick on him."

"But I didn't. I could have hit him, but I didn't."

"I appreciate that, Aura. And thank you. You gave me the idea of how to keep him from slipping away." Gabriela touched her chest, remembering tying Brynmor's tread around the other already within her.

"You like him, though. You do," Aura cooed.

Gabriela scoffed. "I don't think I do. He seems vain and tiresome."

Aura floated beside her over the blankets. "First man you're taking to meet Mama."

"Stop that! I feel bad enough as it is."

"Why, Gabs? You didn't kill him. The steps did all the work of breaking his neck."

Gabriela stared at the plain, whitewashed ceiling. "I wish I knew why you're so often so terrible. We'll be rid of him tomorrow, and you can find something else to be cruel about. Do as I ask and see to the others."

Aura rushed over her with a blast of frigid air to vanish through the wall.

Why am I cursed with her?

As she relaxed into the old starched sheets, Gabriela's mind swam with worry, mainly from a growing dread over what her mother would say about Brynmor. She tried imagining her mother rushing from her library, eager to assist with all the weight of her magical accompaniment. She squeezed her eyes against the moonlight through the cracked window pane. When did she last see her mother outside of her library? She spent every moment there, casually combing through the dusty tomes of every feasible discipline, copying notes to other books in an endless cycle.

Exhaustion won over worry, and Gabriela soon woke to the drone of insects enjoying the morning's growing humidity. Not feeling at all refreshed, she pulled on her boots, pausing for a breath with her hand on the doorknob. The tug of Brynmor's tether was as strong as last night, slowly draining her stamina.

In the hall, voices echoed from below, the loudest of all instantly recognizable as Lord Sebastian.

Fish eyes, I didn't even wait for him to arrive last night.

She glanced back at the bed, debating returning for another fifteen to ninety minutes. No, the sooner she got to her mother, the sooner Brynmor could be severed from her, and things return to normal.

"There she is, sleepy head!" Brynmor boomed as Gabriela stepped into the parlor. He sat between Mister Tanner and Lord Sebastian. The knight wore his leather helmet again.

"You're in a good mood this morning," she said, stopping behind the last seat. "Lord Sebastian, do you still…" She waved across his armor and nodded at Brynmor.

He nodded. "Unfortunately, yes. As I was seeing to the horses last night, I thought to leave our friend in the stable, but what would have kept the rats from eating him?"

Gabriela sat, frowning. "I am sorry for this."

"Nothing to be sorry for, Princess. Nothing a good scrub and incense can't undo."

"You said that was just a term of affection," said Brynmor with a wink.

Lord Sebastian wrung his hands. "I might have told him something of your mother and therefore, by extension, your place in our society."

Gabriela sighed. "It would have come up soon enough when we get home."

"A real princess, then? We would make a grand match," said Brynmor. "That you're the daughter of the queen of the Deadvale is nothing my uncle couldn't overlook with time. Royalty's royalty."

"My mother hasn't used any title like that in my lifetime. Calling me a princess really is just a cute name."

"Don't discount your mother so," said Lord Sebastian. "I've served beside her a long time, including when she would have relished in the thought of mortals from far away knowing of her infamy."

Mister Tanner cleared his throat, or at least he made a sound to resemble it. "Gabriela, would you like some coffee or grits?"

"That would be lovely, yes. Then we should get on our way."

"Well..." The ghost gestured at the other wide doorway from the parlor. "You know where the larder is."

Gabriela knew to expect that and pushed back her seat. Lord Sebastian stood as well.

"I'll get the horses ready. Have you seen Aura this morning?"

Gabriela shook her head. "Maybe she's finally decided to move on."

"Oh, don't say such things. You'll miss her when she's gone."

"I'd love to find out." Gabriela smirked, then cringed at her callous words.

Brynmor jumped up to join her.

"She can't be your real mother, right?"

Gabriela stopped with one hand on the cabinet holding the coffee supplies. "What a terrible thing to say. Of course she's my mother."

"You know what I mean. How could the queen of the dead...?" He waved his hands downward from his pelvis, miming the birthing trajectory.

She slammed an old canister of grounds on the counter. "That's hardly a question for you to ask, Viscount."

He said nothing for a moment, but she felt his gaze bore into her as she filled the kettle from the pump over the sink.

"I see I've struck a nerve," he said at last. "Never mind that, then. We were up talking all night, Gabriela. The barkeep has quite a lot to say on the topic. This is amazing, being a ghost."

"I'm glad you're enjoying it. I'll tell Lord Sebastian to leave you for the rats and save us a lot of trouble."

"I don't know if I'd go that far."

Gabriela held the kettle between her hands, focusing on her magic. For every fiber she tried pushing in to heat the water, two more flowed to Brynmor's tether. She gave up after a few moments. She'd have to settle for a lukewarm breakfast.

A blast of wintery air swept through the kitchen, knocking the canister of coffee to shatter on the tile floor.

"Aura!"

"Looks like she's gone." Brynmor nudged at the grounds with his ghostly boot. "What is she? A sister or something?"

"She's my curse, is what she is. We're leaving."

"Shouldn't you..." Brynmor gestured at the shattered ceramic and grounds.

"The sooner I get home, the sooner you can get back into your body."

CHAPTER 6

ONE GLOVE SHY OF A PAIR

"Leave it." Eleanor tugged gently on the reins, forcing the horse's focus forward, away from the berry bush. Treasure snorted and limped beside her. "We're almost to the stables."

The first tiled roof peaks of Mytara came into view over the tall stalks of wheat. Eleanor knew little of the towns this far south, only that Mytara at the sea's edge was famous for its steep stone steps connecting its three levels.

The wheat ended with a stony grass field surrounding the town, and she spied the stables near the entrance. Another twenty minutes at a slow pace, and she handed her mount's reins to an exasperated man wearing a heavy leather apron.

He whistled, eyes darting over Treasure's sleek, black coat. "Beautiful bit of horseflesh you got here."

"Don't call him that. He threw a shoe on the way here," said Eleanor. "I'll be by to pick him up in a couple of hours."

"Probably'll be longer than that, lady," the man grumbled and ran a hand through his mop of red hair. "My boy's run off in the night. I'm backed up here."

41

"That's unfortunate for you." Eleanor unclasped a saddle bag and tossed it over her shoulder. She leaned to glance over the other horses, seeing neither the marquess' nor those of his men. "Where is the nearest tavern?"

The stable master pointed down the street toward a central statue surrounded by a fountain. "Day's a bit early for drinking alone, eh?"

Eleanor noted the flaking sign featuring an overflowing mug under what might have been a crude seashell. *Just once, I'd like to see an inn with a freshly painted sign.* "And the nearest brothel?"

The man gasped, falling back a step, but recovered with a wry grin and a chuckle. "You're a lady who likes to plot her visit, eh?"

His grin faltered when met with Eleanor's unblinking, tired stare.

He coughed and cleared his throat. "The Butterfly Lounge is on the second level."

"Thank you. I'll be back for my horse in three hours." She pulled a guld piece from the bag over her shoulder and flicked it to the man, turning toward the street before he could catch it. He stammered some reply, but Eleanor strode away without a glance back.

So the marquess has already moved on. This town was supposed to be the whole reason for his trip. Where would he have gone from here?

Eleanor glanced up at the placard hanging over the tavern and pushed in. It was no different than any other in the half-dozen towns she'd been through following the marquess. A bar took up one wall, with tapped kegs and glass bottles of booze behind it. Tables littered the main floor, and stairs led to the second-level balcony surrounding the room with a dozen doors. A few regulars hovered over their mugs as the kitchen banged and clattered in preparation for a lunch rush. Eleanor sniffed, noting that the air was a bit fresher than the last tavern, and went straight to a wide, round table beside an upright piano. She threw her coat across the chair beside her and her hat on its backrest.

She sank into the seat, grateful for the moment of rest after walking most of the distance from Solia. Tossing the saddlebag onto the table, she dug through it for her map, flattening it on the table in front of her. A faint red light flashed near the illustration of Mytara, as she expected. Eleanor next took her compass, setting it in the corner and rotating the map until the needle aligned with the mark on her map. Last, she took out a smaller compass, adjusting the dials on the side before setting it beside Mytara. The needle pointed south.

You better be a few streets over with your horses.

The bartender, a man in his late forties with dark hair graying at the temples, approached. "Luncheon's not ready yet, but we have some cold stew and ciders."

"Are you the owner?"

He tossed a rag over his shoulder. "No, but I may as well be. Is there a problem?"

"Have you seen a well-dressed man with dark hair accompanied by two big men who look like brothers?" Over the time following Brynmor, Eleanor worked to scale back her description of the man. The response was usually some version of, "Oh yes, that handsome chap nearly drank me out of business."

"No," said the bartender. "But the other two might have been here last night. Lighter hair and beards? They were sitting real close, talking real conspiratorially."

"That's them. Only them? Not the dark-haired man, too?"

"Not that I saw." He shook his head. "Not that I was watching too hard all night. They paid for a room and left at first light."

Eleanor sat down the coin purse she had reflexively taken from her bag. "They paid for everything?"

He nodded.

"And you saw them leave?"

He nodded again. "They looked in a rush."

"Any idea where they might have been off to?"

He shook his head. "Not really my business once they've paid up."

"Fair enough. I'll have a cup of that stew and your best whiskey."

"Right away." He turned to return to the bar but paused and pivoted back, an impish grin tracing across his lips. "Was that a cup of stew *and* a cup of whiskey?"

"Sure." Eleanor waved the man off and opened her notebook, starting a fresh page for her exploration of Mytara.

If he's paying his bills, maybe I can finally catch up. Maybe I could get a day off. That the barman didn't see Brynmor along with Jon and Job barely worried Eleanor. The marquess had two ways to introduce himself: with loud fanfare or sly flirting, and he probably chose the second here. *He probably met some local heiress or young man with a suit as nice as his coat and told his men to meet him with the horses in the morning. Of course, they'll be whipped if the duke finds out they let Brynmor out of sight.*

Eleanor set her notebook aside as the barman returned with a bowl and a mug. He set them in front of her, along with a spoon. "That'll be twelve bits, unless you'd like to start a tab."

She pulled out a guld piece and watched the man's eyes widen. "Keep the change if you'll ask around to anyone else that was in here last night. Make sure no one else might have seen the dark-haired man."

"Of course, m'lady. I'll ask my wife and son." He disappeared into the kitchen as quickly as the coin disappeared into his pocket.

Eleanor stirred the stew, breaking up the fatty skin that quickly formed across the top, poking at the floating chunks of overcooked vegetables. It tasted like nothing, but that was better than tasting terrible. After a few spoonfuls, she gave up and picked up the mug in both hands. *What a shame not to serve it in a glass.* She waved the whiskey under her nose, picking out a light honey note. Blowing out a long breath, Eleanor took a sip, holding it on her tongue and breathing in slowly. Pulling her notebook toward her, she flipped to the back half and made a note. "Enchanted Oyster Inn, honey, clove, vanilla? 6/10. Served in a mug 2/10."

The man returned just as Eleanor scraped the last bit of stew from the bowl and knocked back the last of her drink.

"Be careful, m'lady. That's a lot of whiskey for such a slight thing."

She glanced up at the bartender. *Did he comb his hair?* "Any news on the dark-haired man?" Eleanor pushed back her chair and started gathering her things into her bag.

"No, m'lady, but we had two others working last night that won't be back until later. Want me to go find them?"

"No rush. I'll be back through later, I'm sure." Eleanor pulled on her coat, pushed on her hat, and tossed her bags over her shoulder.

Back in the street, Eleanor pulled out the little compass to verify that it still pointed south, toward the sea, toward the next level of the city. Toward the brothel. Of course Brynmor would be there. But where were the horses?

After a couple of steps, she stumbled against a storefront window and fumbled for her notebook, adding to the review line.

"Deceptively strong."

Eleanor put the notebook back and pulled out a flask. Her fingers pulsed with a light green glow over the opening while she spoke a few syllables that were nonsense to anyone without her training. Even with her training, they were nonsense. The academy taught the prayers but not the theory behind them. It was the main reason she quit. Well, one of her top three reasons. But, to perform magic without the prayers to the goddess was profane, so she went through the motions. A few seconds later, she took a quick drink, gagging as the water burned like ice dragging down to her stomach. The unpleasantness lasted only a few seconds more, and when she looked up, a couple on the far side of the street were staring at her.

She continued past the statue and fountain, between buildings and through alleys, until the sky opened to the city's lower levels with a steep set of stairs in front of her.

Well, this doesn't look safe at all.

At the bottom, Eleanor passed through a narrow alley. As she cursed the Mytara city planners, movement in her palm drew her attention. The compass needle pointed back at her.

"What..."

She pivoted back and saw a fine leather glove with rabbit fur lining beside a trash pile. Picking it up, the compass needle twitched to point directly at it.

"Well, you were here."

The dark leather felt strange, slick. She shifted it in her palm, then dropped it to stare down at her fingers, now coated in thick, dark blood. Only then did she notice the smear of blood low on the wall.

"Oh, this definitely isn't good."

Eleanor gathered a few wisps of magic, spinning them into something they most certainly never taught at the academy, before touching a single finger to the glove. A shock rocked through her arm, blasting her vision to a hazy wash of blacks and whites, more shadow than color.

She looked up and recognized the glow of Brynmor by a general swelling of adoration, emotions fed to her by the magics. Next came a hint of shame and the shadow of a second person. The scene rushed by, leaving her with a vague sense of something like sadness. Perhaps loneliness. The emotion continued, unchanging, and Eleanor ended the spell.

"Definitely not good..."

Eleanor blinked until her normal vision returned and let her gaze shift to the stairs nearby, reaching upward with their sharp stone edges. She imagined the marquess bouncing down, breaking a new bone, or rupturing a new organ with each hit.

"Did you fall, or were you pushed? Who was with you, and where are you now?" Her eyes drifted back to the streak of blood on the wall and the pool below it. "And are you dead?"

Eleanor shook the glove a few times to dispel the tracking magics, careful not to splatter blood on her coat. Consulting her compass, it now pointed west.

Please be sitting up in a quality hospital with your men keeping you company.

She wrapped the glove in a bit of canvas from her bag and moved in the direction her compass indicated. Within fifteen minutes, she stood at the city's outer edge, staring at a lonely crossroad. Eleanor had looked at her map often enough to know there was nothing more to the west before hitting the Crack and the Deadvale beyond.

That blood was at least twelve hours old, but his men left only a few hours before I arrived in town. I can't return to the duke with a bloody glove and tell him I lost his nephew.

I haven't lost him, not completely. Not yet.

Eleanor looked down at the compass, closing it into her fist with a grunt.

I can't go into the Deadvale alone.

Her gut twisted as she imagined the coming encounter with the duke, but she needed his resources to continue. Not his guld, but his steel.

"That man better be done with my horse."

CHAPTER 7

A BONEY WAVE

"What's the point of that?" asked Brynmor, pulling Gabriela's focus from the road ten feet in front of her. Lord Sebastian held a long, thin flute between his gauntleted fingers, mimicking the motions of playing.

"What's the point of anything, my good sir?"

"No, I mean, you're just a suit of armor. You can't produce the breath to play that. So why bother with the fiddling?"

Lord Sebastian lowered his flute. "I once could play and play quite well."

"But you can't anymore."

"That's quite rude to draw attention to. I know the instrument well enough to hear myself play it."

"Really? Fascinating." Brynmor hummed thoughtfully. "I played a few stringed things when I was young. My mother said I was quite nearly a prodigy."

"I'm sure she did."

Gabriela returned to watching the road ahead during the awkward pause that followed.

Brynmor, again, broke it.

"What exactly are you, Lord Sebastian? You can't be a real lord."

"Oh, but I am. Lord Sebastian Rafferty, Earl of Farswyth, Knight of the Realm."

"Rafferty? I have Raffertys on my mother's side."

Lord Sebastian chuckled.

"What's funny?"

"Only that you and I likely share some blood, and now all the blood you have left is literally within me." He patted his chestplate. Gabriela bit back her own laugh.

Brynmor sounded less amused by his grumbling grunt. "That's not quite what I meant," he said. "Mister Tanner explained to me in detail the nature of ghosts last night, but you are not a ghost."

"Quite true; I am not."

"So then what? Some sort of cursed armor?"

"Cursed armor... How rude. What do they teach you children these days about etiquette and respecting one's elders?"

"If you won't tell me, I must guess something." Brynmor ran a hand through his hair, shaking back his spectral waves.

"Guessing the unspoken details of someone else's affairs is not yours to do, young man. If I won't tell you, maybe I just don't want to tell you. Maybe I don't yet trust you with the details of my existence. We only just met, and you want me to exposit about myself? If we catch the queen in the right mood, and with a great deal of luck, you'll be gone and on your way back to the uncle you love so dearly before supper. You'll think this last day a fever dream and forget any of us exist. I'd rather focus on keeping you from leaking out of my boots than to prattle on to someone that won't care in another day."

Gabriela kept her eyes forward. She'd always known the knight in armor and never knew him to use such harsh words or such a harsh tone. She would owe him a great favor when they got home, but she couldn't think of what might possibly be enough to show her gratitude for what he was putting up with.

"I'll make you a deal." Lord Sebastian's tone softened after another pause. "If the queen can't or won't help you get back into your feet, I'll show you around the town personally. I'll tell you all about myself and what I might know about your great-grandnan."

"You sound as though you're not sure she will help."

"I would never make assumptions for my queen's will."

"Gab..." Brynmor sped up to keep pace beside her. "Gabriela, your mother will help you—help me—right? You'll tell her that this happened because of you, right?"

Gabriela looked up at the pleading in Brynmor's eyes. She knew anything short of complete uncertainty would be false hope and a lie. "My mother is of a strong will. She would never be convinced of action unless it's her idea."

"She sounds like a cat."

With a flash of sickly green light, Aura burst from the ground directly before them. Brynmor hopped back with a startled gasp, but Gabriela kept walking.

"You can be my forever friend," she cooed and swept close to Brynmor, wrapping a wisp of green around him.

Gabriela rolled her eyes. "Ignore her. That's the best advice I or anyone could give you while you're with us."

Aura trumpeted, zipping up and away, drawing Gabriela's attention forward again. The first hints of Soulhaven peeked between the husks of trees. Within a few minutes, they passed between the decayed ruins of the outer crypts. The party followed the path, weaving over crooked limestone markers and monuments. Swirls of thin mist clung to the ankles of Gabriela and the two horses.

The air hung close, silent, and Gabriela breathed it in deeply.

Home.

"What a gods-awful place." Beside her, Brynmor took several deep, loud inhales. "Why does it smell like nothing here? It looks as though it should stink of something."

"I can't imagine you've smelled much the last day since your nose and lungs are inside of Lord Sebastian now."

"A fact I am only too aware of," called the knight from behind them. "Alas, I also lack the sense of smell, but I have no doubt your nose and lungs have quite an odor at the moment."

"I won't stand for this," said Brynmor. "I won't, and nor should I. I am a noble, heir to the duchy of Melo..."

Gabriela waved at three skeletons leaning against a stone crypt to their right. One lethargically raised an arm in response.

"...dis." Brynmor wiped at his eyes. "Which of the seven hells have you dragged me to? I thought you were an innocent-looking young girl, but I see now I was mistaken. You're some sort of devilspawn. You've brought me for some unjust infernal torture."

Gabriela stopped walking, turning to Brynmor and raising her eyebrows in anticipation of what more he would say.

"I am a just and honorable man." He pounded his fist into his palm. "I demand some trial to prove my devotion to the proper gods."

Gabriela waited a moment until she was sure he had nothing more to say. "Welcome to my home." She bit back a grin, knowing laughing would be inappropriate, but she couldn't help it, looking up at the pleading confusion and anger on his face.

"Why are you laughing?" he grumbled.

She covered her mouth and shook her head. A thought came to her. In her twenty years, how many new people had she met? The occasional well-formed ghost might come and go, but otherwise, she only had her mother, Aura, and Lord Sebastian to converse with. True, she was dear friends with all the skeletons and risen dead with some amount of flesh left, but her discourse with them was generally more one-sided, though often just as fulfilling. Her visit to Mytara was mainly disastrous, but Brynmor would love to hear about her hometown. How could he not?

"I should introduce you to the regular citizens," she said, waving for him to follow her to the trio of skeletons.

"Princess, we shouldn't dally too much," said Lord Sebastian.

"It'll just take a moment," she called back to him.

The three skeletons sat on the ground, leaning against a stone vault. They pivoted their skulls as Gabriela and Brynmor approached, and the one on the right raised his arm in greeting again.

She gestured to each in turn. "Mister and Misses Popkin and Mister Foster, might I introduce Viscount Highgate. We're on our way to see my mother."

The last skeleton in the line, Mister Foster, inclined his skull just a fraction.

"No, he's not a naturally occurring ghost," said Gabriela. "But he is real nobility. We better be on our way. A pleasant day to the three of you."

Gabriela nodded and turned back to where Lord Sebastian waited in the path. Brynmor lingered a moment longer and hurried to catch up.

"They didn't say anything," said Brynmor. "What was the point of that?"

"It would be rude to pass them without a proper greeting."

Brynmor kept looking back as they returned to the path. "They look identical. How are you supposed to tell them apart?"

"Do they?" Gabriela glanced back at the skeletons. "I suppose I've known them so long I can't help but tell them apart. You know, those three have quite the history."

"Why would I know that?"

"Well…" said Gabriela, pushing a stray lock of pale hair behind her ear. "It's really juicy between those three. I almost wonder if I shouldn't tell you."

"Let's get to your mother," said Lord Sebastian from atop Harvey. "You can see to the introductions afterward."

They continued between the crypts, and Gabriela lowered her voice to a conspiratorial tone.

"Mister Popkin and Mister Foster were stationed together in the war, where they became quite close, if you know what I mean."

"No, I'm not sure I do," said Brynmor. "Which war was that?"

Gabriela paused to consider the question. She never thought to ask the three. "The War of Rubies," she said with confidence.

"Princess…" Lord Sebastian said in a warning tone.

"The War of Rubies was over three hundred years ago," said Brynmor. "Those skeletons looked good for sitting out in the open that long."

"Was it that long ago?" asked Gabriela. Her history books spoke of it being far more recent. "They only came out of their crypt in the last five years."

Lord Sebastian made a loud throat-clearing noise. "Tell me, good sir, how are you both viscount and marquess? I should think such titles would conflict with one another."

"Not at all," said Brynmor. "I was born a viscount but inherited the title of marquess when I became my uncle's sole heir."

"How very needlessly complex. Back in my day, a person would only use their highest title."

"What was your highest title, Lord Sebastian? Something above an earl? I don't remember you from my history lessons."

The knight chuckled. "Are you wondering which of us outranks the other here? I assure you that matters very little in the Deadvale."

"Maybe so," said Brynmor. "Yet there must be some structure, some hierarchy if Gabriela's mother is called the queen."

"No." Lord Sebastian's tone was again stern, distant. "We serve our queen equally. Only she and her will matter this side of the Crack."

Rubble lined the path, evidence of once-tall buildings. Gabriela noticed movement but resisted the urge to introduce Brynmor to her other friends in town. Skeletons, and a few with some flesh left, shambled along on their business in the distance, but strangely not a single ghost. Eventually, the path turned to a cobblestone road leading into a wide town center. A steepled building dominated the north side, while smaller stone and wood structures surrounded the other edges.

As they approached the large building, Brynmor slowly scanned the front, focusing on the overlaid circles forming a crescent moon high in the stained glass some forty feet up.

"What is the symbol of Elysara doing in the Deadvale? Or a church, for that matter?"

"This is Mama's library," answered Gabriela.

"Soulhaven was once a bastion of worship for your goddess's followers," said Lord Sebastian.

"It's all crypts. I would have guessed we were coming into the edges of Crystalwood Gardens," said Brynmor.

"Ah, Crystalwood," said Lord Sebastian, nostalgia ringing in his voice. "That is a place to store bodies. Soulhaven was a place to revere them."

"Never heard of it."

"Your ignorance has no effect on reality, good sir. You go ahead to your mother, Princess. I'll drop off the horses and join you momentarily."

Gabriela watched him leave and paused with a hand on the library's door handle. Brynmor's inane questions about why he was a ghost, and what it meant to be a ghost, and why it was so important that he not be a ghost anymore occupied her every thought since they left the inn a few hours ago. She hadn't taken a moment to consider how to start the conversation with her mother and convince her to carry out such a feat.

Oh well. She tugged the door open, feeling the chill from within wash over her.

Tomes and scrolls were stacked nearly to the ceiling of the wide vestibule in haphazard piles, lit by oozing tallow candles that Gabriela never noticed get any smaller. Racks against the walls sagged under the weight of the books tossed to face every direction, arranged to completely fill the space between shelves. Tables held stacks of loose parchment, quills, ink bottles, and, of course, more books.

"Did a cyclone pass through here?" Brynmor asked.

"This is how Mama likes it. Don't touch anything. She knows exactly where everything belongs."

"Can I even move anything? I'm a ghost."

"I haven't forgotten. Still, don't. She's probably in one of the back rooms."

She pressed open the door to the main library, or church, as Brynmor thought it was. Sunlight filtered through the stained glass window dominating the back wall, illuminating the vast space as untidy as the vestibule.

"How does anyone find anything in here?" Brynmor reached for a stack of books.

"Don't! Mama has a system."

"Is that my tiny back already?" echoed the low, smooth voice from around distant mountains of parchment. The queen glided into sight, a thousand-page tome in one hand with another, slightly smaller one open on top of it. Her dark dress swept the stone flagons, her hair piled high and laced with gems. She barely looked up as she strode forward, icy mist trailing from her eyes as she moved.

Gabriela rushed forward. "I brought a few spirits back with me, and, Mama, this is Viscount Brynmor Highgate. Brynmor, my mother, Queen Venica Marwol."

"Venica?" Brynmor gasped, shrinking back a step.

"I needn't remind you, my dearest," said Venica without glancing up from her books, "to see to the outer crypts. You know you will be one of the few unaffected by the solstice."

"Yes, Mama. And I needn't remind you that saying you needn't remind me is essentially a reminder."

Venica hummed. She looked back at the book in her hands and turned to leave.

"Mama, wait!"

The queen turned back, focusing on Brynmor as if seeing him for the first time. "Tell me, my tiny, why is there a ghost in my chambers?" She narrowed her icy eyes. "One so well formed and with a fetter to you?"

"That's why I've come. I—"

"You were to retrieve the Lost in town. Why is this one tethered to you?"

"That's what I'm trying to explain!"

"I should hope so. Please do. Don't let me stop you."

"This is Viscount Brynmor Highgate. We met in town and... and there was an accident. I snared his ghost so you could help him."

Venica set her books on the table beside her, keeping her back to Gabriela. "I see. How do you think I could help?"

"Resurrection. Lord Sebastian has his body. I mean, he has Brynmor's, not his own, obviously... Please, Mama."

"Resurrection? Where did you learn that word?" Venica turned, her fingers traced the delicate locket on a chain around her neck.

"It was in one of your books here, somewhere. It's magic that can bring someone back to life, right?"

"That is the theory," said Venica.

"Is there more to it than that? You've told me over and over that magic is little more than an expression of confidence. I'm sure you can do it, Mama, so you must be able to."

"He is handsome, I suppose. Is his body in decent condition?"

"Decent enough. It's in one piece." Gabriela tried to swallow, but her mouth felt suddenly dry. She knew her mother was working her into a trap.

"And it's maintained with the appropriate Repose magics?"

Gabriela's breath caught in her throat. There it was. "Fish eyes, I forgot."

"Then the chance of resurrection is slim, as it is, since you've left the body to rot. I'll remind you to always cast a Repose upon a body before traveling with it."

"I know. I forgot."

"If you're so keen on keeping him around, I could animate his body to join your other friends."

"Mama! Don't be vulgar."

Venica sighed. "You ask for a grand piece of magic, my dearest. To restore one's life, once it is over, is nothing to be done lightly."

"But this was an accident. It wasn't his time."

Venica turned. "You would know this?"

"Mama, please. He's an important man."

"All men think they are important."

"He's the ward of the duke. He says his uncle can bring war on us."

Venica considered the statement while drawing one hand's nails across the other's palm. "Gabriela, my love, your problem does not require a solution involving one of the grandest feats of magic, one never, to my knowledge, performed successfully. It requires a shovel."

Gabriela staggered back, stunned by the callous statement and her mother's wry grin. "Then you won't help?"

"If I stopped to resurrect every person that dies that happens to have a title, I would never have time for anything else."

"My uncle will bring the king's armies and wipe out the Deadvale when he learns what's happened to me," said Brynmor.

Venica hummed thoughtfully. "You say you have his body. Did anyone see you leave with it?"

Gabriela considered the question. "I don't think so. His body was hidden in Lord Sebastian while we were in town."

"Unless someone saw his ghost, your trouble can, again, be solved with a shovel. This duke will have no reason to suspect he's here."

Gabriela balled her fist, sighing out her frustration. "If nothing else, can you secure him so he can be untethered from me?"

Venica took a few steps toward them, leaning forward. "I see you have intermingled his fetter with Aura's. Sloppy, but this is a quality effort for your experience. There is little need to untether him, my dearest."

"What? Why? He can't go that far from me, and he's draining away my magic."

"He appears to be a near complete expression but is missing all the key stabilizing magic. That must be done at the time of death, not days later."

"What does that mean?" Brynmor asked.

Venica looked at Brynmor, then back at Gabriela. "His existence relies upon the magic you feed him, my dearest. Come the solstice that will prove insufficient, and he will move on."

"Can't you do anything?"

Venica turned, striding toward the table with her book. "There may be something in an ancient text, but it is never something I've come upon, that I recall. To purposefully rip a ghost from a body as it dies and tether it to your magic is... unnatural." She touched her locket again.

"My uncle will know," Brynmor called out as Venica was about to disappear around the heaps of tomes. "My men will track my disappearance, as well as any other agents my uncle has dispatched to follow me. The duke will bring a war to wash over the Deadvale and burn it to cinders."

Venica paused at the doorway. "If your vaunted duke wishes war, nothing I will do can stop him."

"You won't stand a chance against the king's paladins."

Venica scoffed, disappearing around the corner.

"She's mad!" Brynmor shouted.

"I don't know why I would have expected anything different." Gabriela's eyes darted over the towers of tomes.

"So, she's always like this? Gloriously unhelpful?"

"She only ever tries to protect me."

"How does leaving me dead protect you? And what's this about the solstice?"

"You really don't listen very well, do you? Mama says your connection to me is the only thing keeping you around. Come the solstice, I won't have enough magic to sustain that."

"So... what do we do?"

Gabriela turned fully to him, looking over his ghostly form. "I don't think *we* can do much. My mother's the only one here with the power to resurrect you. If she won't do it, it won't get done."

"There must be someone else with her level of power."

"I don't know of anyone as strong as Mama."

"Must they be as strong as she? Is she the only one in the whole of the world with the power to do this?"

"It's not just about power as in the strength of magic, Brynmor. Mama's the only one that knows how to do this, or at least has access to it somewhere in this library. We won't find someone else who knows how to perform a resurrection. Especially not in time."

"What about something in all these books? Maybe you could piece it together. You seem resourceful."

"The solstice is less than a week away. I can't find the right tomes *and* master some magic that has never before been performed in that time."

"Not with that attitude, you can't. Come on, Gabriela. You owe me to at least try."

"I owe you?"

"You pushed me to my death!"

"You were touching my face!"

"A cheek as soft as yours begs to be touched. Gabriela, please."

His eyes widened in poorly disguised begging. It probably worked on everyone in every bar and brothel he entered. And Gabriela cursed herself that it was starting to work on her.

"Fine, I'll try. But!" She cut off Brynmor's excited response. "I'm not doing this for you. Or not *just* for you. I can probably figure it out if I find the right book, and Mama has lots of books. Let's go talk to Lord Sebastian first."

CHAPTER 8

HE'S DEAD, I THINK

Eleanor rode Treasure hard. Fear for the horse's wellbeing was slightly less than what the duke would say and do upon hearing her news.

The dead have the marquess. They intend some sacrilegious ritual.

No, I don't know that. I got the impression of him falling down those ghastly stairs, there was a lot of blood, and his trail led toward the Deadvale. That's all. And I can't tell him the first bit because who would believe my magic visions?

They raced through the lowlands, mud sucking at Treasure's hooves. Eleanor prayed to all the deities she knew the names of that the horse wouldn't trip or throw another shoe. Finally, when the beast sounded ready to heave his last breath, the parapets of Montker Abbey rose over the marshes. Perhaps knowing he could soon rest, Treasure rallied for a last burst of speed.

A groom and footman met her in the gravel dooryard. Eleanor nearly fell from the horse as the groom took the reigns to let the poor horse walk it out.

"Where's the duke?" she gasped.

"Miss Lane," said the footman with a dismissive sniff. "His Grace is quite busy. You may wait in the servant's hall, and he will be informed of your arrival."

"My news can't wait. Take me to him."

The butler stepped from the door, prim in starched black and white, taking in the scene instantly. "What's all this commotion? Miss Lane, you're covered in mud."

Eleanor pulled off her hat and marched to glare up at the butler, grabbing the sleeve of his perfectly cut jacket. "Edwards, take me to the duke immediately. What I have to tell him can't wait."

Edwards shook her off and tugged at his cuff to straighten the fabric. "Very well, Miss Lane. Follow me."

He turned, folding his hands behind his back, and set a painfully slow pace through the house. The grand staircase trimmed with royal red carpet, crystal chandeliers with a thousand candles, suits of armor from across the ages, and tapestries from across the world were nothing to her. She'd seen it all in her previous visits, and the only thing that mattered now was divesting herself of the knowledge of Brynmor's fate.

The butler guided her through the library to the small dining room. Duke Highgate sat at the head of the table shrouded in white lace. As they entered, he looked up from selecting a piece of chicken on a platter held by a footman.

"Your Grace," said Edwards. "Miss Eleanor Lane."

The duke set the utensils back in the tray and waved the footman back. Rarely out of his military blues, Duke Rhys Highgate leaned back in his chair and stroked a finger along the length of his mustache.

"Miss Lane," he said with a loud breath. "Quite surprising to see you in my home, tracking mud on my floors."

Eleanor glanced down at the mud up to her thighs. That didn't matter. Floors could be cleaned.

"Your Grace, I come with news that cannot wait."

The duke leaned forward, picking up a chicken wing and ripping the bones apart. "Correct me if I am mistaken, Miss Lane, but I believe I have you in my employ, and pay you quite well, according to my accountants, for a solitary job."

Eleanor stammered for a response. "Yes, Your Grace. To ensure the integrity of Viscount Brynmor's, ah, social interactions."

The duke bit into the chicken. Grease dripped across the back of his hand and over his rings. "Why, then, am I paying you for your job when you are clearly in dereliction of it?"

"Your Grace?"

"The marquess is not here, so why are you?" He took another juicy bite.

"Your Grace, the marquess is… Viscount Brynmor is…" The words were right there but refused to be said.

Duke Highgate tossed down his chicken, pounding a fist against the table. "Dammit it, girl. He's what?"

"He's dead!" She sucked in a breath to amend her statement, that she only *assumed* he was *at least* gravely injured, but instead exhaled it in a puff.

The footmen gasped, but the duke only stared at her, unblinking. After a moment, he ran his tongue over his teeth, under his lips, with a loud sucking noise.

The side door opened with a click, and a woman in heavy blue and white plate armor entered. Eleanor knew her immediately by reputation, Commander Valoria Ravell, hero of the Battle of Wilkins Field. She didn't expect a woman of such repute, with such a lengthy history of victories, to look so young. Ravell's dark skin looked untouched by the years and stress of her accomplishments. Her hair, shaved close on her right and tinged with crimson highlights, swept to her shoulder.

Ravell stopped beside the duke's chair. "Is everything alright in here, Your Grace?" Her eyes never wavered from Eleanor's.

"That is yet to be determined," said the duke. "Miss Lane has just given me some distressing news. It seems the marquess has died while in her care."

Eleanor opened her mouth to argue the point but bit her lips closed.

"How did it happen?" He leaned forward and picked up his chicken.

Eleanor cleared her throat. "I don't exactly know, Your Grace. I believe there was an accident, and he fell down the steps connecting the levels in Mytara. I couldn't find his men, but I was able to track the marquess using magic."

"Hard to believe anyone that fell down those stairs would walk away." The duke dropped the bones and picked a fresh piece to tear apart.

"I don't think he walked away. I..." She took a quick, deep breath. "I tracked the marquess toward the Crack, toward the Deadvale."

"What of his men? Missing or dead as well? Or did they take him to that cursed realm?"

"His men were seen leaving town quickly, and all their horses were gone from the stables. I assume they learned of the marquess' fate and fled."

"You there," said the duke around a mouthful of chicken, nodding his chin at the distraught footman. "See that his men are hanged when found. Go, spread the notice."

The footmen bowed and fled through the door the commander had entered through.

"So, we finally come to war." Duke Highgate snapped up his napkin to wipe his hands slowly, methodically. His eyes bore into the plate in front of him. "They came across our unprotected border, killed my nephew, and absconded with his body. Now they mean to desecrate him further."

"That isn't what I said. We can't know who is at fault or what happened—"

"It isn't, Miss Lane? My beloved nephew is dead, and his body is now across the Crack? Agents of the Deadvale are to blame for all of this. Ravell!"

"What? No I—"

The commander stepped forward with a single clink from her armor. "Yes, Your Grace."

The duke jumped at her immediate response and looked up at the soldier beside him. "The next course of action is clear. The king will require proof of my nephew's demise. You will accompany Miss Lane into the Deadvale. Track these fiends. Find the marquess' body and return it to me for the proper death rituals."

"Yes, Your Grace."

Eleanor's heart leaped to her throat, and she stepped back. "I can't go to the Deadvale! I'm no soldier! I'm a mage, a tinkerer."

"That is exactly why you are in my employ, Miss Lane. You are a mage, a tinker, and have the means to track my nephew. Might I remind you how near you were to bearing the brand of a heretic before I lifted you up?"

Eleanor glanced at Ravell but couldn't hold the other woman's stern gaze.

The duke took a long draw of wine from his goblet, spilling it down his cheeks. He wiped at it with a napkin. "Rumor is the king has new information making him more receptive to an assault against the Deadvale. He only needs one more nudge in the right direction." He smirked, causing a chill to chase down Eleanor's back.

"What information?" she asked.

"Nothing that should concern you. You will leave at once," said the duke, tossing his napkin over his plate. "We can only guess at the plans the dead may hold, but should they intend to raise my nephew as some soulless abomination, I needn't be explicit in what you must do, Ravell. Return my nephew's *body* to me."

For saying he needn't be explicit, Eleanor couldn't see a second way to interpret that command. She would return the marquess' body no matter its state when they found it.

Chapter 9

Stoking the Fires

A blast of cold air knocked loose parchment from the desk.

"You're not making this any faster," Gabriela groaned.

"You promised me a story," said Aura as she drifted forward through the wall.

"Brynmor only has a couple of days. I don't have time to read to you."

"You promised, Gabs." The stack of books shuddered.

"Aura!" Gabriela slammed her palm against the woodgrain. "Stop this! My time to do something about Brynmor is limited. You, of all, should appreciate that."

"Why do you like him more than me? What's he got that's so good?"

Gabriela looked reflexively back at Brynmor sitting in a chaise behind them. He examined the nails of his ungloved hand.

"Fetch me a file," he said when he noticed the attention on him.

Gabriela sighed. "You could be helping."

Brynmor scoffed. "I'd only get in your way with all this book nonsense. I'm more of a man of action, charm, and intrigue."

"He's an idiot," said Aura with a giggle. "You left me for him?"

"I didn't leave anyone for anyone else," said Gabriela.

"He's still an idiot." Aura flew through the wall with another chill breeze.

Gabriela rubbed her face with both hands and returned her attention to the tome before her. Found near the top of a nearly toppling stack of seemingly unrelated books, it described the resurrection of a third-century mystic, among other stories. Though the language felt dated, there was far too much dialog for a manuscript teaching a magical technique.

"What is it between you two?" asked Brynmor.

"Aura?"

"No, you and Mister Foster from the crypts outside." He rolled his eyes. "Yes, her. You obviously don't care a fig for her; her existence seems focused on getting under your skin. Send her away."

"I can't do that."

"Of course you can. Call for her, and I'll do it for you."

"No, I mean, I really can't. Aura is bonded to me just like you are, just better. Without that connection, she would move on. I would never force that on anyone. Besides, as annoying as she may be, I've known her my whole life. I don't exactly have that many to talk with around here."

"Move on?" Brynmor raised an eyebrow.

"I thought you stayed up all night talking to Mister Tanner in the inn. What did you discuss, if not the cycle of ghosts?"

"Nothing appropriate to repeat to a young girl." He returned his attention to his nails.

"Young girl?" Gabriela stood up too fast, knocking the chair back to send another pile of books tumbling. "You seemed quite interested in me back in Mytara, and now I'm just a young girl?"

"Come now, don't get hysterical." Brynmor glanced at her, then back to his nails.

"Coming from the man that won't stop looking at his nails."

"They look dirty."

"You're dead!"

"What is with all the commotion in here?" Queen Venica glided from behind a rack of mismatched scroll casings. She held a rolled piece of vellum in both hands as she looked over the books scattered from the overthrown chair. "Careful, my tiny. Some of those are quite irreplaceable."

A retort hung on Gabriela's tongue, something about not leaving irreplaceable tomes stacked on the floor, but she left it unsaid. "Sorry to disturb you, Mama."

Brynmor gracefully stood with a bow. "The fault is mine, good lady. I spoke out of turn and disrupted the princess's concentration."

Venica's frosty eyes moved over Brynmor with a thoughtful hum before she turned to Gabriela. "I thought this matter resolved. Why is he here?" She strode to the desk, setting down the vellum to pick up the book Gabriela had been reading.

"He's tethered to me. If that breaks, he moves on."

"No, I mean, why is he in my library? I have strict rules regarding strangers entering my library."

"I..." Gabriela stammered, looking between her mother and Brynmor. "I'm learning what's involved in resurrection magic. Maybe I can do it myself." She took a deep breath, rolling back her shoulders to stand a little taller before her mother.

Venica hummed again and looked down at the book in her hands. "*The Adventures of Basil the Thrice Damned*," she read. "This is your resource?"

"It's the first I found. I don't know how you find anything in this nest." Gabriela waved her hands over the teetering stacks and awkwardly crammed, uneven shelves.

"Everything has its place, as does everyone. Like everything else I see you read, the frivolous stories in this book have no place in your head, and this ghost has no place in my library. I fail to see how I can make myself any clearer." She set down the book to pick up the vellum.

Gabriela moved around her mother to stand between her and Brynmor. "He needs me, Mama. You said so yourself. At the solstice, he will move on."

"That is the natural order of things, my love. Most are lucky enough to never be in the state... the... marquess is currently in."

"Brynmor. His name is Brynmor. Viscount Brynmor Highgate, the Marquess of Melodis. His death will mean war, Mama. The king and his paladins will sweep across the Crack, laying everything to a final rest."

Venica stared at Gabriela for a long moment, then finally sighed, laying down her rolled vellum. "I see this is important to you."

"It is, Mama. Very."

"Then I suppose I ought to make an effort to make it important to me, as well."

"Thank you, Mama." Gabriela could hardly ask for more.

"You're quite sure about this war business?"

"Without the slightest doubt," said Brynmor. "My uncle has spies and informants across the continent. They will report back to him. The duke's retribution will be swift and absolute."

Venica's focus never wavered from her daughter. "Do you believe all that?"

"I do," Gabriela nodded. "At least, why would he lie?"

"My sweet girl." Venica put a cold palm on Gabriela's cheek. "All men lie; it is in their deepest natures. The question should not be *if* he is lying, but *why* he is. I have enough experience with the king's paladins to know they are not to be trifled with. Even if this ghost only spun a story to be reunited with his body, it may be worth the effort if his resurrection can keep back the king's forces."

"So, it is possible?" asked Gabriela, feeling the hope surge in her chest.

"Of course. That it has not been done does not mean it cannot be done."

"And you'll do it?" Gabriela tried to keep her voice from rising too high in pitch.

"I spoil you, but it shows my love is genuine. Very well." Venica sighed, picking up her roll of vellum yet again. "I will do this for you if only to demonstrate the folly in attempting the research yourself."

"Thank you, Mama!" Gabriela moved to hug her but stopped at seeing her mother's dour look.

"Leaving town near the solstice is hardly ideal, but I will risk it for you."

"Leave town?" Gabriela's shoulders sank. She hadn't considered having to leave home again. Not so soon, at least. "Why? You can't do it here?"

Venica slowly shook her head. "Were it possible, I would perform all tasks from the comfort of my library. Alas, there are necessary reagents, and we lack the time to send others to collect them."

"What kind of reagents?" asked Brynmor.

The queen glanced at him, then back at her daughter. "Return to your duties about town while I gather the requisite notes."

"Yes, Mama. Thank you."

Gabriela spun to leave, but Brynmor paused to place his ungloved hand across his chest and bow deeply. "I speak for my uncle and the king when I offer my most solemn thanks, Dark Lady."

Venica turned her frosty gaze to him, exhaling a loud breath. "Your thanks mean little to me. You are nothing but an interruption. My daughter may feel for your plight, but I act only for her and to prevent further annoyances your death may bring upon my people."

"Annoyances?" Brynmor balled his gloved hand into a fist.

Gabriela rushed between him and her mother. "Come now, Brynmor," she laughed, pushing him back and glancing over her shoulder at her mother. "Mama needs the space to focus. I'll show you the gardens."

"After you see to the braziers in the catacombs," Venica said.

"Yes, of course, Mama!" She kept pushing Brynmor until they stood alone on the other side of the door to the library.

"Stop that, I say!" Brynmor waved at her hands, but his arms passed through hers. "This is entirely unfair," he pouted.

Gabriela pulled away. "Watch your tone with her! You should be honored she's doing this at all."

"Honored?" Brynmor scoffed. "You must forget my station. It is she that should be honored to perform this service."

"It's a wonder your head can fit inside Lord Sebastian's helmet. Come on. I have things to do."

"More menial tasks? For being a princess, you hardly have the life of one."

"Nothing is menial that needs to be done," said Gabriela, quoting one of Lord Sebastian's favorite bits of wisdom.

"Well, lead the way, I suppose." Brynmor gestured away from the door. "As if I have any option but to follow as you sweep the stables or polish the silver or whatnot."

"Carmel's the only living pony, and I'm the only one that eats in town. Well, Harvey now, too, but he won't be staying," Gabriela said as they passed through the double doors and back into the yard of the manor house. She frowned at the sky of darkening gray clouds and wondered how the day could have slipped away so quickly.

"I don't care for how you said the only *living* horse," said Brynmor at her side.

"Why's that? It's not like we need others. Most horses don't like to be ridden or led by dead things. Your horse seems to be the exception."

"Harvey is remarkably well-bred and trained," Brynmor said with a sniff of agreement. "What is your mother researching, anyway? I thought she didn't know about any details regarding resurrection."

"Well, maybe she thought of something."

Gabriela crossed to a squat stone building with its iron portcullis mostly raised and rusted in place. Over the entry was an intricately carved image of a woman with a half-skull mask standing watch over a line of souls marching to their final rest; Elphame, the goddess of death herself. Gabriela reached to touch the worn carving as she passed under it, as she always did. Beyond, steep stairs cut a sharp twist into the ground, and she kept her left hand on the inner wall, humming to herself while descending the fifty feet to the main chamber below.

Lit by the white and blue flames licking from the brazier set into the center of the floor, the walls of the wide vestibule were dotted by six evenly spaced darkened halls. Between each were six alcoves, some empty, some with crumbling relics on display stands.

Gabriela crossed the floor made of the lids of the burial vaults below and knelt by the brazier. Taking up the iron poker laid beside it, she adjusted the pale blue coals.

"I hope your mother didn't mean to check deeper into this horrid place," said Brynmor. "There's just the brazier right here?"

"Horrid place?" Gabriela looked across the carved busts and reliefs with flaking paint, the shattered urns with bits of misplaced bone. "Why would you say that?"

"Never mind. What are you doing?"

"Come the solstice, all the dead must find somewhere safe for a few days. They'll start to make their way back here as long as the brazier doesn't go out, which it never should, anyway."

Brynmor stepped near to kneel beside her and raised his palms to the ghost fire. "I feel it. It's warm. So very warm."

"Of course it is, to you. I don't feel much. Here comes someone now."

They turned to the irregular click of bone on stone. An ancient skeleton, missing most of one hand and half its ribs, with moss spotting what remained, stepped from the stairs into the vestibule.

Brynmor gasped and slid behind Gabriela.

"It's only Miss Honeywell." She looked back at Brynmor, rolling her eyes at him. "Good evening, Miss Honeywell." She waved.

The skeleton ignored her to shamble down the first corridor on the left.

"Gods and saints," Brynmor whispered.

"That's fine. I'm used to them not always waving back. Her niche is down that way. Unless she's forgotten something for her night on the town, she's returning to settle in for the solstice. Miss Honeywell is always concerned about being late for anything. You know what they say, 'On time is already late!' She's probably one of the first here."

"These creatures amble about uncontrolled?"

"Uncontrolled? Of course no one controls them."

"My tutors told me of the necromancers, death mages, that roam the Deadvale, raising the legions of dead, twisting them to their ranks."

"Interesting." Gabriela tapped a finger to her chin. "Well, that's not how it works here. All the dead you see have naturally risen, and Mama and I leave them to their business, only interfering to keep them safe."

"Like feral pets."

Gabriela snickered. "You say the strangest things, Brynmor." She set down the iron poker, brushing her hands over her dress. "Follow me. The next catacombs are about a fifteen-minute walk."

Descending the stairs to the next underground crypt led the pair to a nearly identical chamber. Gabriela knelt by the blue-white flame of the brazier while listing off the residents and a few of their hobbies or other defining attributes.

"The Barnett brothers are down here. They rarely come out, though. They were hanged for murder, you see. Falsely accused, if you ask me, but what's done is done. Anyway, their skulls don't stay on all the time." She paused, realizing

Brynmor hadn't said anything in minutes, and looked up at him. "Something wrong?"

The marquess rubbed at his face. "Your stories are endless."

"It's a big town, and I know everyone here. Well, a deep town, if not big." Gabriela beamed.

"And how... how do you know all this? How do you know Lady Holt raised prize-winning dogs? She was just a skeleton with a few scraps of hair clinging to her skull. She didn't say a word. She can't talk; she's just a skeleton."

"*Just* a skeleton?" Gabriela scoffed. "Maybe if you spend more time without your body, you'll learn to hear without your ears."

She stared at Brynmor for a long moment before poking angrily at the pale coals.

"You're an odd one, Gabriela. Very odd."

"I can say with certainty that there's nothing odd about me. We're all a product of our circumstances. Lord Sebastian told me that. Just because I'm different than you or what you expect doesn't mean there's anything wrong with me."

Brynmor chewed his lip and narrowed an eye. "Being odd isn't a bad thing; not necessarily. I suppose I'm accustomed to figuring a person out more quickly than I am figuring out you. You're... complex."

Gabriela's smile returned. "That, I'll take as a compliment."

"How many more catacombs are there?"

"Two. Then you get to watch me eat dinner and..." Gabriela let the thought trail as the silent terror crept forward. Last night, the unique magic of the Guardian Arms let Brynmor wander farther from her and stay in the company of Mister Tanner. Tonight, however, he would be tethered close by. So very close by.

"What is it?" he asked after a long moment of her staring blankly into the flames.

"Nothing," she said quickly. *A screen. I can put a screen beside my bed and a chair for him to sit in on the other side. Not that he needs a chair, but he'll want one, and it's the hospitable thing to offer.*

Gabriela set the iron poker back and stood, not meeting Brynmor's gaze. "I'm sorry the nights will be rather boring for you."

"I don't understand."

"Oh, nothing. Don't worry about it." Gabriela stood, brushing her hands together. "Shall we carry on to the next catacomb?" She moved swiftly past Brynmor, feeling his tether tighten, then release. His ghostly fingers gripped uselessly at her elbow, only chilling her with his touch.

"What do you mean, Gabriela?" he asked.

She turned, shaking from his touch. "We're in this situation because you overstepped your bounds."

"I remember things differently, but continue."

Gabriela's nails bit into her palms. "We're about to spend a close night together, and I would like some assurances that you will remain... honorable."

"My word! I am little if not a man of honor! I take great offense you would even—"

"If you peek at me even once as I slumber, we're done. I'll rip out your tether, and you can meet Elysara or Lady Elphame."

Brynmor's mouth moved silently. "Of course, my lady," he finally said.

CHAPTER 10

THE QUEST ACCEPTED

G abriela woke to a young girl made of translucent light floating beside her bed, a breeze felt only by her tugging at her frayed summer dress.

"Queen... Venica..." hissed the girl.

Pushing a palm into her eye, Gabriela yawned. "Thank you, Ivy."

The girl drifted backward and faded into the blackness.

"Gods and saints, what was that, now?" Brynmor's voice came from behind, and Gabriela snatched the bedding to her neck. He peeked from around the floral screen, his face glowing a soft white in the last light of the moon.

"Don't look!"

"What was that?"

Gabriela followed Brynmor's wide eyes to where the other spirit faded into nothing. "Ivy? She's my mother's messenger. Well, one of her messengers."

"You have other ghosts that randomly hover over you while you sleep?"

"It's not uncommon." She waved for Brynmor to retreat behind the screen, to stand and wrap herself in a silk dressing robe when he did. "Lord Sebastian says that just after the event that caused the Crack, there were so many ghosts in the world, you couldn't get dressed without three watching you."

"Well, I'm glad there are fewer now."

"And Ivy isn't a ghost, not like you are. She's the collection of conscious energy from several individuals combined into an amalgamation capable of deciding when to move on."

"What in all the hells does that mean?"

"Usually, when a person or some of the more intelligent or emotional animals die, they move on right away. Sometimes, they leave behind bits of their awareness, and very rarely, they stick around almost completely. Mama tasked me to collect some stray ghost fragments from Mytara. She lumps them together into something that can decide to move on."

"Lumping together ghosts into some... I don't even know what. That sounds monstrous."

"Not at all! She's been at it for years across the Deadvale. Without her efforts, there would be six ghosts to watch you pee."

"That really seems to bother you."

Gabriela paused to consider the statement. "And it doesn't bother you?"

"Not as such a high priority." Brynmor paused and tugged at his hair. "Your mother. Why are we having this conversation when she has some news for me?"

"Because it's a perfectly valid conversation to have. The overwhelming majority of people, according to my mother, can't see ghosts. They can't even sense them more than a feeling of unease. Imagine how many ghosts were watching you do every little thing."

"I find myself quite content in ignorance. Can you *please* take me to your mother?"

"I envy you that, being so willfully ignorant, now knowing how many ghosts surely watched you do everything."

Brynmor rubbed his face. "What can I say to end this conversation?"

Gabriela frowned at the ghost peeking around the screen. "I don't see why you need to be rude about it. Stay behind there while I get dressed."

Brynmor disappeared, as requested. "Not that I have any interest in such an odd girl."

"You seemed perfectly interested in me at the top of the stairs."

"That was..." Brynmor chuckled wryly. "A different life, it seems."

Gabriela slipped from the bed, tugging off her sleeping gown to pull a fresh blouse over her head. She cinched a long skirt around her waist and stepped into her scuffed leather boots before calling Brynmor to follow her.

"Last night was miserable," he said as they walked through the otherwise empty, dusty halls of the manor. "I had nothing to do but stare at the ceiling. I couldn't even get close enough to the window to watch the moon."

"Watch it do what?"

He looked down at her with a hard blink.

"I think I know what you mean," said Gabriela. "Mama says ghosts experience time differently than do the living. Well, I read that somewhere and asked Mama to confirm. She didn't so much confirm as didn't deny it."

"Meaning what?"

"I love how you ask so many questions."

Brynmor tossed up his hands and ran one through his hair. "I wouldn't have to if you ever gave a straight answer."

"Mama says she once knew a mage that said asking questions is a sign of weakness, to admit ignorance in a topic. But you've already admitted to your ignorance, so I guess that's all to be expected."

"I do hope your mother has good news. I'd hate to be an imposition to you for one day further."

Gabriela looked up at him striding beside her, his arms now crossed in front of his chest. The nerves and trepidation she felt only yesterday at this stranger taking such interest in her had already faded. "Oh, you're not an imposition, Brynmor. Not really. I actually am growing rather fond of talking so much. You're a good listener."

"I am a captive audience, for sure."

"The skeletons are great listeners, too, but their responses are more... implied."

The pair left the main doors of the manor and, with morning mist swirling around her ankles, crossed the yard to the library. A single skeleton wandered in the distance but didn't respond to Gabriela's wave.

"Back to the question of the perception of time," said Brynmor.

"Oh, that, yes. Mama's studies imply the passage of time is only noticed because of the rhythms of the living body. You don't have that right now, so you have nothing to mark the passage of time. A century might flow by without notice, or a night might last an eternity."

"As might this conversation," Brynmor grunted in response. "That's nice that your mother taught you so much."

"Well…" Gabriela paused with a hand on the library door. "Not directly, not always. She made sure I always had books, most of which she wrote, so that's like she taught me herself. Lord Sebastian saw to my social needs to ensure I grew into a proper lady." She lifted the hem of her skirt with her free hand and curtsied.

"What a labor, and what a result." Brynmor's eyes flicked to the library door.

"Thank you. Lord Sebastian is nothing if not fully dedicated to his duties. He—"

"Open the door!"

Gabriela bit her lip, shying half a step from the ghostly noble. "No need to be cranky. I thought we were having a good little chat."

"One we can continue when I'm back in my body with an unbroken neck and wearing two gloves."

"Right, yes, sorry. I sometimes get a little excited. It happens every time there's someone new in town, but they usually don't talk back as much as you do."

She tugged the heavy door just enough to squeeze through and pulled it shut behind her. Brynmor followed, not seeming to notice the door clipping through his shoulder.

The library antechamber was in complete disarray, even more than normal. Many of the usual uneven stacks of tomes were toppled, littering the floor along with unrolled vellum maps and curling scrolls.

"Mama?"

Ivy floated through a stack to stop a few inches from Gabriela's face. "Queen… Venica," she gurgled.

Brynmor backed away. "Gods and saints," he mumbled.

Gabriela looked back at him, noticing how he tapped three fingers to his chest. "What's that about? I keep catching you doing it."

"A Niclaos Ward?" Brynmor stopped and glanced down at his hand, holding the three fingers up in front of his face. "What's the question?"

Gabriela mimicked the gesture, tapping three fingers on her chest. "Does that do something? I don't feel anything."

"It's to... I forget you must have been raised with profane magics. Of course, you wouldn't know the holy wards and ways."

"That's so adorable that you think tapping your chest would call your gods to action. I almost hope Mama can't help you so we can spend more time together. You're fascinating." Gabriela grinned and turned back to Ivy. "Lead the way, dear."

The amalgamation of ghost energy led the pair through two chambers, passable by a narrow path carved through the heaps of old tomes. They entered a three-story-tall room with a wall of leaded stained glass catching the early morning light.

Venica sat behind a narrow table jumbled with more books. She looked up as they entered.

"Gabriela, my love. How did you slumber?"

"I slumbered well, Mama. Thank you. It looks like you've fairly torn the library apart overnight."

"Yes." Venica rose smoothly, gliding around the table to lean against it. Her fingers rose to caress the silver locket at her throat. "It might be soon that I must invest time in my organization. I have gathered my notes on how we may deal with this unfortunate ghost if that still holds your interest."

"It is. I mean, it does."

"Very much, yes," Brynmor added beside her.

Venica exhaled, long and loud, at him and focused back on her daughter. "Perhaps reserve your enthusiasm while I list for you the requirements. They may alter your decision."

Gabriela chewed her lip. She knew the feat of resurrection would be well within her mother's ability, but the hesitation in her voice worried her.

"The first is the issue of reagents," said Venica, raising a long, thin finger to tick off the details. "We require a corpse. Naturally, a corpse makes the entire process simpler. Next, a ghost or sufficient ghostly or spiritual energy to imbue the corpse with something similar to life. That we have a corpse and ghost that were once of the same person vastly simplifies the process. I saw to the corpse last night, and it is in decent enough, though not ideal, condition. It is in the next room."

Brynmor took a few steps in the direction Venica gestured. "May I see it? Me?" he asked.

"No," said Venica. "The next material requirement is, as I have interpreted it, the remains from an ancestor. This aids in tethering the ghost to the body while... You should be making a note of all this."

Gabriela snatched a piece of parchment from another table to start a list. "Ghost... body... old bones," she mumbled while writing. "What else?"

"Divine blood," said Venica, drumming her fingers together.

Gabriela added it to her list.

"Divine blood?" asked Brynmor. "What does that even mean? Blood from a god?"

Venica tore her gaze from Gabriela to look his way. "Or one blessed by a god. The final requirement is to perform the ritual in a place of great power. Write that down. I have located an ancestor of the deceased. We will go first to Crystalwood Gardens, then to the Devil's Pit for divine blood, and perform the ritual at a nearby fae ring."

With the soft click of his leather boots, Lord Sebastian entered the room from the direction Venica indicated earlier about Brynmor's corpse.

"Good morning, Lord Sebastian," Gabriela beamed.

"And a good morning to you, Princess." He bowed, taking off his helmet to show he was again empty.

"Divine blood, fae rings..." Brynmor gaped.

"The blood might sound difficult, but the devils aren't really that bad," said Lord Sebastian. "They may easily be convinced to barter away some, if they don't willingly donate it. The fae ring is just a circle of stones out in the open, nothing special. The fae are all long gone."

Venica slowly turned to Lord Sebastian, fixating her cold stare on him.

"That isn't to mean this quest won't be fraught with peril," he said quickly. "The fae ring is positioned over a nexus of wild energy."

"Who is the ancestor?" Gabriela asked.

Venica's frosty gaze remained on the leather-clad knight.

Lord Sebastian bowed again, this time to Brynmor. "My dearest great-great-grandson."

"What?" Brynmor staggered back a step. "Impossible, inconceivable. I have studied my family's tree, and while your surname may appear, you are not my ancestor."

"On paper, no," said Lord Sebastian. "But my brother, Estrane, is. He was so often away for wars and business."

"Your brother Estrane..."

"The nights were colder, longer, and lonelier back then." Lord Sebastian sighed fondly.

"No..." Brynmor shook his head.

"Lord Sebastian," said Venica, "is interred at Crystalwood Gardens and has graciously offered the necessary scrapings to continue the ritual."

The armored knight shrugged. "It is my pleasure to help where I can. Not like I'm using those bones anymore."

"I have enchanted the corpse to preserve it as we travel. Lord Sebastian has graciously offered to carry the body."

"And act as a bodyguard where needed." Lord Sebastian clenched his fist with the creak and rub of supple leather.

"This quest will be good for you, my tiny. You will see more of our world and fully appreciate the awesome magic you so flippantly wish to harness. We leave immediately," said Venica. "We have precious little time before the solstice, and every moment spent here is one not spent in rest preparing for the wane of magic. Ivy, see to the stables. Prepare Carmel and Darius along with the new horse." The ghost messenger left soundlessly, drifting through the wall of stained glass. "Gabriela, my love, put together a satchel of your required trappings."

"Yes, Mama." Gabriela turned to leave, to wind through the rooms with narrow paths between the books. She noticed a dull pang of sadness as she walked with Brynmor at her side. In seeing Ivy, she realized the other regular ghost that had been suspiciously absent since yesterday. As much as she complained about Aura being a pest, Gabriela worried about any ghost that went a period without contact.

Once they entered the yard, she glanced at Brynmor, seeing the expectant look on his face.

"What?" she asked.

"What do you mean *what*? Haven't you been listening to a thing I've said the last five minutes?"

"Apparently not." She looked down at her empty hands, only then remembering the sheet of notes she had left in the library.

"I'm a bastard! The descendant of one, at least. My life is a lie. No, I'm sure Sebastian is lying. He may have known my some-great grandnan, but he's making it up for attention."

"*Lord* Sebastian does not lie. He has his moments of fun and exaggeration but would never utter a base lie. So what if you're a bastard? A twice-great-grand bastard? What will that change?"

"It changes everything. I wouldn't expect you to understand."

"If you say." Gabriela shrugged. "Mama didn't say how long this will take. Will we be gone overnight or for weeks? Will we be staying somewhere for the solstice? Fish eyes, I should have asked."

"That's your concern? I'm having a crisis of patronage, and you worry about how many skirts to pack?"

"And blouses, yes. My bag is only so large."

CHAPTER 11

AN UNCOMFORTABLE PAIR

It had been miles since Eleanor last looked up from the device in her hands. This particular puzzle box, made by her father, was turning out to be his most infuriatingly perfect creation yet. She only glanced up when she noticed Treasure slowing beneath her.

Ahead, Commander Valoria Ravell lead the pair, finally out of the marshlands. Eleanor's worries and fretting over what she could say to hold the attention of one such as Commander Ravell seemed like wasted energy now. The two had barely said a word since leaving Montker Abbey at first light.

Commander Ravell looked back at Eleanor, waiting for her to pull up beside her.

"Consult your workings," she said.

Eleanor twisted to take the map from her saddlebag and unfold it enough to see the dully pulsing red point. After carefully orienting it to true north, she set the smaller compass on it, watching the needle settle. It pointed a few degrees north of due west.

"Odd," Eleanor mumbled.

"Explain," said Ravell.

"The marquess is moving in a direction nearly perpendicular to ours."

"When and where will we intercept him?"

Eleanor ran a finger north along the map, frowning at the first, most obvious, option. "Crystalwood Gardens."

"The cemetery. Of course the dead would take him there for their rituals."

"I can't be certain; it's just a guess. A good guess, but a guess."

"That will have to do, Miss Lane. If we cut around the Ebonwood, we can be at the eastern edge of the grounds by this time tomorrow. How far away is the marquess?"

"I can't tell distance, only direction. I can sort of estimate it based on the angular difference between compass readings, but that's mathematics I wasn't prepared for; I wasn't marking the proper notes to work that out. And you can call me Eleanor."

"There is little reason to relax our formalities, Miss Lane." Ravell tugged the reigns to steer her steed north. "We will ride hard but cannot exhaust the horses in case their speed is needed in the cemetery."

Eleanor nodded along but wasn't sure the words were meant for her. She tucked away the map and her father's puzzle box, noticing Ravell's lingering eye as she did. A quick glance at the sun showed the pair could get at least another three hours closer to the cemetery tonight. Three hours of utter silence.

Ravell spurred her horse to a canter, and Eleanor squeezed her legs to encourage Treasure to match the pace. The miles passed more quickly in the higher, drier land now they were clear of the Murkwallow Marshlands surrounding the Abbey. Eleanor debated taking out the puzzle again, thinking about it until she no longer paid attention to the path Ravell chose. She imagined the interlocking gears and knobs, switches and sliding panels. It would be impossible to solve as a pure mental exercise; her father wove too many pieces together, and there would be no way to unravel them without having the box in her hand.

Still, Eleanor envisioned what little progress she already made, combined with what she knew of solving her father's previous work. This new puzzle employed some of his old tricks, yet was still unique.

"Why are you smiling?" Ravell asked, snapping Eleanor from her thoughts to realize they'd again slowed to a walk.

Eleanor shook her head, not realizing she'd been grinning, thinking about the toy.

"It's nothing," she said. "My mind was just drifting as we rode."

Ravell frowned. "This mission could easily determine the fate of the duchy and kingdom. Do not allow your focus to stray."

Don't you tell me what to do. "I won't. There's not much to do while we travel, so I'm keeping my mind sharp."

"Is that a concern? Your mind dulling suddenly as we travel? So much that you fantasize about a toy rather than watch to guide your horse around rocks and pits?"

Eleanor glanced down at her hands. She must have been unconsciously moving them as she thought about the puzzle. "Treasure's a great horse. I barely have to guide him."

"I would never doubt the skill of the duke's men that trained it, but nonetheless, keep your eye focused ahead."

Eleanor clenched the saddle's pommel, chewing back the rising anger at being scolded like a child, even if it was from a military commander whose reputation saturated the room before her. Eleanor achieved her position through her merits and deserved the respect that came with that. She knew when to drive away the distractions for a goal, and traveling between locations where there was nothing but speculation on the other end was not such a time.

"When we camp," Ravell said a little quieter, more gently. "I should like to see the device that holds your attention."

Eleanor's eyes flicked to the saddle bag behind her containing, among other things, the puzzle and map. Ravell was already staring ahead by the time she looked back.

The silence hung between them again, but Eleanor risked breaking it. "Have you been to the Gardens?"

When there was no response, Eleanor watched the severe angles of the commander's jaw and nose, debating repeating the question.

"That is not a question to ask someone who has served," said Ravell at last.

"I take it you were stationed there to hold back the dead?" asked Eleanor.

"It is the first tour for every green cadet." Ravell kept her glassy eyes forward as she spoke. "And for many, their last. If a soldier possesses nerve enough to hold rank against a surge of risen dead, they can surely be trusted on any line in the kingdom."

Eleanor drummed her fingers on the saddle's pommel, seeing no clear route to turn the conversation from such grim statements. Though she fully accepted the fault for bringing it up in the first place.

"We will walk for an hour before making camp," said Ravell, pulling her horse to a stop and throwing a leg over to hop to the ground.

Eleanor followed suit. Her eye flicked to the saddlebag again, but this time with thoughts of the map within. In less than twelve hours, they'd enter Crystalwood Gardens. The sprawling boneyard, larger than most cities, was the site of dozens of brutal, bloody battles against the dead over the last two centuries.

Eleanor was not excited.

CHAPTER 12

IN SEARCH OF A KIOLIST

L ord Sebastian alternated between humming and whistling a jaunty tune. It wasn't anything Gabriela remembered hearing before, but perhaps the knight was composing something from the back of Brynmor's horse. She'd never asked exactly how a person whose only physical form was a set of well-polished leather armor might produce a whistle, but then, how could he talk at all? Her skeletal friends back home never spoke, at least not audibly, but they said enough with subtle body language. The cock of their pelvis as they stood or how high they lifted their feet as they walked told all the stories she needed to know about their lives.

As Gabriela understood it, the knight kept moving using very different magic than her boney friends. Magic she didn't yet understand, but not that she'd even tried to. Her mother kept a healthy stack of literature on Gabriela's reading list and assured her she would learn about the higher levels of magic once she was ready. Gabriela wondered when she would ever be ready for something at the level of adhering a person to a set of animated armor, but trusted her mother would let her know when and if she was.

Ahead, Venica led the party, riding Darius sidesaddle, her long, pale hair gathered in a loose braid and covered by a wide-brimmed hat. Lord Sebastian rode Harvey a dozen paces behind Gabriela, with Brynmor's lightly enchanted corpse again tucked away behind his chest-plate and under his helmet. To Gabriela's silent relief, Aura ignored the trail to rush through the scrubby grass, disturbing loose rocks and any wildlife she could find. That left Brynmor to sulk beside Gabriela. Still clinging to the mortal ways of movement, he walked a few feet off the trail, just at the range of the magic tethering the two of them.

"Chin up, Brynmor," said Gabriela. "We'll be at the Crystalwood Gardens soon enough. We get what we need there, then on to the fae ring. We'll have you back in your body and all wrongs forgiven before you know it."

Brynmor glanced back at Lord Sebastian, still humming and whistling away, at Gabriela, then back at the ground before him. "What's the point? I'm not who I thought I was. If the ritual requires an ancestor, and he…" He jerked a thumb back at the knight encasing his body, "…works for the ritual, then it's true. I'm the spawn of a bastard."

"No one seems to have noticed. You don't have to tell anyone, and I certainly won't."

"But I'll know, Gabriela. I'll know. Don't you see? My life, all my titles, everything is built on a lie."

"Seriously, Brynmor. If no one's pointed it out before, no one ever will. I'm sure there are bastards hanging on every branch and leaf of your family tree." She patted his shoulder.

"I don't expect you would understand."

Carmel whinnied, picking up on Brynmor's distress. Gabriela stroked the pony's neck. "I guess I don't know enough about noble bloodlines to see why it matters all that much. You learning some truth about your family tree doesn't change anything about who you are."

"Says the girl who doesn't know her parents."

"What…" Gabriela glanced at her mother, then back to Brynmor. "What does that mean? Yes, I don't know my father, but Mama—"

"Is the local queen of the dead, Gab. Queen Venica has been the star of folklore for generations. She's an ancient and powerful sorceress and clearly cannot be your actual birth mother."

Gabriela's fingers brushed at the stitching of Carmel's saddle. "That's hurtful."

"I'm sorry. Maybe once this is done, it would be good for you to leave the Deadvale. Come live with your own people."

"You want me to live with..." Gabriela's fingers froze when she understood the obvious, more profound meaning of Brynmor's offer. "I don't think it appropriate for me to come live with you. We only just met."

"Is that what... No, you..." Brynmor stammered.

"We have arrived," said Venica.

Gabriela looked ahead to the steep incline blocking any view of what lay beyond. The horses trudged on without hesitation, and at the top of the hill, the ground again fell away to a valley beyond. Crystalwood Gardens stretched to the horizon, intertwining paths cutting around massive mausoleums and above-ground crypts. Trees, vines, and moss fought to reclaim the cement and limestone, and after decades without use, nature was winning.

Carving a jagged line through the center, uncaring of whose graves it let sink into its bottomless nothing, was the Crack. Nature on their side was blackened and dry, but the distant shore held a green vibrancy that seemed to Gabriela almost obscene in a boneyard.

"Lord Sebastian's resting place is on the far side of the Crack," Venica said. "There is a crossing not far from where we now stand. I will lead us there and await your return."

"Await our return? You're not going with us, Mama?"

"No, my tiny. As I have told you before, the magics that sustain me require I remain on this side. You must needs cross without me and venture with Lord Sebastian at your side."

Gabriela chewed her lip while again brushing the saddle's stitching. "I guess I knew that." Her eyes traced a line weaving through the mottled coffins and crypts, to the Crack and beyond. "Lord Sebastian, how far into the other side is your... are you?"

"A valid question, Princess. It shouldn't be far if the Crack has not widened or shifted. Maybe a half hour's walk."

"That doesn't sound too bad," said Gabriela, looking again at her mother. What dangers could pop up in the round-trip hour apart?

"Look for a mausoleum with the winged star," said the knight.

Brynmor's attention snapped to Lord Sebastian. "Winged star? You were a Kiolist?"

"And I proudly am still," Lord Sebastian said with a waving flourish of his gloved hand.

Brynmor kept his eyes locked on the knight while sidling closer to Gabriela and lowering his voice to a conspiratorial tone. "I don't know how I feel about this. You know what they say about Kiolists."

"I don't know what they say about Kiolists," Gabriela said, not matching the other's low volume. "As I'm sure you've put together by now, Viscount, much of my knowledge of the world's politics is slightly outdated. Please, enlighten me."

Brynmor coughed, backing away a step. "They are regarded as... liberal with their social, political, and financial agendas. I was not aware any were allowed to be interred in Crystalwood Gardens, with the Ninth Grand Matriarch's vocal stance on Kiolists."

"Ninth?" Lord Sebastian laughed. "They were only on the second back in my day. Kiolists helped fund the start of your modern Reformed Church."

Brynmor raised a hand, cutting off anything further from the knight. "This is too much. To learn I am the probable descendant of a bastard, a Kiolist, *and* a slanderer against the Church. I... can't."

Lord Sebastian shrugged and turned to Venica. "Might I ask that you refresh your spells before we cross the Crack, Mum? I'd hate for our bigoted friend's corpse to seize up at a critical moment."

Venica sighed but nodded. "Unless... Gabriela, my love, this is yet another chance to eliminate this annoyance. The Gardens contain the greatest ossuaries in the world. The viscount should be honored to be laid to rest in any of them, beside the greatest minds and commanders of history."

"I'm sorry, Mama, but no. We must carry on with the resurrection to avoid consequences with his uncle."

"Do you, though?" The voice drifted from the air before Gabriela, and Aura faded into view. "I could snip him from you. I could do it while you nap, and you'd never know it was me." She tapped together both hands' index and middle fingers, mimicking scissors. "Snip, snip, snip."

"Stop that, Aura." Gabriela shifted to stand between the ghostly girl and Brynmor. "If anything happens to him, I'll know to blame you."

Aura tucked her snippy hands behind her back. "What if it really is an accident? What if I have nothing to do with him moving on?"

"Then you had best make sure that doesn't happen."

"Well," said Lord Sebastian, clapping his gauntlets together. "That's all settled now. Shall we go into the Gardens? Would you like me to take the lead, Mum?"

"No," said Venica. Darius started walking again, encouraging the other horses to follow. For a horse that had died decades ago, he still moved gracefully.

"Quiet," Aura said in a loud whisper. "So quiet. Quiet like the inn."

Darius slowed, and Venica turned on her saddle to face the ghost. "What do you mean by that, Aura?" Her fingers drifted to touch her locket.

Aura shrank back, wringing her hands together to speak in an actual whisper. "At the inn, all the ghosties were gone."

Venica considered the statement a moment before turning next to Gabriela. "Why is this the first I have heard of the matter?"

"I told you when I got back, Mama."

"When?"

"Just after introducing Brynmor. Or maybe it was before that?" Gabriela paused to remember the sequence of events in her mind. "Yes, after that. I mean, I meant to."

"You are quite certain of that? This was not another of your practiced conversations?"

Now that her mother had introduced doubt, Gabriela couldn't help but wonder if it had only been what she had planned to say.

Venica waved her off and turned back to the sprawling city of the dead. "It may be nothing or simply related to the solstice. Aura is correct. I sense only a fraction of the ghosts since last I visited the Gardens."

"When was that, Mum?" asked Lord Sebastian.

Venica did not reply except to click her tongue once, and Darius started walking again.

Gabriela lengthened the gap to her mother and brought Carmel beside Harvey.

"Is it that serious? The missing ghosts?" she asked the knight, keeping her voice low.

Lord Sebastian hummed thoughtfully. "I wouldn't dare speculate, myself. If your mother is concerned, I would be too."

Gabriela's hometown of Soulhaven was essentially a series of linked necropolises, with skeletons and others with a bit of flesh left to them freely roaming. Despite that, the home crypts were neat and orderly compared to the Crystalwood Gardens. Here, nearly every sarcophagus and mausoleum looked shattered and forced open. They passed solid iron gates ripped from their hinges, and crypts smashed open from the inside.

"By all the gods and saints," Brynmor said, tapping his chest.

"Fat lot they'll help you here," Lord Sebastian chuckled.

"The graves," Brynmor said, waving as they passed them. "They're all broken open."

"Haven't you been to the Gardens before?" Gabriela asked. "I'd think a big fancy marquess would have, for sure."

"I have, some years ago. Though it was from some distance as we passed on the other side of the Crack."

"The dead were eager for a stretch," said Lord Sebastian. "I doubt you could blame them."

Gabriela followed Brynmor's gaze across the landscape of shattered tombs as the ground slowly sloped downward.

"My tutors told me about their rising, but there must have been thousands," said Brynmor.

"Tens of thousands or more," said Lord Sebastian. "All fumbling around with no ill will, causing terror in the hearts of the king's people. Blessed be that the paladins were a marginally greater force."

Ahead, Darius stopped beside a steep hill of grass to their left. At its base, a tunnel bore into the darkness within.

"I leave you here," said Venica. "I have business to attend to. The bridge across the Crack is straight ahead by less time than a single flicker of the Eternal Flame."

"What's that, now?" asked Brynmor.

"A half hour," Gabriela hissed. "Shush."

Lord Sebastian dismounted and helped his queen to the ground. He removed his helmet, exposing Brynmor's lolling head, his wavy hair crusted with dried blood. Gabriela noticed the ghost marquess turn away with a fist in his mouth.

Venica swept a hand slowly across the air, gathering a filament of blue-white magic. She twisted the other arm and knotted the string before pressing it into Brynmor's forehead. His skin pulsed briefly with a more vibrant tone before settling back to a sullen hue. Lord Sebastian pushed his helmet back on.

The queen turned to her daughter. "Remain close to Lord Sebastian. Do not stop to talk with ghosts, risen skeletons, mummies, or the unlikely living person. Retrieve a sample of his remains and come straight back to this point. Wait for me here, should I still be beneath, but do not come in after me."

Gabriela swallowed hard, and Venica turned to the armored knight. "Lord Sebastian, keep her safe and see that my will is adhered to."

He raised a fist and bowed stiffly at the waist. "Yes, Mum."

Gabriela winced, watching the sharp bow. "All this movement can't be good for poor Brynmor's corpse. Maybe we should leave it here? It's not like someone will come by and accidentally bury him while we're gone."

"If I have a say in it, I'd rather my mortal shell stay near me," said Brynmor.

"It's not up to you, good sir," said Lord Sebastian. "Though that isn't a terrible idea. What do you say, Mum?"

Venica sighed. "We stand surrounded by a hundred thousand graves shattered by their inhabitants rising by the magics of the Deadvale. What will you do when upon your return, you find the viscount's body has stood and wandered away?"

"Excellent. Yes, of course, Mum."

"Can that happen?" Brynmor hissed.

"Don't worry," said Gabriela. "If it does, Lord Sebastian's strong. He'll keep it... you... from getting away."

Venica took a small pack from her steed's saddlebag and, without a word, glided to the mound's tunnel.

"Well then." Lord Sebastian clapped his gloves together. "Shall we? I must say, I'm rather excited for this. I can't remember when I last visited my grave." He hoisted himself onto Harvey's back.

"I never imagined hearing a man say those words outside of a dramatic play or an insane asylum," said Brynmor.

Gabriela watched her mother disappear into the burial mound's maw. "I know this is my fault that we're doing any of this, but I wasn't clear on why I must cross the Crack. Can't you go on your own, Lord Sebastian?"

"And let you stand here, missing all the fun?"

"I'm trying to ask a serious question. The last time I crossed it, things didn't end well."

"Right." Lord Sebastian made the sound of clearing his throat. "I think your mother is concerned I might get distracted. Unless robbers have been through... Well... There are some shiny things in my tomb. That aside, I readily admit my ability to remain focused is not my strongest attribute."

Gabriela grinned, thinking how readily she'd agree to that very statement. His whimsy might be one of her favorite things about the knight, but she knew how it grated on her mother. Which, to be honest, only added to his charm. How could anyone dare defy the Dread Queen Venica, Mistress of the Veil, Champion of the Deadvale? Her mother had so many grand titles, all predating Gabriela's life.

Not that she would ever let her mother hear her think such titles. She kept those secrets with the skeletons and ghosts at home, and she was good at keeping secrets.

"Well, come along," said Lord Sebastian, nudging Harvey. "The sooner we start, the sooner we return. The marquess will only get deader the longer we dally."

"Must everything be a joke with you?" Brynmor moaned.

"Yes. I am a Kiolist, after all." Lord Sebastian tapped his helmet in salute.

Gabriela didn't know enough about the different religions or ways of life to understand the conflict but appreciated the fun the old knight was having. She paid little mind to the passage of time, so focused she was on the intricate carvings over each smashed door and crumbling wall. Lord Sebastian and Brynmor bickered ahead of her, but Gabriela only thought of who would have risen from each crypt. What were their stories in life? And what new adventures had they been up to since? Did they have goals and ambitions?

Luckily, Carmel was paying attention and stopped before running into Harvey's backend. Gabriela shook from her reveries to look up at Brynmor's groaning complaints.

"Another tiny bridge? What do you have against a stout construction of iron?" He stood at the edge of the Crack, only a few dozen feet across at this point, near what might have once been a great spanning bridge. Now, the wood and mud structure looked like the dry vines held it together more than anything built with purpose.

"What is your worry, good sir? It's unlikely you'll fall to your death."

Brynmor said nothing but leaned to peer into the depths.

"You should leave the horses here," said Brynmor.

"Pish," said Lord Sebastian, dropping to the ground. "Sappers tried to take down this bridge decades ago. Look, you can see the burn marks from their explosions." He pointed to logs underfoot as they crossed. "That they failed is a testament to the quality of past generations. The horses will be fine."

A log cracked, and he stumbled to keep his footing.

"Never mind that. We'll be at my tomb forthwith."

Safe on the other side, Gabriela paused to glance around. The tombs on this side of the Crack were pristine, other than a usual level of wear from age. That wasn't what caught her attention, however.

"Princess? Is something the matter?"

"That was too easy. Where is Aura?"

As if hearing her name whispered, the ghost appeared in a flash of green light.

"Aura, where have—"

"We're not alone," gasped the ghost, her eyes unnaturally wide.

"Not alone?" Lord Sebastian stepped nearer. "Who did you see?"

Aura held up a waggling finger on each hand. "Two ladies coming this way. On horses. One looks scary."

"Coming this way..." Lord Sebastian glanced at Gabriela. Despite his helm, she could sense his concern. "Last I knew, the living folk kept their patrols to the edges. I wouldn't think anyone would come this far in. Aura, keep an eye on them, please. Do what you can to steer them from us."

Aura grinned a little too wide than would look natural for a living person, tilting her head with a quick nod. She slid backward, disappearing in a blend of mist.

"Two ladies on horses, a scary one," said Lord Sebastian, turning to Brynmor. "Friends of yours, good sir?"

"Certainly not by that description alone."

"Naturally. Come then, let's make all haste. I'd rather not encounter a scary lady while smuggling a pompous, fifteen-stone man inside me."

"Thirteen," Brynmor grumbled.

Lord Sebastian patted his belly with both hands. "Right, yes, no matter. Let's be on with it."

CHAPTER 13

PINNED IN THE CRYPT

"He's near." Eleanor consulted her compass. She hadn't gone more than a few seconds without checking at it over the last hour.

Ravell half glanced at her, then back to lead her mount through the twisting paths between crypts. As they entered this section of the Gardens not long after noon, the commander explained how she had been stationed farther north, and that this area was foreign to her. Not that a map or previous experience would have helped much, given how the place snaked and branched like a labyrinth. Eleanor gave a silent thanks that the church decreed cremation was now the appropriate form of corpse disposal. A cemetery's just a waste of space.

A stone head toppled from a building's roof, rolling into their path. Ravell's horse nickered, but she kept it from reacting further.

"I don't know if this is a good idea, Commander. If the dead have him, aren't we meeting them where they're strongest?"

Ravell rolled her neck. "If the marquess is as near as you claim, as you have been claiming for the last hour, he is on this side of the Crack or close to it. I would not venture deep into the Deadvale without a dozen paladins at my command."

Then this entire mission should have waited until we had those paladins from the king. Highgate isn't making much effort to get his nephew back.

"So you're saying it's now or never," said Eleanor. "What if I was wrong about everything? Maybe it wasn't agents of the Deadvale that took the marquess. Maybe whoever kidnapped him just fled into the Deadvale. No, maybe he wasn't even kidnapped. Maybe he just wanted to escape his duties, and me, and fled into the Deadvale. He's just crossing back here."

"No one would think to escape *into* the Deadvale, Miss Lane. No one of sound mind would cross the Crack unless they are of the other side."

Despite the warmth of the afternoon sun and clear sky, a sudden blast of freezing air slammed into Eleanor's side, nearly tossing her from Treasure. She clawed for the saddle horn, but the horse bucked, and she lost grip. Eleanor landed hard on her side, her head missing the edge of a sarcophagus by inches.

Treasure bolted back the way they'd come.

Ahead, Commander Ravell's horse bucked. She tossed herself from the saddle, landing in a smooth roll, as the horse streaked by Eleanor, its eyes white with terror.

"By the goddess and all the saints." Ravell pushed to her feet and offered a hand down to Eleanor. "What in all the hells was that?" She stopped to sniff at the air.

Eleanor could smell it too, something like a pile of vegetables long forgotten in the back of the cellar. She held a palm across her nose. "What is that?"

Ravell ignored the question, craning her neck with poorly disguised anger toward where the horses had disappeared. "There runs our food and supplies."

And my map and a dozen guld worth of dust and reagents. And all the guld, for that matter. Eleanor patted the satchel at her hip, glad to have not lost everything. It contained her jeweler's tools, representing most of her magic craft. "Were there anything other than skeletons and husks at the front lines, Commander?"

Ravell slowly turned her attention back to Eleanor. "Is that not enough?"

"I mean..." Eleanor waved her hands, trying to find the word. Realizing she still held her compass, she tucked it in her satchel. "Non-corporeal things. Spirits."

Ravell rolled her eyes dramatically. "Nonsense. Come, you said we were close. The horses will wait for us outside the Gardens." She didn't meet Eleanor's eyes as she drew her sword, an unwieldy thing of dark steel, and turned to continue deeper into the cemetery.

Eleanor glanced back toward the horses. She distrusted burial sites as much as the next sane person, but the clear blue sky and heavy sword in the commander's confident grip calmed her nerves for a while. The fetid cabbage stink lingered, along with a chill that the sun did nothing to warm, eliciting a shiver up her arms. There was a reason anyone who died in living memory was cremated. Now she stood surrounded by the quiet dead that, just by chance, were buried on the side of the Crack that hadn't become the Deadvale.

She shook out the tingling in her hands and jogged after Ravell, pulling her compass from her bag. The needle twitched wildly, vibrating erratically over almost a full radian.

"Comman—"

Ravell clasped her free hand over Eleanor's mouth and wrenched them both to huddle against the smooth side of a sarcophagus. Only then did she glance up from the brass compass and hear the nearby voices.

"Maybe it's good that she hasn't come back yet? Maybe she scared them off," came the voice like a young woman's. They sounded no more than twenty feet away.

"Perhaps something shiny attracted her attention," said a deep voice, crisp and lofty, immediately reminding Eleanor of the duke, if the duke had any mirth in his tone.

There was a pause, silent, except for Eleanor's blood pounding in her ears. Ravell finally released her hand, adjusting her crouch to perhaps spring to action.

"Ha, yes indeed, good sir," said the man. His laugh sounded hollow and forced. "The marquess may be on to something, Princess."

Eleanor froze and noticed Ravell tense just as quickly.

Marquess? Why couldn't I hear Brynmor's response if he's there?

Ravell pivoted, pointed two fingers at her eyes, then at Eleanor's, then waved her hand as if tossing something over the tomb separating them from the speakers.

Eleanor nodded, catching the meaning. She unsnapped the pouch at her hip as quickly as she dared, taking out a single smooth stone. After a prayer she'd repeated a thousand times, she closed her right eye and touched the stone to her eyelid, then tossed the stone gently around the edge of the sarcophagus. Closing her left and opening her right, it took a heartbeat to orient to the image sent to her from the stone.

Mostly upside-down, inverted left to right, and in a grainy grayscale, she saw two figures huddled behind a coffin and two others standing before a crypt entrance. Tied off beside them were a pony and a dark horse that Eleanor recognized immediately, despite the fuzzy image, as the marquess'. She focused on the two for a moment. A girl with long, light hair wearing an odd frilly dress and a taller person in a complete set of ornate, antique leather armor covering every inch of skin, complete with a helmet. An odd darkness took up space beside the pair, but there was no sign of the marquess.

She shook out of the vision, blinking back to full color and the commander's expectant countenance. Unsure of the proper military sign language, Eleanor held up two fingers and shook her head once. She could hardly mime the horses as well.

Ravell nodded, tightening the grip on her sword. With a sharp inhale, she leaped to her feet, vaulting over the tomb. "Go no farther, dastardly..."

Eleanor peeked over the edge to see the commander alone in front of the crypt door. The horses whinnied once but otherwise ignored them.

"Who did you see, Miss Lane?"

"A man in leather armor and a young woman."

"Were either armed?"

"I didn't see a sword or the like on either. They may have daggers."

"Or profane magics. Where did they go?" Ravell asked, relaxing her stance.

The pair looked to the open crypt.

"Kiolists," Ravell said, noting the winged star over the door. She made no effort to hide the disdain in her tone. "You heard them speak of the marquess, Miss Lane?"

Eleanor nodded, stepping around to approach Brynmor's horse. "I saw only the woman and man. The marquess must have slipped into the crypt ahead of the pair."

"That must be it. The two forced the marquess ahead of them. He is likely terrified, meekly speaking his words. That is why we could not hear him. Viscount

Brynmor may be of noble blood but does not possess all his uncle's more noble characteristics." Ravell paused, grimacing, adding quickly, "Do not repeat what I have said."

Eleanor nodded again, biting back a grin at finally seeing cracks in the commander's shell. Apparently, she wasn't completely, irrevocably loyal to the upper class.

Ravell sheathed her sword. "They have gone for something below. We will lead the horses away and prepare an ambush."

Eleanor approached the crypt's door to read the plaque. "There are a few noble house names here," she said.

Ravell grunted. "The royal line has not always been the most discerning. Not like it is today." Her eyes flitted to the winged star before she moved to untie the horses.

It was an argument Eleanor had heard and participated in dozens of times. While it wasn't the main reason they asked her to leave the academy, it was certainly one of them. The public debate was always over Kiolists not expressing their belief and devotion to the goddess Elysara. They chose instead for happiness derived from within rather than from the goddess, which everyone knew was just silly. How could anyone truly be happy if the goddess didn't make them so?

The larger issue came when Kiolists and others performed magic without first speaking a prayer to the goddess. That was the profane magic that caused the Crack and Deadvale, if the church's scholars were to be believed.

"Lane!" Ravell hissed.

Eleanor jumped and ran to join Ravell around the corner of another crypt.

CHAPTER 14

LORD SEBASTIAN OFFERS A HAND

Gabriela shivered, rubbing her hands against her forearms. "I'm sorry you're in a place like this, Lord Sebastian." The steep, curling stairs from the surface left the trio in a chamber smaller than her bedroom. Brass plaques lined the walls while seven stone caskets choked the floor space.

"Sorry? Why is that?"

"It's just so..." Gabriela turned a slow circle to collect her thoughts. "Dead."

Lord Sebastian laughed. "That is, as hard as it is to believe, an attribute most people look for in a grave. 'Restful' may be a better term."

She shrugged, staying close to the stairs.

"This must be surreal for you," said Brynmor.

Lord Sebastian moved to one of the stone caskets, spreading his gloved hands over the top. "Perhaps a bit. It reminds me a little of going back to visit your childhood home. You know things will be different, but you hope to see some spark of recognition."

"Your grave is like your childhood home?"

"No," Lord Sebastian chuckled. "No, that would be silly. I mean that I hope to see some recognition in what remains of my remains."

Brynmor's face twisted with disgust as he took a step backward.

"Might you give me a hand, Princess?"

Gabriela shuffled forward to put her hands beside the knight's. The engraving across the top read, "Sebastian Filmont Rafferty, Son and Brother," with a date range below.

"Just son and brother?" she asked. "Don't they usually say beloved or cherished?"

"Hardly surprising. I'm sure they paid by the letter and didn't want to waste my fortune here."

"Fortune?" Brynmor asked, stepping forward again, eyebrows lifted.

"Nevermind that. Princess?"

Gabriela shoved against the lid beside the knight. As she was about to suggest needing some tool to lift it first, the lid lurched a few inches.

"Having to take care of you within me does little to make this easier, good sir," Lord Sebastian grunted. Gabriela looked over at him, wondering not for the first time why the armored knight would ever get winded or exhausted. Perhaps it was all performative.

"It would have been fine to carry me on a litter," said Brynmor. "I can't imagine all the wear you're putting on my joints in there."

"I would be more worried about my hair, were I you."

"What?" Brynmor moaned.

"Worry not."

Lord Sebastian kept his helmet turned upward as he and Gabriela gave the lid another shove. She looked down at a collapsed and shattered skeleton garbed in scraps of dull cloth. No jewelry or adornments sparkled from the gray dust.

With a long, audible breath, Lord Sebastian looked down, then steadied himself on the edge of his coffin.

"I jest," he whispered, "but it is humbling. I have carried on as a suit of armor for decades, where I have surely grown and changed. Would anyone recognize me from when I wore flesh?"

Gabriela put her hand over his leather gauntlet and squeezed.

"What if the process that bound me such changed me irrevocably? What if who I am now is nothing like this man was in life?" The knight pushed back to stand a bit taller. "Well, either my grave was burgled, or my next of kin ignored my wishlist of things to be buried with. Sorry for the disappointment. It looks like it's just me in there."

"You're all we came for, Lord Sebastian." Gabriela tried to sound comforting but worried her delivery was flat. She cleared her throat. "Mama didn't tell me how much we need."

"A speck will do, Mum said. I thought she was rather clear on that."

Gabriela frowned, not remembering her mother saying anything of the sort.

"Best to be over-prepared." Lord Sebastian reached into his coffin, taking his left hand in both of his gloves. He turned, offering it to Gabriela, who quickly fumbled a bag from her belt. "That was my second favorite hand. I don't think I like the marquess quite enough to give him my best."

A low hiss cut the silence as green light flooded the stone coffin.

"Get out of there, Aura," Lord Sebastian scolded.

She rose through the lid, circled the room once in a blur, and settled between the three. She held her fists to her mouth, holding back a wracking giggle.

"What is it, Aura?" Gabriela asked. "And where were you? Did you get the two off our trail?"

"Their horsies go skitter away."

"And did the ladies go on them?" Lord Sebastian asked.

"No." Aura paused with her mouth agape, then grinned and continued. "The scary one almost saw me. I think she saw him." She jerked a thumb at Brynmor.

Gabriela and Lord Sebastian glanced at each other and back to Aura. "What? How?" Gabriela asked.

"Magic." The ghost waggled her fingers.

"I wonder who they are," said Gabriela.

"Tall lady." Aura waved a hand over her head. "Shiny, shiny armor and a big sword. Pretty hair. Short lady." Her hand waved at waist level. "Big hat. Lots of fancy metal things."

"This is bad," said Brynmor. "The tall lady, does she have dark skin?"

Aura scratched her head with both hands. "Colors are hard."

Brynmor rubbed a hand over his jaw. "This is... Perhaps very good, perhaps disastrous."

105

"You know the women by that description?" asked Lord Sebastian.

"Agents of my uncle, Commander Valoria Ravell and Miss Eleanor Lane. That they are here means my uncle is aware of my disappearance. That it is only the two of them means he isn't fully alarmed. He doesn't know what happened to me."

"What do we do?" asked Gabriela.

"They will want your body at all costs," said Lord Sebastian. "They will have no interest in allowing our plans for a resurrection ritual to continue. Mayhap we can throw them off. Tell them they just missed you."

Brynmor shook his head. "Miss Lane is an artificer with a trove of magic items used to track and spy on me."

"Artificer?" Gabriela asked.

"She creates magic gadgets. Useful, as my uncle would agree, but borderline profane." He waved a hand to continue. "The point is I, or rather you, Lord Sebastian, would not fool her. Her devices would point straight at you, at what's within you."

"You," said Lord Sebastian, patting his chest plate.

"Perhaps I can speak with them? Convince them to abandon whatever brings them here."

Gabriela scoffed. "I doubt they can see and hear ghosts as I can. How does Miss Eleanor track you? Do you wear an enchanted bracelet? Maybe I can counter it."

Brynmor shrugged. "Maybe one of my rings? I never worried much because Miss Lane did an excellent job as an assistant of sorts. It's Commander Ravell with her that causes me to worry."

He turned away again when Lord Sebastian tugged off his left glove, exposing Brynmor's gloved hand. Gabriela prodded his fingers through the leather, feeling the metal rings on each digit.

"How do you close your fist with such huge rings?" She asked. "I don't sense any magic from them, though maybe I don't know what to look for. Where else can I check?"

Brynmor whirled on her with his gloved hand raised. "I'll thank you to keep your hands from me!"

Gabriela raised a hand to brush her knuckles across Brynmor's ghostly cheek. "I wish I remembered exactly what you said to me at the top of the steps, or I'd repeat it unironically now." She grinned.

Brynmor twisted his face from her touch.

Lord Sebastian chuckled, then cleared his throat. "Enough flirting, you two. Aura, where are the two women now?"

When there was no immediate response, the three glanced around the tomb.

"Aura?" Gabriela called. After another few heartbeats, she let out a long sigh. "For being fettered to me, she sure does come and go as she pleases."

"Her leash is lengthy," said Lord Sebastian.

"That and she likes to hide in plain sight," said Gabriela.

Brynmor stamped his foot, making no noise. "We can't stand around in a tomb all day. We must return to your mother, Gabriela. Now, how can we get past the women? Lord Sebastian, can you fight?"

"Of course I can fight." He pulled his leather gauntlet back over Brynmor's corpse hand. "I was a knight of the realm, proficient in martial and magical warfare."

"Excellent, then you can hold them back, at least for a moment while—"

"But I have no weapon and can't use magic in this form. Even if I suddenly could use magic, I haven't in centuries. My skills would be quite rusty."

Brynmor balled his fists with an annoyed grunt. "Some protector you are that doesn't even carry a sword!"

"Well," Lord Sebastian leaned down to peek into his coffin. "I was supposed to be buried with my two magic swords and a handful of shiny trinkets, but it's just me in there."

"Just me in there..." Gabriela repeated, a smile growing across her lips. "That gives me an idea. Let's try out your skills as a silver-tongued bard, Lord Sebastian."

"I don't know where you're going with this, but I'm all in."

CHAPTER 15

SWIRLING EDDIES

"How long has it been?" Ravell drummed her nails on her knee.

Eleanor pulled out her brass pocket watch embossed with her father's initials. "Twenty-four minutes." The pony stamped his foot beside her.

"What could be taking them?" Ravell's fingers twitched, drumming a staccato on her sword's pommel, the blade resting across her knees. Eleanor caught herself staring at it as they huddled, legs cramping, across from the crypt's entrance. The cutting edge of the length of dark steel was an odd, wavy design, and its end, rather than coming to a point good for stabbing, was squared off. "Maybe there's another exit."

Eleanor didn't think there would be, but didn't know enough about mortuary architecture to speak up.

"Maybe they mean to stay the night down there?" Eleanor offered.

Ravell grunted. "Who knows what foul plans they have for the marquess. You are certain about your instrumentation?"

Eleanor had checked her compass and the enchantments set up on it a dozen times in the last day. She was as sure about their accuracy as she was about anything else. "Extremely certain."

"I must take action," Ravell announced, pushing on her knees to stand. She immediately dropped again when echoing voices reached them from the crypt's entrance. The man in full leather armor emerged, followed by the young woman with pale hair a few years younger than Eleanor. She laughed and pushed at the man's arm.

"Oh, Lord Brynmor, you are hilarious," she said rather loudly, wiping a tear from her eye.

"Hello then, where have the horses gone to?" The man's scratchy voice sounded muffled behind the helmet. He whistled, making Harvey nicker restlessly.

Ravell stood, her huge sword ready. Eleanor rose a heartbeat later.

"What is the meaning of this? What have you done with Viscount Brynmor Highgate?" the commander called.

"Commander Valoria Ravell, what a pleasant surprise and honor to see you here!" said the man with overflowing excitement. "And Miss Eleanor Lane. It seems you've caught up with me at last."

Eleanor opened her mouth to respond but wasn't sure what to say. She glanced down at the compass still in her hand, confirming it pointed at the man in full leather armor.

"Where is the marquess?" said Ravell with a step forward, raising her sword an inch. The girl shied behind the man.

"Whatever do you mean, Commander? Tis I. This armor is new, of course. A present from the local royalty." He spun a quick circle. "Ah, might I introduce Lady Gabriela Marwol. Lady Marwol, Commander Valoria Ravell and Miss Eleanor Lane. They work for my uncle, the duke I told you about."

Could it be? It does sound oddly like him, perhaps with a head cold muffled by the full-face helmet. The Brynmor I know would never wear something to obscure his hair.

"What happened to you in Mytara, Lord Highgate? I found... My trail went oddly cold," said Eleanor. The discarded leather glove nearly called out from her pocket.

"Nothing of interest," he said, whistling again. Harvey pulled at the lead loosely wrapped around a tombstone decoration, freeing himself to clomp over to the man. The pony followed. "I met Lady Marwol, who arranged for this mastercraft armor, and she has since been taking me on a stunning tour of this province. Please, Commander, lower your sword."

That sounds like the marquess, but he sounded like a completely different man before they entered the crypt. What about the glove and the vision of him falling down the stairs? If he has new armor, maybe someone made off with his old duds, only to quickly meet their demise?

That possibility hit Eleanor hard. Of course the marquess was fine. All that blood belonged to someone else. Someone stole his glove and then died. The marquess told Jon and Job to take a few days off, and they, always anxious to shirk responsibility, did. Eleanor rushed back to the duke with false information, stirring up all this commotion because of her untested magic.

Ravell's blade lowered slightly, but she kept it firmly in her grip. "I never heard about local royalty in the outer provinces, My Lord. This is very odd. Might I see you take off your helmet?"

Viscount Brynmor scoffed. "How dare you presume to give me orders. You may certainly not, specifically now, because you asked. How very presumptuous. I have the better part of a mind to speak with your superiors about this impropriety."

Lady Marwol gently elbowed Viscount Brynmor.

"Right, we must be off," said the marquess, hoisting himself onto Harvey's back and Lady Marwol mounted her pony. "Commander, you may return to my uncle with a full report of my well-being. Tell him my mission to the south is meeting with grand success; it's quite life-changing here. Miss Lane, you may take some time for yourself. I'll be back to Mytara sometime after the solstice." Lady Marwol started toward the Crack atop her pony, and Viscount Highgate twitched the reins to start Harvey after her.

Ravell glanced sidelong at Eleanor, and she could read the distrust in the commander's eyes. The commander jogged in front of the viscount's horse, stopping him with a hand on his nose. "Marquess, I cannot allow this. By order of the duke, I am to return you to his presence immediately."

"Again with presuming to give me orders," the viscount scoffed. "Have you a written notice of my uncle's demands?"

Eleanor had all the papers to allow her free movement about the duchy and surrounding provinces. However, she'd left it all in Treasure's bag, and there was nothing specific to the duke's most recent orders. She assumed the commander lacked such written authority as well, especially with how non-specific the duke was about the condition of his nephew's well-being.

"My Lord," Eleanor called, jogging up beside Commander Ravell. "I insist you tell us where you are going. My tracking magics are faltering this close to the Deadvale, and we should all agree about not crossing the Crack."

The viscount scoffed behind his helmet. "Come now, Miss Lane. I don't need you treating me like you're my nanny. Besides, that would be a discourteous insult to Lady Marwol. I trust her to lead me wherever her tour takes us. Everything is in hand."

"Nothing is *in hand* this close to the Crack and Deadvale, My Lord," said Ravell.

"Lady Marwol!" Eleanor shouted after the woman on her pony. "Please, come speak with us."

The young woman glanced back but didn't slow her mount.

"If you willingly refuse your uncle's orders," said Ravell, "I insist you have an escort in case of risen dead."

The viscount tutted. "If you insist, but you must follow on foot." He swung the reins to guide his horse around the two.

"My Lord!" Ravell hissed, lunging forward to put a hand on the viscount's boot. "By your uncle's name, I cannot allow you to go off to such obvious danger with this mystery woman."

Viscount Brynmor stared down at her hand until she plucked it away. "I go where I must for my station, for my uncle's, the duke's, name and honor. So be it if you believe Lady Marwol has ensorcelled me with her wiley enchantments. I will continue on my tour, and I suspect you will continue to harass me. You have no jurisdiction over me, just as I, apparently, have none over you." Harvey continued after the pony.

Ensorcelled? Enchantments? Not that I often hear the marquess speak, but those are larger words that I thought would come out of him.

Ravell fell into step a few paces behind the horse. "My Lord, your uncle's command was clear."

"As were his to me. It seems we are at an impasse," called the viscount without glancing back.

Eleanor jogged up beside her. "What do we do, Commander? We can't let him follow some mystery woman into the Deadvale, right?"

Ravell chewed her lip, her brow pinched with thought and concern. "No," she breathed. "If the marquess seems set on crossing the Crack, I will escalate my efforts. My duties are to the duke before the marquess, but I see a benefit to understanding this situation and how it may play out."

"What if the marquess spurs his horse to a gallop?"

"I considered that. We take the Lady Marwol as a prisoner—her pony couldn't be that fast—and use your devices to locate the marquess again."

Eleanor grimaced at the thought of taking the unknown noble prisoner but appreciated the commander having a plan in place.

"They won't outrun me." Ravell swept back the tunic from her right hip, putting her hand on the butt of another weapon there. A pistol? Eleanor stumbled a step at seeing it, wavering somewhere between awe that the commander would have access to such a rare weapon, fear for the terrible destruction she heard they could cause, both to victim and user, and an itching desire to disassemble the firearm to sketch its components carefully. The chemical properties of black powder especially intrigued her.

She tore her eyes from the pearl inlay curling through the heavy maple. *Surely she couldn't mean to shoot the marquess or this Lady Marwol. Who could this young woman be? What if the viscount's flippant remark about her ensorcelling him was some poorly coded cry for help?*

Most of Eleanor's tools and reagents ran off with her horse, but not everything. She put her compass back in the safety of her hip pouch to pull out her wire goggles. By some stroke of luck or a specific blessing from one or more goddesses, they were saved from shattering in her fall from horseback. She fished in the pouch for the interchangeable lenses, which hadn't fared as well. They had all come free of the small carrying pouch, and the first two she removed were cracked and worthless. She dropped those in her wake with a curse. The next lens, a nearly opaque red, was what she was looking for, and it showed no signs of damage. She slipped it into the right frame of her goggles with a solid snap and mumbled a prayer to the goddess.

Eleanor kept her right eye closed while pulling the wire of the frames around her ears. After a steadying breath, she swapped her eyes.

The world pitched with crimson swirls. Whorls of sluggish energy spiraled beneath her feet, collecting into eddies like foamy waves at low tide.

The very essence of magic, the goddess's gift given form.

With a deep breath, she looked forward again, seeing the commander as a dim smudge a few paces ahead. Beyond her, the viscount atop his horse made her stumble a step. He radiated a brilliant green, brighter than a Mabon tree. But more, Lady Marwol shone just as bright, if not more so, with two filaments of energy trailing from her, both ending in dark smudges.

I need to modify my lenses once we stop walking. Her mind left the fantasies of dissecting Ravell's firearm to consider how she might detect the truth about the armored viscount's aura and this mystery woman. *I've never seen armor so saturated with magic. What would the purpose even be?* She hoped for a chance to scan the interior of the armor for runes or circles of power.

The swirling eddies of magic slowed their spin with each step, and Eleanor knew action would soon be needed. There were few magical theoreticians throughout history, but Eleanor once posited the direction of magic's flow would reverse itself beyond the Crack. The lenses she used to view the world's magic were unique, and the enchantments powering them were exceptionally rare. While part of her looked forward to exploring the thesis that resulted in her expulsion from the academy, the commander made clear what actions she would take before then.

"We are within a quarter mile of the Crack," Ravell whispered. "Prepare yourself."

Eleanor couldn't guess what the commander intended her to do but kept any questions to herself. Still walking with only one eye open, she slid a finger along the edge of her glasses, reducing the effect of the magic sense, and making it easier to see the debris on the path before her.

The eddies of magic were swirling faster, growing brighter, despite the adjustment to her glasses. This wasn't right. They should be slowing as the Crack—

Magic flowed into Lady Marwol, spiraling along the ground in tight rivers, arching up the pony to pour into the young woman. It left her in pulsing waves the color of dried seaweed.

Eleanor switched eyes, grabbing Ravell's arm, but missed in the resulting disorientation from the sudden shift in her vision.

"She's casting a spell!" she yelled, too late. The ground lurched once, throwing Eleanor to her knees. Lady Marwol and the marquess whipped their mounts to a gallop in the same instant. Ravell ripped the pistol from its holster, leveled her aim, and with a single deafening crack, the back of Viscount Bynmor's helm burst apart. He only glanced back, unphased by the head wound.

Ravell threw down the firearm, pulling her sword in a smooth motion as she sprinted after the horses. Eleanor pushed up to give chase but saw in her red lens how magic reverberated from the crypts surrounding their path. Motion to her right, a skeletal hand clawing from a patch of grass. Ravell saw it, too, slowing her pace. A half dozen skeletons shuffled from tombs on either side of the path. Behind the pair, too. They were surrounded. Beyond, the two crossed the Crack on a thin bridge.

Eleanor thought she saw another figure on the far side, but the dead pressed closer, denser. Rotted forms with scraps of hair and clothing hanging from their broken forms, some with patches of gray skin clinging, lurched to form a tight circle around them. Eleanor bumped her back against the commander's, helplessly considering what work of magic could be effective in this situation. She thought of none that didn't require an hour's preparation and especially none she had the reagents for in her pouch.

Unless...

Eleanor watched the magic pulsing from the risen dead.

"Why do they not attack?" The commander's voice sounded strained, even with a slight tinge of fear.

No, she can't be afraid.

But the commander was correct. The dead maintained their posture, swaying slightly out of sword range.

"Go for the marquess as I create a path."

Back-to-back, Eleanor could feel the commander tensing, ready to spring to action. It had to be now.

"Wait," said Eleanor

She channeled the energy into herself, gagging at the revolting taint of the dead. There was just so much magic in such a small area. Her little toys and trinkets required a splash of magic to animate. She enchanted her compass and other tools over weeks or months. This was an onslaught, a tidal wave of magic slamming against her, and all she could do was channel it upward in a worthless beam of light.

Is this the true power of the profane? This waste of magic?

Eleanor barely began to bleed off the awesome glut of power when the skeletons dropped like dolls with their strings cut. They collapsed in heaps around the pair, their bones clattering off to mix with every other body around them, creating a ten-foot-long ossuary ring.

"Brilliant show, Miss Lane," Ravell beamed. "After them."

Eleanor watched the commander scramble across the bones with surprising dexterity for a person wearing plate armor.

I only began to bleed off the magic. Our rescue had nothing to do with my effort. Still...

"Miss Lane!" Ravell shouted, shaking Eleanor from her thoughts. Beyond the mound of bones, the commander waved her to follow. Maybe two hundred feet more was the Crack, narrower here and with an unsafe bridge spanning it. There was no sign of the marquess or mystery magic woman.

"This is beyond us, Commander," she said, picking across the bones more carefully than Ravell had. "They've gone into the Deadvale, and the marquess is clearly compromised. We should report back to the duke. He can call for the king's paladins."

Ravell sheathed her sword as she closed the distance between them. "My orders are clear, Miss Lane. As loathe as I may be to enter the Deadvale, I have no choice. Nor do you. I require your magics to follow, and if the marquess is ensorcelled, it happened when it was your duty to protect him."

"My job was never about protecting Brynmor, not physically. I'm not a guard. I only clean up his messes and keep him from the gossip papers." She turned, circling the ring of bone, stooping to pick up the discarded pistol. "I won't go in there." She hoped the firm set of her jaw and the fists on her hips matched her fierce intention.

"You would let *Viscount* Brynmor and the entirety of the Highgate line die for your cowardice?"

Eleanor crossed her arms. "This isn't cowardice. There's nothing cowardly about it, Commander. This is beyond my pay grade and, quite frankly, not my job. You exist on the dream of loyalty, but I get a monthly stipend for a job done. Going above and beyond gets me nothing."

Ravell stroked a thumb across her lips, eyes narrowing to consider Eleanor. "Is it only about guld, Miss Lane? The duke would see you well compensated for the return of his nephew."

Eleanor held up the pistol, noticing the scuffs along the barrel and hairline crack in the grip from the commander's hasty discarding of something that no longer served her. "You halfway blew off his head. Are you prepared to go against whatever terrible profane magics are at play here?" She dropped the pistol into her pouch, gesturing at the mounds of bones. "She raised a small army while riding a pony at full speed. How do you intend to fight her if she chooses to attack, not just delay us? Following is pointless. Brynmor is gone, raised as some terrible agent of the dead."

Commander Ravell said nothing. After a few breaths, she closed her eyes and turned away. "May I borrow your compass?"

"It wouldn't do you any good. It requires constant monitoring."

"Such monitoring that requires training or your special touch, I assume?"

Eleanor nodded. "It took me most of a year to make this. It's very delicate."

Ravell sucked in a quick breath. "I admire your conviction, Miss Lane. I basely disagree with your decision but appreciate how you adhere to it. Please, then, return to Duke Highgate. Tell him what has occurred and petition for the king's paladins. Farewell... Eleanor."

She never met Eleanor's gaze as she turned back toward the bridge spanning the Crack.

Is she seriously trying to guilt me into risking everything to save a dead man? A man hardly worth saving while alive? And using my first name like that? Who would think a storied military commander would use emotional manipulation as a tactic?

Eleanor watched the commander through a few more paces, her fists balling, yet she didn't immediately turn away.

She's going to her death. I don't care how masterful she may be with that sword; she's going against unknown forces of the dead.

That is, if she doesn't immediately lose them in the Deadvale, to wander helplessly until she starves. And she would starve. She's too bullheaded to admit she can't find food on the other side of the Crack.

With Lady Marwol's spell ended, the eddies of magic resumed their natural flow, clearly slowing the closer Eleanor followed them toward the Crack. She saw herself standing at the front of a packed auditorium, a handful of her least favorite professors in the front row, the dean himself sitting in the center wearing a resplendent white robe he bought just for this occasion, all in rapt attention. They hung on every word as she described in excruciating detail the operation of magic on the other side of the Crack, casting new light on the nature of magic outside of the divine. At least, in theory. They sat through the delivery of her paper, exited quietly, and asked her to leave the academy less than a week later.

The duke took a chance in hiring her when no one else would. Not that she owed anything to the man, but perhaps she owed herself the chance to test her theories, to fully break from the molds all those professors tried to pour her into.

Eleanor mumbled a curse, striking after the commander. "Valoria, wait up."

Chapter 16

Tugs on the Ghosties

"F aster, Princess, faster!" Lord Sebastian's encouragement was utterly unnecessary.

"Fast, fast, faster we go!" Aura's trilling, even less so.

"Gods and saints," said Brynmor beside her, apparently forgetting he thought he had to walk, as he floated beside Carmel, facing backward. "What did you do?"

Gabriela couldn't look back. Looking back meant having to answer that question. The dark powers came too quickly, too easily, flooding into her like a burst levee and surging out just as rapidly. She barely had a chance to shape the magic as it ripped by her, pulsing into the unbroken graves and crypts.

She focused instead on the bridge directly ahead, urging more speed from Carmel than she ever had before. Beyond the Crack, her mother stood beside Darius. She held her horse's reins in one hand, but in the other, she held some object high overhead. A skull?

Their horses' hooves beat across the bridge without the concerns from their previous crossing.

The pair pulled up beside her.

"Mother! We— They— We have to run!"

"Gabriela," Venica said smoothly in contrast to Gabriela's breathless rambling. "What manner of trouble besets you? Who are those women?"

"Agents of my uncle," gasped Brynmor, inexplicably out of breath. "They mean to recover my body."

Venica circled Lord Sebastian, tutting, "They did this to you?"

Gabriela gasped at the ragged hole in the back of her knight's helm, exposing Brynmor's wavy hair. She couldn't discern any damage to the body.

"We must away." Venica smoothly swung onto Darius, placing the skull that looked a little too square to be human under a blanket.

Gabriela could feel Carmel's flank burning under her legs, but he obeyed when urged to gallop after the others. One dead and the other a purebred noble horse. She knew her old pony couldn't keep up.

"Mama, Carmel, he's exhausted!"

Gabriela yelled to be heard over pounding hooves, but her mother replied as quietly as always. "Channel vitality into him, my tiny. It will be nothing compared to the feat you attempted across the Crack."

The subtle dig was hard to miss, what she *attempted*, not what she succeeded in doing. Gabriela pulled a stream of power, imagining it as strength and energy, before breathing it into the pony below her. Carmel's gait immediately steadied into a stronger rhythm. She kept the magic going at a trickle, worrying what too much might do. Even with Brynmor's tether tugging at her and the power she'd channeled in the boneyard, the power came easily now.

The three horses wove through the Crystalwood Gardens, taking a different path that would deposit them somewhere farther north. Gabriela wasn't sure of where this fae ring lay but trusted her mother's navigation.

Lord Sebastian fell in beside her. "That was a fantastic display back there, Princess!"

"Was it?"

"Certainly, yes. You raised a small army that allowed us to escape without further conflict. I would classify that as fantastic."

"Did I do it, though? Mama was working on this side of the bridge. We probably had the same idea, and she cast through me."

Lord Sebastian hummed. "Is that possible?"

Gabriela shrugged. "It was a lot more power rushing through me than ever before, so that must be it. What about you? Your head, does it hurt?"

"You know I'm beyond pain." Lord Sebastian chuckled. "It's just a leather helmet; it can be mended. Though much more power in that blaster and she might have turned me into a dullahan! I only hope there's enough of the good viscount's head left in me to make all this worth it."

The marquess groaned from Gabriela's other side.

"I'm sorry, Brynmor," she said. "I keep forgetting how distressing this must all be for you."

"I never imagined a person thinking nothing of the line between life and death," he scoffed.

"No, but you've met my friends and mother. Who were those women? More of your girlfiends?"

Lord Sebastian snickered to her other side.

"Hardly!" Brynmor's voice verged on shrill. "Those two would never... Wait, what did you call them?"

"Girlfiends?"

"I think you mean girlfriends."

Gabriela shrugged. "So, they're that?"

Brynmor rubbed his gloved hand across his face. "As I said, they are my uncle's agents. Miss Lane is a sort of fixer, sent to follow in my wake. She attends to bureaucratic matters below my station."

"It is my understanding that magic is rare outside the clergy," said Lord Sebastian. "Or at least it was. Is that no longer the case? Or is Miss Lane some sister or priestess?"

"That hasn't been true for almost fifty years," Brynmor said with a snort. "The magic academy, Aetheria, accepts adepts without requiring they take the vows."

"So sorry. My information isn't regularly updated here. And the warrior woman?"

"Commander Ravell served with my uncle during the Ironcliff Campaigns. She is his most loyal servant. Now that you've posed as me, they'll either rush back to my uncle to return with a host of the king's paladins or..."

"Or?" asked Gabriela.

"Or they'll simply follow us."

"Slow, slow with no horse, horse," Aura tittered.

"Maybe," said Brynmor. "But Ravell is an unstoppable force."

"So, not your girlfriends?" Gabriela asked, just to be clear.

"You try my patience."

"Why not, though? They're both pretty, I think."

"I'm not the sort to take lasting partners, if you catch my meaning."

"I don't."

"Of course you don't." Brynmor let out a long, loud sigh. "Lord Sebastian, maybe you could explain it to your princess?"

"I could, but I'm having more fun watching you be uncomfortable."

"Of course, you're a Kiolist. It doesn't matter for now, Gabriela."

She raised a hand to cover her laugh. "Lord Sebastian's right. You're fun when you're flustered, Brynmor. You can call me Gab."

"Gab, that's..." he paused, brow pinching with thought. "I haven't heard anyone call you that."

"No, you're the first."

The sun slipped to the horizon as the three horses cantered from the Crystalwood Gardens and continued north. The moons rose as waxing blinding beacons, reminding Gabriela they would soon be full come the solstice. And with that, a near freeze to the magics that fettered Brynmor's ghost to this plane.

After an hour-long lull of the group passing by miles of dead trees and abandoned villages and farmhouses, Gabriela broke the silence. "Where is everyone? I imagine those with bodies found a place to settle down for the solstice, but where are the ghosts?"

Ahead, Darius slowed, taking a slow circle to face the other horses.

"Aura, Viscount, do you feel unusual?" asked Venica.

"I hardly know how to answer that," said Brynmor.

Aura faded into sight beside him, shaking her head. "Something wants me, but Gabs wants me more."

Darius stepped nearer. Venica narrowed her icy gaze down at the poltergeist. "Wants you in what way, my sweet?"

Aura whirled, spinning in a rapid circle, stopping just as suddenly to point both arms in a direction perpendicular to their route. "That way."

"That is not what..." Venica paused, following Aura's waggling fingers. Her gaze trailed to the distant horizon as a hand gripped the brooch at her throat. Gabriela could only assume by the descriptions she'd read in books that it was fear in her mother's wide eyes and slack jaw.

"What is it, Mum?" Lord Sebastian asked.

Venica looked up at the rising moons while tracing a nail along the strung gems of her necklaces. "We must needs alter our priorities."

"How so?"

She looked past Lord Sebastian to Gabriela. "How certain are you of reactions from this man's relation?"

"You mean, how will his uncle react to his death?" asked Gabriela.

"There is no doubt of it," Brynmor answered. "Commander Ravell's presence proves my uncle is suspect of something. He's ached for the king's approval for war ever since his family..."

Venica edged Darius nearer. "Continue."

"Since his family, my family, was killed by the dead." His voice caught in his throat.

"Rubbish." Venica turned away, dismissing him with a wave. "A greater threat unveils in the west."

"What's in the west?" asked Gabriela.

"Mama's home," Aura whispered when no one else responded.

"Eldrisil? Your tower?" asked Lord Sebastian. "We'd be better squaring off against a legion of holy paladins than to go against *him*, Mum. You vowed never to return."

"That I did, Lord Sebastian."

"What does all this mean?" Gabriela asked when the silence between the two began to stretch. "What tower, Mama? Who's there?"

"Your mother wasn't always the loving, benevolent student of arts and history that she is today," said Lord Sebastian. "Her past is dark and twisted, full of sordid trysts and—"

"That is enough, Lord Sebastian." Venica turned Darius to face them again. "I cannot ignore this development. Gabriela, the path ahead imposes too great of a danger. You will return to Soulhaven as we bury the viscount's corpse at the roadside. It is with some small regret I admit the mission to resurrect him must end in failure."

"Mama, no!"

"Roadside?" Brynmor gasped.

"At least let him be taken back to the Gardens or a plot in Soulhaven, Mum," said Lord Sebastian. "He is nobility, after all."

"It will *not* be taken to Soulhaven. This matter is not for debate," said Venica. "If the corpse is tracked, it must be discarded. You will not lead these women to our home, nor will you return to their waiting arms. Lord Sebastian, aid in the burial, see my daughter home, and make haste to the tower. I may require you." Darius pivoted westward and shot off at a gallop.

Lord Sebastian held out his hands, gloved palms up. "She might have at least first magicked us a hole in the dirt."

"This won't stand!" Brynmor yelled.

"You heard her, my good sir, and our queen's will shan't be ignored."

"She really means for me to just go home?" said Gabriela. "To just give up on days of effort? To go back on my promise to Brynmor?"

"No one can accuse you of a lack of effort, Princess. You should feel good for trying."

"What of the duke? What of the war and the king's paladins?"

"It may seem your mother is brushing that matter off, but I've no doubt she has some deep plan to deal with it all."

Brynmor growled his frustration. "You always think the best of everyone, don't you?"

"You say that as if it were a bad thing. Unless you had a spade in your saddlebag, I hope you won't mind a shallow grave." Lord Sebastian paused to laugh to himself. "Silly me, those women will find your body quickly enough. We may as well lean it against a tree stump with an arm propped up in greeting."

"No," Gabriela said with a determination that surprised even her. "The fae ring was just a place with enough power to fuel the spell, right?"

Lord Sebastian nodded, then shrugged. "That and it's a lovely vista."

"What do you know about this tower?" she asked.

"It was your mother's old home. She led quite a different life before you came into it. Before you and... well, yes. Before you."

"It's a place of power, like the fae ring?"

"Oh, a hundred times over. It's the center of the Deadvale, after all. The center of the world, in a lot of ways. Not geographically, but in terms of... Oh no, Princess. No, no, no."

Gabriela nodded along with the knight's words. "We have what we need. Your hand, his ghost, his body. Well, most of what we need. I don't know where to get divine blood. We'll follow Mama and have her do the resurrection at the tower. It will probably be even easier there than at the fae ring, right?"

"I mean, yes, it would be easier, but you don't know what you ask, Princess. Your mother's tower isn't some abandoned tavern we can walk into."

"What's there?" Brynmor asked before Gabriela could. "What's so terrifying?"

"Interplanar traps and creatures designed to kill you from the inside out. Not even you are safe as you are, good sir. But none of that compares to *who* is in the tower. The only being able to defeat Queen Venica Marwol holds residence and stewardship over it since she fled twenty years ago."

"No! Not him!" Aura moaned.

"Hush, Aura. You're not helping," said the knight.

"His eyes." Aura swooped close so her nose was inches from Gabriela's. "Those eyes..." Her form shimmered at the edges.

Gabriela waved her back. "Who? Who is so terrible? Does Aura know this person?"

"Aura has been in the tower before." Lord Sebastian tapped his fingertips together. "She has met him."

"What? How? When? I thought she was just a few years older than me when she... when she was bonded to me."

"I really shouldn't say more on that, Princess. Those are questions for your mother to answer. But the gentleman at the tower is Ser Oswin Mourningsword, former First Brother of the Order of Six and Eight. The order of paladins railed against your mother for decades, but Ser Mourningsword was the only one to make it to the queen's throne room."

"It was considered a great honor to be sent to die against the tower," said Brynmor. "They stopped doing that a bit before I was born. It's a good thing, as I briefly considered becoming a paladin. I probably would have been sent to die by now. What a waste."

"You? A paladin?" Lord Sebastian chuckled. "I can tell you're a man of little faith or experience as a ruler to think it a waste to sacrifice oneself to protect others."

"Who did they protect? I don't think a single one ever returned to tell their tales."

"You said you considered becoming a paladin, so they clearly inspired someone."

"Mama had a throne room?" Gabriela asked.

Brynmor gaped at her, rubbing his hands over his face.

Lord Sebastian pulled off his left glove, exposing Brynmor's limp gloved hand. "We should leave the horse with the body. I'd rather have as few reasons for these women or their patron to continue after us. Perhaps a note of apologies as well? Would you mind penning that while I extricate the marquess? Good sir, you can help with phrases that may calm their anger."

"This is absurd," said Brynmor, cringing and turning away as Lord Sebastian pulled off his helmet. "Gab is right. There is no choice but to continue with this plan. Failure will only lead to war. From what I've seen so far of the Deadvale, a very short war, but a war."

"How does the back of his head look, Princess?"

The viscount's dark, wavy hair was charred and matted, but she saw no damage to the scalp. "I think your helmet did its job."

"Like the rest of my armor, my helm's job is to look fabulous. A job it does quite well."

"Please!" Brynmor yelled, stamping a foot soundlessly.

"Sorry," said Gabriela. "I'm going, Lord Sebastian. Put Brynmor's corpse on Carmel if you must, but I'm going to Mama's tower. If it's anything like her library at home, there must be the details of the spells I need. I'll do this myself, but I won't give up."

Lord Sebastian paused from unbuckling the straps at his shoulder. "Strong words, Princess. You really mean to defy your mother's direct command?"

"I mean to keep my word and see this mission to the end."

Lord Sebastian drummed his fingers on the edge of his helmet. "You put me in a pickle! I like pickles. Well, I used to like pickles, but I suppose I still would. Did you forget about my warning regarding interplanar traps and monsters? Not to mention the fallen paladin that's likely now driven mad from the constant onslaught of power flowing through Eldrisil?"

"Most of that last one is new," Brynmor grumbled.

Gabriela crossed her arms. "Mama has always fed me half-truths. Giving just enough details to get by. She should have been clear and explicit about the dangers if she thought I would stay away. She should have told me about this paladin and the tower."

"My details about dangers aren't enough?" Lord Sebastian mimicked her body language.

"No."

He uncrossed his arms. "Well then. Pickles it is. Your mother would most certainly *not* be pleased to see you approaching beside me."

"So you'll come with me?"

"Or you with me. Semantics, really. It wounds me that you think I might let you go unchaperoned. Besides, she bade me join her; maybe I'm just fulfilling her wishes out of order? If your mother asks, and she will, could you say you coerced me in some way? Perhaps a threat? Or no, we'll approach the tower from two sides, so she won't know I knew you came, only that I seem to have forgotten about the viscount within."

"None of that matters," said Brynmor. "Once we are there, it will be too late to stop. The queen will have no choice but to help."

"My queen is never forced into a choice that does not suit her." Lord Sebastian's tone was firm yet somehow rehearsed. "Need I remind us of the fine ladies trailing us? We should be on our way." He tightened his straps and replaced his helmet and glove before pulling onto Harvey's back. With a kick, he was off after Venica.

Gabriela pulled at the power to again feed vitality into Carmel. The poor pony wasn't used to so much action in a day.

CHAPTER 17

RED PAINT

"Will you even be able to put that thing back together?"

Eleanor ignored the commander's grumbling, focusing instead on the delicate inner mechanics of her compass. It lay in pieces across Ravell's cloak spread flat on the dusty ground. As she theorized, the flow of magic this side of the Crack played havoc on the most fragile bits. Eleanor took out each fine needle and spring, gingerly cleaning them with a soft rag, before placing them on the other side of the cloak. She held up one of the three tiny crystals vital to the compass, frowning at the hairline crack visible in the fading evening light.

"It's damaged, probably from my fall from horseback. It won't be as accurate, but it will work."

"Quickly then, we must track them as far into the night as possible."

"And so we encounter them in the dark, exhausted?" Eleanor started the careful assembly process, and her father's words rang in her head. "A rushed job is a bad job," he would say. Her father was never one for grand works of poetry, just phrases he would repeat over and over. His work as a toymaker was slow, and his products prohibitively expensive, but no one would ever comment against their quality or ingenuity.

She rotated the glass faceplate with a satisfying click and traced a finger across it with a muttered prayer, infusing it again with the magic needed for a day's work. The brass needle pivoted to point north and a little west.

"We're still going in the right direction," she reported, gathering the commander's cloak and standing. Stretching the kinks from her back from hunching for the last hour, she surveyed the ruined village. Nature-ravaged huts, a well, a church. Nothing special.

Ravell slung the cloak across her back, fastening it at the shoulders. "How far away?"

"I thought I made it clear I can't tell that. The marquess is moving at one rate, and we at another, both at different headings. It's too much math. By the time I worked it out, he'd be miles away."

"A shame. You would be able to calculate it, were you prepared?"

"Sure," Eleanor shrugged.

"Impressive. Let us be off."

Eleanor put her rag and handful of fine tools back into the pouch at her hip. Her fingers brushed the wire rims of her goggles within. The dark blurs surrounding Lady Marwol still plagued her thoughts.

"I don't think we should carry on too late tonight. I have work I'd like to get done that I can't do while walking and watching the compass."

"And I have the work of rescuing the marquess," said Ravell. Much of the kindness shown as they left Crystalwood Gardens had evaporated in the hours since.

"My work will help us to understand what's happened here," said Eleanor. "If Lady Marwol is an agent of the dead, we must unravel what hold she has over the marquess before dragging him back to the duke."

"Is that a task for you? Your dossier reads you were ejected from Aetheria. I should have asked Duke Highgate to send a properly qualified magic user to aid me."

Eleanor snapped the compass's protective shell closed. Her parents and relatives never understood why she left the academy, so why should some random military grunt, as high ranking and decorated as Commander Ravell might be? Eleanor had long ago stopped caring, yet the casual brushing off of her past still stung. "Perhaps you should have. You're welcome to submit your petition to the duke. I've no real need to continue beside you, guiding your way, to conduct my research." She turned away to hide her grin. It was petty, she knew, to threaten to take away her help in the same breath as enumerating it, but damn if it wasn't satisfying.

"I would ask a favor of you, Miss Lane," Ravell said. "When I served in the Ironcliff Campaigns, the priests and mages I served beside were all the same petty, childish sort. They held their noses high, looking down at us from their supposed station nearer to Elysara. I wondered if that was only how they acted near the battlefield. Do me the favor of proving me wrong."

"Petty?" Eleanor forced her fists to loosen. "You think me petty? You— What was that?"

It came again, the sound of claws scrabbling on stone. The women whirled, searching for the source, eyes darting across the ruined buildings. A crow landed on the edge of the central well, screaming a greeting, or warning.

Ravell pulled her sword, flourishing it in the useless twirls that Eleanor always saw swordsmen use. "We are not alone. Can you magicly detect anyone?"

"That's why I need to stop and reconfigure my lenses. There are magic forces—"

Scrape. Scrape.

The crow screamed and fled as a pasty, skeletal hand slapped onto the well's lip. Another followed it, then the head, wrapped in the threadbare coverings of a field worker from one of Eleanor's early history books. She could only stare in amazement as another pair of rotten hands clambered over the edge of the well, but that wasn't the only place with the sound of scratching. Another skeleton pulled itself from the collapsed hut to their right.

Ravell had no problems with inaction. Her sword flashed across those crawling from the well, severing their dry joints so they fell with a clatter. She flashed to the one, now three, crawling from the hut, arcing the blade across their ribs. They collapsed but still attempted to advance with bony digits digging into the dry ground, legs twitching a few feet away.

More shambled from the buildings, struggling out from under the weight of fallen roofs. Ravell ran at each as they got clear, dark sword shining in the dying evening light. She raised her blade to the next but paused.

They must have been children decades ago, three of them. Missing ribs or an arm, their ragged clothes trailed behind their arrhythmic gait. Ravell moved backward as they advanced, keeping her sword high.

"By the goddess and all the saints…"

Eleanor couldn't guess how she had missed it before; the flaked red paint slashed across the rotted door behind the risen children. This was a plague town. Or had been a lifetime ago. As a child of ten years, Eleanor's elderly, mostly blind aunt gave her a textbook on obscure diseases, confusing it for one on herbs. Now every terrible illness of the last four centuries flooded her mind. Which would be worse, which might have survived in the soil or the bones or—

"Ravell! Leave them and run!"

"I must destroy them first." Ravell backed a step from the children, bumping her heel against the well.

"No, leave them! This was a plague town. Who knows if they still have the infection."

That broke Ravell's attention. She glanced again at the children standing idly by the hut before fleeing after Eleanor. When they were a few hundred feet from the village's center, the stitch forming in Eleanor's side forced her to slow. Ravell trotted back to her, finally replacing the sword on her back.

"The children, they're gone," said the commander.

Eleanor squinted into the village, seeing no sign of the animated skeletons, apart from the remains of those the commander cut apart.

"Maybe they went back into hiding," said Eleanor.

"Awaiting the next unsuspecting traveler."

Eleanor watched the commander in profile for a breath. "How did that compare to battling the risen dead in the Gardens early in your career?"

She intended it as an honest question but realized the underlying jab. *Did you wage war against a bunch of children?*

Ravell heard it too, by how her lip twisted to a snarl. "You see mindless shambling husks animated by what lingering magics formed the Deadvale. In the north, they were armed and armored, controlled and supported by death mages."

"Death mages?" Eleanor, of course, heard tales of the twisted sorcerers with magic enough to rip the souls from their victims, but she'd never met someone who implied to have gone against one on the battlefield.

"You mock me?"

"What? No, of course not. Despite what you think you know of my past, I am proud of why I left Aetheria. I am a passionate arcane researcher who would love to hear about your encounters with death mages. Though not while still in sight of a plague town harboring risen dead."

"So you will continue with me to retrieve the marquess?"

Eleanor removed her oversized leather hat, slapping it against her thigh to shake off the dust. Ravell's expression was no softer than before. She stared with the same cold emotion, impatient for a reply. Eleanor took a deep breath, tugging the hat back over her dark hair.

"Fine, yes I will, though I can't say why. I don't do this out of loyalty to the duke, definitely not for Brynmor, and I've already absolved myself of any harm that comes to you in the Deadvale."

"Remember which of us will be doing the protecting when necessary." Ravell adjusted a plate arm guard as if to accentuate her combat prowess.

"We have yet to get started on the right foot together, have we, commander?"

CHAPTER 18

THE SWEEPING VISTAS OF THE MISTY MIRE

"Fish eyes!"

Gabriela's outburst stopped Lord Sebastian's humming. "What is it, Princess?"

"I didn't check on the Morgans before we left Soulhaven. They always have the hardest time around the solstice."

"They'll be fine; never you worry."

"I know. I just can't help it sometimes."

"And empathy is a fine trait to cultivate." Lord Sebastian pulled on the reins, stopping Harvey. "Might we, since we're on the topic, take a moment to refresh the enchantments on the good viscount's mortal remains? I worry the jaunt from the Deadvale might have weakened them."

Gabriela frowned. "We'll need Mama for that. I don't know those spells."

"Neither did you know how to channel vitality into Carmel, not until your mother told you to do it. You didn't need a description of the process then."

Brynmor stepped between them. "Is that honestly a worry? That my... That the enchantments would fail after only a few moments out of the Deadvale?"

"You mustn't forget Lady Marwol's grand display of magic, raising the slumbering dead. That may have done something."

"I don't know," said Gabriela, pulling at each of her fingers. "What if I mess it up? Or mess up Mama's work?"

"Can that happen?" Brynmor asked.

"Quiet," Lord Sebastian hushed him. "Come then, Princess, give it a go." He removed his helmet to let Brynmor's head flop to the left.

She was used to seeing the viscount's semi-translucent ghost, but it barely did his physical body justice. Gabriela couldn't resist admiring Brynmor's strong jaw. His pronounced cheeks and orbital bones. She could imagine the shape of his skull with perfect clarity. Gabriela kept that to herself. Brynmor seemed touchy about so many perfectly natural topics.

She reached to cup a palm against his cheek, coarse with stubble, noticing his ghost didn't turn away this time. Other than a cut across his cheek and forehead, he looked as though he could be asleep. Maybe his cheeks were a bit ashen, not that she had much experience for comparison.

"I don't know, Lord Sebastian." She pulled her hand back and tugged at her fingers again. "Isn't there a lot that could go wrong?"

"Oh pish, you must at least give it a try."

"I rather think a lot could go wrong," Brynmor moaned.

Lord Sebastian waved off Brynmor with his own floppy hand. "You watched your mother do it, and it seemed simple enough. Just do your best. I believe in you, Princess."

"You believe anyone is capable of greatness, don't you?" asked Gabriela.

"To a detriment," Brynmor grumbled.

Gabriela breathed deeply, focusing her power as she always did, imagining Brynmor as he was when they first met. His wavy hair swayed in the gentle breeze, and the slightest blush reddened his cheeks from the day's long ride. She also imagined that flash of power as he touched her, his eyes wide with horror as he fell back into the nothing. No, that wasn't useful; back to the pink cheeks and perfectly rehearsed smile. Gabriela felt her power rise, that old familiar darkness that flowed from the twisting rivers of magic in the world. Yet, as she pushed that power out onto Brynmor, something else seemed to cloud it, causing the spell to fizzle.

She pulled her hand away, frowning. "So much for that."

Lord Sebastian flopped Brynmor's hand over, drawing it closer to his face. Gabriela knew the lives of everyone in town but never asked the knight how he perceived the world without eyes or a body.

"I wouldn't be so sure of that, Princess. You may have done it as well as your mother."

"You're just being nice."

"I see no difference," said Brynmor.

"Not that you know what to look for, good sir—"

Gabriela felt a sudden tug on her tether to Brynmor, pulling the wind from her. His ghost faded and flickered until she recovered.

"Princess, what happened?"

"I don't know." Gabriela wiped a hand across her sweaty brow. "I couldn't breathe for a moment." She kept a steadying hand on Carmel before waving the knight back. "I'll be fine."

"This is too much to ask of you. I shouldn't have suggested you try that spell. The tether tying the marquess to you is causing a drain on your body and magic. It will only worsen until we reach the tower. Come, your mother escapes while the viscount's girlfiends gain on us."

Brynmor's lip curled with restrained annoyance, and Gabriela bit back her grin at seeing it. The man was so easily riled up, and the range of emotions was oddly satisfying to watch play out across his face. His lip tightened, and his eyes narrowed while he tapped his fingers against his palms with both hands. Viscount Brynmor Highgate was not one of the stoic nobles Gabriela read about in dozens of books in her mother's library. Even despite his current condition, Brynmor was the most animated and vibrant person she'd met.

"Princess?" Lord Sebastian asked, ready to pull the helmet back in place.

"Hmm? Were you talking?"

He pushed his leather helmet over Brynmor's head. "I was just saying again how we should be on our way. If I remember my geography from here, and I may not, the most direct route to your mother's tower will take us through the Misty Mire."

Gabriela gasped. "I've always wanted to visit the Misty Mire. It's in so many romance books."

"Specifically the Devil's Pit, or at least very near it," Lord Sebastian finished.

Brynmor stumbled, looking ready to collapse. "I'm sorry, the what? We're actually going there?"

"Yes, but never worry your pretty head about it. I could never imagine the residents would dare harm a party related to the queen."

Gabriela snapped her fingers. "We needed something from there, remember, Brynmor? Divine blood. Mama listed it off in her library."

"So that I'm clear," Brynmor tapped his hands together. "Are we talking actual devils here? Beings of pure maleficence from mythology? Because I've seen a lot over the last few days and think I need to prepare myself if that is where we're going."

Lord Sebastian shrugged. "What a flowery description. Maybe don't use those exact words when we encounter one."

"The reagent was *divine* blood," said Brynmor. "Not devil blood."

"Semantics," said Lord Sebastian. "They're all just two sides of the same coin. Or, not a coin, that's too rigid. A marble, perhaps. Yes, I like that. Divinity is a marble. Two points may be direct opposites, but there are myriad points in between. Gradients of divinity."

Brynmor grunted, running a hand through his wavy hair. He shook his head, and his hair looked as perfect as it always did.

The sun had just set by the time they reached the edge of The Misty Mire. It still lit the west with a blaze of pink and orange as the nearly-full moons rose. Gabriela's breath caught, looking down at the sweeping valley that inspired some of the loftiest, wordiest pieces of romantic literature she had ever read. With icy rivers fed from the Frostfang Range to the north and warmer air flowing from the west, the low mist clung to the tall grasses and low willows year-round. Some of the most prolific poets in history waxed in depth about the rising or setting sun and moons. Knowing all that, Gabriela wanted to immediately feel transported as those old, dead bards had, to forget her troubles, at least for a moment. Other than a few fireflies pulsing in the mist, there was nothing much of interest from what she could see in the moonlight.

"What about this Devil's Pit?" Brynmor asked from beside her.

Lord Sebastian swung a leg over Harvey, dropping to the ground. "I will go see to that. I'll ask if your mother's been through." He flexed the digits of his right hand. "Now that we will be going to Eldrisil, it may not be a bad idea to put the good viscount's body on the back of his horse to free up my mobility."

"I like the idea of not seeing it," said Brynmor. "And as long my body is within you, I doubt it will fall off the horse and into a ravine or whatnot."

"Yes, good sir, and your comfort is paramount to our quest."

"Who could guess what Commander Ravell and Miss Lane would do should they catch up and see me slumped over the horse's rear."

"My, my, my good sir, you are positively glutted with not bad points today. Stay here a moment. I shan't be long."

Gabriela dug through Carmel's bags, unwrapping a bar of compressed nuts and dried fruits.

"What is this Devil's Pit about?" Brynmor asked, watching Lord Sebastian pick his way around puddles, disappearing into the mist.

"I'm not sure," said Gabriela around a mouthful. "He told me about how when the Deadvale erupted, creatures from outside our world were drawn to the inversion of energy or something. A few made it here, and a couple of those never left."

"Why have I never heard of any of this?"

Gabriela shrugged. "I don't know about the failings of your education. Mama says your church has done a lot to make people afraid to cross the Crack, so you'd have no one to tell about what happens on this side."

"I suppose I can't fault that." He shook his head violently. "Who cares about that. Why are there devils in this world, and why has your knight gone so casually to speak with one?"

"Why can't you ever ask just one question at a time? I think there's only one devil in this pit. If Mama had come through here, they probably would have noticed. Lord Sebastian can find out how long ago and whatnot."

"Sounds like a friendly, helpful devil."

"Most are if you come at them the right way, so I've read." She finished her snack, wiping her hands on the wrapped napkin, and replacing it in the side bag. "How are you? Anything else since the problem with the Repose spell?"

Brynmor raised his ungloved hand, flexing his fingers to a fist. "I don't think so, but I find my memory growing hazy as if I'm living in a fog."

"Well…" Looking around, she stopped herself from correcting him with a joke. "You're doing much better than Aura, but she's been a ghost longer."

The second moon crested the mountains to the east, outlining Brynmor's translucent form from behind. His long jacket and trousers were stark against his halo glow.

"What is the story with Aura?"

Gabriela shook her gaze to the ground, realizing she'd been staring at Brynmor's wavy hair.

"She's always near but not always present, if that makes sense."

"It does not."

"Ghosts are usually bound to a time, unable to notice its passage, like Mister Tanner. He can tell you what he's done and learned since being a ghost caring for his inn and the others he's met, but he couldn't tell you what happened a week ago versus ten years ago. It's all the same."

Brynmor stared at her, blinking slowly. "I see. Since you mentioned that our second morning together, I have noticed it."

"Ghosts like Mister Tanner are bound to a place. Those who visit him wander freely. Aura is fettered to me, and it changes her attributes as a ghost. Though hers is far more secure, with a longer rope. Now you're fettered to me, as well."

"That doesn't explain who Aura is."

"I don't know. Mama fettered her to me when I was a baby but never told me more."

"What?" Brynmor staggered a step backward. "Your mother bound a madwoman to you?"

"Aura isn't mad. She's usually completely cheery."

"Mad as in insane, not angry," said Brynmor.

Gabriela chewed her lip, trying to push down the general feeling of sadness she often got when thinking about the ghost. "Can we not talk about Aura? Tell me about you. You said you're not one for long-term relationships. Why's that?"

Brynmor stepped a little nearer, gazing down at her. Gabriela remembered the smoky gray of his eyes from when he looked down at her at the top of the stairs, a color she'd never imagined would look so... attractive.

"Nobles such as myself are expected to marry for political fortune, not love." He reached for her hand with his ungloved one. "In all my travels across the kingdom, visiting every duchy and meeting the most fascinating people, I've never met one I thought I might love."

Gabriela squeezed his hand, savoring that slight resistance as she slid a finger over the signet ring on his index finger. Even in his ghostly form, she felt the tickle of hair on the back of his hand.

"Oh?" She swallowed hard. "And are you looking for someone to love?"

"I would prefer that. If I could, for example, fall in love with a princess, someone my uncle would approve of, that would be ideal."

"How long would you have to know someone before you knew you might love them?"

"What are you two lovebirds discussing?" Lord Sebastian stepped from the mist.

"Lovebirds?" Gabriela and Brynmor said in unison, each shifting away from the other.

"It was nothing of the sort," Brynmor continued.

Aura appeared in a flash of green. "Me, me! They were talking about me!"

"You are marvelously interesting, Aura," Lord Sebastian beamed. "We could talk about you for days."

"Success?" Gabriela asked.

"Yes. They said your mother passed by not long ago. They were horrified not knowing she would be in the area, or they would have prepared some reception. They also wanted to do the same for you, Princess, but I said we're on a tight timeline."

Gabriela frowned. "I wish we had time to meet your friend."

"More of an acquaintance, I would say."

"Well, no matter. Give me their blood sample, and I'll keep it with the other reagents."

The knight remained quiet.

"Lord Sebastian?"

"Fish eyes," he grumbled, opening his hands to show they were empty. "I guess you'll get to meet them, after all."

Gabriela dragged a hand over her cheek. "Let's go."

CHAPTER 19

THE LAWYER'S PIT

Lord Sebastian took Harvey's lead and directed them into the mists. "How are you faring, Princess? The horses are looking fatigued, so you must be too. Not to compare your looks with the horses; you know that was not my intention. We should settle for the night."

Gabriela stifled a yawn with the back of her hand. "Absolutely not. Mama needs us. We'll ride through the night if we must."

Lord Sebastian considered her, drumming his fingers together. "I never imagined myself saying this, but no. You're exhausted. The horses are exhausted. This whole plot to fix the marquess would be for nothing if you cannot maintain his tether. A few hours rest. That's all we need."

"What of the women chasing us?"

"Aura saw to their horses. With how hard we rode to get here, they are far behind us. If they continue through the night, they'll only get lost in the Misty Mire."

Gabriela held back another yawn. "Very well. Just a quick rest. Do you suppose your acquaintance would bunk us for the night?"

"Oh." Lord Sebastian pulled Harvey to a stop. "Yes, of course, brilliant. Their place is not the largest, as you might imagine, but they'd be honored to share The Devil's Pit with royalty. They'll be the talk of the office."

"Office?" asked Brynmor.

"Ask them yourself. Follow me. It's not far now."

With the last remnants of the sun gone, the sky around the moons and stars was an inky black. After a few moments, a single candle's light pierced the mist ahead, and the moons' light outlined a mud and straw construction, barely seven feet tall at the peak. The candle shone from the single window on the front, but there was no movement within.

"This is The Devil's Pit?" Brynmor rolled his eyes.

"Technically, yes," said Lord Sebastian. "Be respectful, or you can stay the night out here."

"I don't think there's much risk of reaching the end of my tether to Gab, even if she's in the back garden."

Gabriela cracked a smile, knocking thrice at the simple door that was only as tall as her neck.

"State your name," called the deep growl from within.

The knight cleared his throat. "Tis I again, Executor. I am joined by Princess Gabriela Marwol and Viscount Brynmor Highgate."

The door opened immediately. Standing barely taller than Lord Sebastian's knee, candlelight framed a creature with crimson skin and a shock of orange hair. Their heavy cloth traveling cloak was closed with a silver clasp at their throat, and horns twisted a few inches over their hair, ending in a tiny flicker of flame. They fumbled to remove their delicate spectacles.

"Is that a..." Brynmor asked from behind Gabriela.

"Executor Smithies," they replied in a deep, smoky voice. "Princess, it is an honor." They inclined their head just a fraction.

"Executor," Gabriela returned the nod. "The honor is mutual. I apologize for continuing to interrupt your evening."

"Not at all, My Grace. What can I do for you?"

"Lord Sebastian tells us my mother, Queen Marwol, passed through not long ago?" Gabriela asked. "Did she say anything to you?"

"No, My Grace. The queen rode without pause. Her dread beast's hooves beat within a stone's toss of here."

"She rides to Eldrisil," said Lord Sebastian.

"Something at her tower is summoning ghosts," said Gabriela. "She abandoned the mission to resurrect Brynmor in a heartbeat of discovering that."

"She would willingly return to the fallen paladin? This must be dire." Executor Smithies tapped their cloak's clasp.

"Right, the paladin." Gabriela snapped her fingers. "I forgot about him when you mentioned Mama had a throne room. Mourningwood?"

"Mourningsword," Lord Sebastian corrected her. "Ser Oswin Mourningsword. You seriously forgot about him? He nearly defeated your mother. I suppose, in many ways, he did. It might not be a bad idea to take our time, to allow your mother the opportunity to deal with him before we arrive."

At that, Gabriela wanted to rush forward to help her mother, but fought back another yawn. "We've been riding for hours without pause since some messy business in the Crystalwood Gardens earlier. Could I impose on your hospitality to slumber here for the night?"

"Well said, Princess," Lord Sebastian whispered.

"You came all the way from the Gardens in a day?" asked Executor Smithies. "Your steeds must be worn ragged. Yes, of course, you are welcome here." They pivoted aside to wave Gabriela and the others in. "Excuse the mess. I wasn't expecting company."

Gabriela ducked to enter the tiny house. A small bed to her left was immaculately made, giving her an image of Smithies ironing the sheets after fitting them around the mattress. Ahead, a chair sat in front of a cold hearth, and at the right end of the tiny cabin was a mountain of neatly stacked parchment and ledgers. The only thing adorning the walls was a long piece of parchment with a stylized skull at the top, lines of text in a language Gabriela couldn't read, and a half dozen signatures and brands at the bottom.

Gabriela's hair brushed the ceiling, and Lord Sebastian squatted to fit into the cramped room.

Brynmor peaked in from around the doorframe. "The Devil's Pit, hmm? Just a flowery name for a lawyer's hovel?"

"Oh, I'm not a full lawyer," said Executor Smithies. "And it isn't just a name. Pardon me, Princess." Gabriela stepped off the rug in the room's center as the imp rolled it up, exposing a circular iron grate about two feet across. They gestured to the sharply cut hole piercing into the world. Gabriela leaned closer, seeing no hint of a bottom, but the warm breath wafting in the room smelled of sulfur and something else she couldn't identify.

"By all the gods and saints," Brynmor breathed. "Does that connect to the hells?"

The devil smirked. "It does connect down to the bedrock of your world, the same firmament at the base of the Crack, but there is no such place as what you call a hell."

"Well, that simply can't be true," said Brynmor, looking to the others for backup and getting none. "No, the hells clearly exist, or what would the gods of the heavens battle against? Just because your very deep hole doesn't reach a hell means nothing."

Smithies waited for Brynmor to finish. "I see you are tethered by magic to Princess Gabriela. Sever that and find out for yourself that nothing awaits you."

Brynmor shrank out of sight at the threat.

"Please help yourself to the bed, Princess. If you don't mind, please, I need the candlelight a little longer. I'm on a bit of a deadline."

"Nothing to worry about, Executor. I'm just going to see to the horses," said Gabriela.

"I can do that, Princess," said Lord Sebastian. "You stay and rest."

"Wait, blood." Gabriela whirled on the Executor. "Mama said divine blood was one of the components of resurrection magic. Could I ask for a vial of yours?"

Brynmor scoffed.

Executor Smithies covered a grin with their hand. "While I appreciate that flattery, Princess Gabriela, it would take more blood than I have to reach the power needed for your spell's needs."

"Then that's it," said Brynmor, waving his hands over his head, not noticing how they passed through the ceiling. "Where else are we going to find divine blood?"

"Do not despair so easily, young ghost," said Executor Smithies. "I may lack the strength you require, but others would be more than sufficient."

"Others?" asked Brynmor.

The devil-not-full-lawyer gestured to the pit in their living room.

"You can't mean to..." started Lord Sebastian.

Executor Smithies slowly nodded. "I stand guardian to the portals. It would only take a drop from those below."

"Portals?" Gabriela asked.

"To what your young ghost friend believes are the hells," they explained. "Other planes and realms brush against this one. Aside from my never-ending paperwork, I also monitor to ensure nothing untoward comes through."

"Untoward? And what would you do if that happened?" Brynmor's eyes moved over the short devil. "What could you do against one that came through, as powerful as you say they are?"

"Never you mind about my work. My blood may be ill-fit for magic, but I am no slouch regarding combat."

"Well, Princess, if you're not too tired, shall we get some devil blood before hitting the sack for the night?"

"I don't know what that entails, but sure," she said, leaning nearer to the hole again. "How do we get down safely?"

"Just hop down," said Executor Smithies. "When you're done down there, find the same place and hop up."

Lord Sebastian moved beside her, also leaning over the pit. "Mayhap I should go without you, Princess. It doesn't look too inviting."

"It doesn't look like anything," she said.

"This is insanity—" Brynmor's words distorted as Gabriela hopped into the pit, and he was dragged behind.

CHAPTER 20

JUST A DROP WILL DO

Brynmor was still screaming beside her when Lord Sebastian landed gently on Gabriela's other side. They stood in a square cavern reeking of sulfur, but also of something else... Mint? A thin shaft of light cut through the darkness to illuminate the trio as Gabriela's skin prickled with sweat from the growing heat.

Quartet.

Aura wailed, flashing into existence, her green light strobing across the rocky walls. "No, no, bad, bad!"

"It's fine, Aura," Gabriela tried to calm her. "We just need..." Her eyes adjusted to the dim light, noticing the faint red glow from the cavern's only apparent exit. Just beyond, the light glinted gold against something piled on the ground.

Lord Sebastian held out an arm to keep her behind him as they approached, stepping from the beam of light. Gabriela's eyes quickly adjusted further, making the source of the shining clear.

Armor.

Aura twirled and disappeared into the wall with a puff of green light.

"By all the gods and saints," Brynmor whispered. Outside their tiny chamber, suits of embellished armor glinting gold and silver littered the next room. At least two score of them. "Paladins." The armored bodies continued into the darkness beyond the reach of Brynmor's glow and the light behind them.

"I don't suppose we could take a peck of their blood?" mused Lord Sebastian. "Though I can't imagine they have any left."

"What are they doing here?" asked Brynmor. "Elysara protect. Some are centuries old."

Lord Sebastian shrugged. "The church has fought against what it perceives as the other side of the marble since forever. They must have at some point been able to send their warriors here, hoping to fight back whatever inhabits this place."

"We can't fight something that killed all these paladins," said Gabriela. "If that's what we're supposed to do down here."

Lord Sebastian bent to pull a winged helmet from one paladin, exposing their dry and brittle skull. Strands of hair may have once been held back in a leather strap fell free now. He slid the helm over his own before taking up the holy warrior's mace and shield.

"Sacrilege," Brynmor muttered.

"You have so many strong opinions, good sir. It's a wonder you can keep track of them all."

"Stealing from the dead should be universal," said Brynmor. "That goes double for Elysara's holy warriors."

"That seems a waste." Gabriela tried to pick up a mace but quickly abandoned it for a smaller hammer. "The dead back home have no problem with sharing anything and everything. The concept of property and ownership seems exclusive to the living."

"How sage of you, Princess."

Heat washed over them with a breeze from somewhere deeper in the caverns, along with the scent of fresh mint. The paladins' armor shuddered, the metal joints clanking in a rising din. Gabriela held the war hammer a little closer against her chest when she noticed the ground quiver below her boots.

"Who..." reverberated a slow voice on the wind.

Gabriela glanced at Lord Sebastian, who shrugged and waved the mace into the dark. She cleared her throat. "I am Princess Gabriela Marwol, come to ask a boon of you."

"Five come. Armed. Ask for a boon," said the voice from the darkness.

"Five?"

Lord Sebastian tapped a finger to his leather chest plate.

"Oh, you're counting Brynmor twice." She held up her hammer, feeling suddenly foolish to think it would do her any good, and knelt to set it down. Red and orange pulsed deep in the distance, growing brighter with each breath.

Lord Sebastian dropped the mace and held the shield with both arms while shifting to stand between Gabriela and the slowly igniting fire. "We may want to be more direct, Princess."

The flickering light resolved into a horned skull wreathed in flames. A shadow stalked before it, walking upright, but broader and impossibly muscled.

Gabriela froze. The heroines in her books were often besieged by fears she found mundane, but the growing sight of this creature struck her with inexplicable terror. Primal dread gnawed at the base of her spine, making her hands shake. Brynmor's tether tugged at her back, but she couldn't take her eyes off the creature, already far too large to be real, yet it was still so far away. It illuminated the armor of dozens more paladins as it waded through them, uncaring.

"You are no warrior," it said, now near enough for Gabriela to see its eyes, like two holes straight through its scaled head to shine hellfire from the skull behind it.

Gabriela sucked in a quick breath of sulfur and mint. "I am not. *We* are not. We have not come to fight." She fluttered a few fingers toward Lord Sebastian, who dropped the mace with a clatter.

"Pity. Have you come as a sacrifice?"

"No. Not a sacrifice. We, er, I was hoping for a small favor of you."

It stopped advancing, and Gabriela had to crane her neck to look it in the eye. It looked thirty feet tall but still stood well beyond the reach of Brynmor's ghost light.

"No favor is small when asked of Malphas, Dread Lord of Desolation, Prince of Ruin, Sovereign of the Abyssal Monarch."

"Perhaps he's right, Princess," whispered Lord Sebastian. "I think we've disturbed the good demon prince quite enough."

"Can we have a little of your blood?" The words rushed from her.

Flames crackled. Perhaps it was laughing?

"You are insignificant to ask that of the Harbinger of Torment."

She swallowed hard. "Executor Smithies sent us."

"The jailor." The demon lord growled, again advancing toward them. "They think to flaunt their power over me."

"Let's go, Princess!" Lord Sebastian grabbed her elbow.

"But we haven't—"

"I know you," said Malphas.

Lord Sebastian's tug lessened.

"I don't see how that could be," said Lord Sebastian. Gabriela recognized something in his voice she'd never heard from the knight before: fear.

"You rode at her side," Malphas hissed. "That woman that failed me; lied to me. Drove me to the madness that left me here imprisoned."

Lord Sebastian tugged her through the fallen paladins, toward the chamber with the light beam. Malphas continued to grow in her vision. The paladins here never stood a chance; they were sent to die. Sacrificed to show the church attempted to fight back the forces on the other side of the moral marble.

Heat washed over them again, stinging her nose as she breathed, just as Lord Sebastian half dragged Gabriela toward the entrance chamber.

"We need its blood for the ritual," she protested.

"It's no good if you're dead!"

Gabriela wrenched from his grip. She stood in the doorway with a sea of long-dead paladins between them and Prince Malphas. All his grand titles fit, as a primal desire to flee rose in her chest with each step he took forward, growing ever larger in her view. She understood that her group fared no chance in subduing the being for a drop of blood, and he clearly would not freely give it, especially with the added animosity he held for Lord Sebastian. They would leave empty-handed. Gabriela would have one question answered.

Was it me or Mama?

She reached for her power, feeling the slick sheen coating it here, but beneath, it was no different than at home. Urged by Lord Sebastian's frantic words at her side and the approaching demon, she wove that power into a net she cast out in front of her.

"Aid me," she commanded.

Nothing happened.

Malphas's heat slammed into her again as the ground quaked with another step. The armor shifted around the demon's feet, causing him to stumble.

The first paladin struggled to their feet, raising a long sword in practiced hands.

Then, as one, they all stood, weapons directed at Malphas. He batted one aside as three others swung at his legs. They looked like toys surrounding the behemoth.

Malphas waded a step forward, flaming eyes fixed on Gabriela. Eyes that burned with unnatural hate that bored through her, freezing her legs with fear. The demon roared, ripping a short sword from his leg and swatting away the paladin that landed the attack. Lord Sebastian wrenched off the plate helmet to throw into the fray just as Malphas launched the sword at Gabriela. By a stroke of luck beyond what any goddess could predict, the two collided mid-air, diverting the sword just enough to strike the wall beside her. She scooped it off the floor as the knight shoved her back into the room and the light. "Hop!"

She did.

• • • ● • ● • ● • •

Her cheek stung. Pushing to hands and knees, Gabriela looked down at the rug while trying to piece events together. Had she asked a demon prince for blood? Had she raised an army of the dead to move against him? She looked at the rusted and chipped short sword in her hand glistening with wet, black blood.

She heard humming and looked up to see Executor Smithies entering the hut. They rushed to her, helping her to stand with surprisingly strong arms. "I didn't expect you back so quickly, my lady. Were you successful?"

"Where's Lord Sebastian?" The house was otherwise empty. No, Brynmor sat hugging his knees with his face buried in his hands. He wasn't there a moment ago, she was sure.

"Well, that was the very definition of harrowing!" said Lord Sebastian behind her. He stood as tall as he could in the short room, dusting himself off. "You're not hurt, are you, Princess?"

Without a word, Brynmor stood and left the hut.

"No," she said. "At least, I don't think so."

"Executor Smithies," Lord Sebastian started. "I must say, you certainly under-sold who you intended us to get a blood sample from. Malphas the Many Titled was far from keen to see us."

"Malphas? I do apologize. He shouldn't be so near the entrance."

"He seemed to think we'd met before."

Executor Smithies crinkled their brow. "I'm surprised you could have forgotten such a name, Lord Sebastian."

Gabriela felt her forehead and wiped the sweat from it on her dress. "Excuse me." She handed the sword to the knight and stepped into the cool night air that took her breath away from the sudden shock of it. She hadn't noticed the stifling heat of the tiny hut from the hell below it until she was out of it.

Brynmor stood before Harvey, extending a hand to the horse's long nose. The horse sniffed at the air, his ears swiveling with confusion.

"My world is crumbling around me," he said.

Hoping some routine would help calm her mind, Gabriela took a brush from Carmel's bag.

Harvey shook away from Brynmor's hand. "Ghosts, profane magic, devils and demons. The goddess has forsaken this world; forsaken me."

"I suppose I've lived a sheltered life," said Gabriela. "My books only say so much and I expected things beyond my ken out here, but not... Malphas."

"Smithies says the hells don't exist, but wherever that beast comes from is close enough. And you. You're a powerful death mage. Though I suppose we knew that after what you did to me."

"I wasn't sure I could do that."

"You did it at the cemetery. Why not again?"

"I thought that was Mama." Gabriela huffed out a quick, loud breath. "We'll be out of here at first light. Maybe by the time those women catch up, you'll be back in your body, and this can all be forgotten." She brushed Carmel's neck as her pony stooped to pull at the tall grass.

Brynmor lowered to a squat, rubbing his hands through his wavy hair.

Gabriela stopped brushing and stepped nearer. "What is it?"

"My uncle, he doesn't care about me. He's my only family, and I his, and he doesn't care if I'm alive or not."

"That can't be true. He sent those two women after you."

"Miss Lane is always after me, so she hardly counts. If he were truly worried, he would have sent a squad of the king's paladins, not a single swordswoman."

"Maybe..." Gabriela chewed her lip. "Maybe the army of paladins will come later. Maybe he was so worried for you that he immediately sent all those on hand."

"You're exactly correct about that, Gab. Uncle Rhys can't get the paladins without proof of the dead's aggression. He's tried for years. He sent who he had to get my... corpse... back to help him petition for the war he wants."

Gabriela squatted beside him. "Why does he want a war? The dead stay on this side of the Crack, never bothering anyone."

"That's not true, Gab. The dead may not be aggressive, not on their own, but they do wander across the Crack." He looked up at her, and though his features were washed out in swirls of blue and white in the moons' glow, she felt the piercing gray of his eyes. "I was only a few years old when my uncle lost his family, and he blames the dead for it. For fifteen years, he's pleaded with the king to call a war to eradicate anything moving in the Deadvale. Dropping my body at the king's feet may be the last thing he needs to get what he wants."

"Why is your uncle so mad at us? How did he lose his family?"

"My parents died of plague when I was weeks old, so I have always been a ward of my uncle. Then, when I was four years old, we were traveling the duchy, staying in a town near the Crack. The dead attacked and started a fire, but my uncle and his men could only save me."

"What a shame. You say the dead started the fire? Not that a fire started in an attempt to fight them off?"

"What are you implying? They died because the dead attacked."

"That doesn't like something they'd do. But I'm sorry, continue."

"He lost his wife and three children, leaving him with only me. He blames me for their deaths. A fact he reminds me of often."

"Like you reminding me of my part in your death."

155

He rose to stand, speaking slowly. "Maybe that wasn't, strictly speaking, the most productive."

She stood as well. "The uncle that resents your survival will want to use your death to get the war of vengeance he's wanted for fifteen years. Yet you were still surveying Mytara, doing his will."

"By the gods, Gab, I sound pathetic when you say it like that. There may be some truth in it. I don't like the man, but he's all I have. I love him, in some weird way, and I want him to love me."

"Why?"

Brynmor floundered for a response, opening and closing his mouth like a ghost fish out of water. "How are you any better?"

"What about me?"

"Your mother clearly has no respect for you. She called your plans silly, dismissing them. Then she shoved you aside to take over when she saw you wouldn't give up. Now she's sent you away without explanation. Good on you for denying her will. It makes me want to do something against my uncle. Why do you put up with it?"

"She just wants to keep me safe. It's a dangerous world, and she loves me."

"Look at you now, without her. You just stood against a demon prince and walked away with his blood."

She couldn't stop the smile. It had all been wild luck, but wasn't most success?

"Have you wondered who your real parents are? Or were?" Brynmor asked.

Gabriela squinted at the marquess. "How do you mean?"

Brynmor puffed out his cheeks. "How can Queen Venica, a dead sorceress, be your birth mother?"

"Dead? Mama isn't dead. She used to read to me and Aura. I'd put my head on her chest and hear her heart with one ear and the story with the other. She might look closer to you inside Lord Sebastian, a little gray around the edges, but..." She waved off the dialog and wiped a tear from her cheek. "I've seen the lengths she has gone through for me. She is my mother."

"Hmm, very well. There's something admirable to that."

"It seems we have more in common than we thought. We both want approval that might never come." She took his gloved hands in hers with a squeeze.

"How can you do that?" he asked, looking down at her hand, raising it to hold with both of his.

"I just can? I don't know. Mama says people believe in their gods and saints, but for most, that's a hope, not objective truth. I don't *believe* in ghosts. I know they exist, so I can see and touch them."

"You see beyond the natural world just by sheer force of will?"

"What's beyond natural? Ghosts are completely natural."

"Princess?" said Lord Sebastian from behind. "You should rest. I can keep the marquess company and watch for his girlfriends."

"They're not my—" Brynmor let out a long breath. "Good night, Gab." He raised her hand to kiss the back of it.

Back in the heat of the hut, Gabriela eyed the portal leading to Malphas' realm. She half expected a flaming, clawed hand to grasp from the pit to drag the demon prince into her world. She curled on her side, facing the wall in Executor Smithies' short bed. The back of her hand tingled where Brynmor pressed his ghostly lips to it, and she found herself grinning, tracing a circle around the spot as she drifted to sleep.

CHAPTER 21

THE PUZZLE BOX

"Of course they thought to lose us in a bog." Commander Ravell paused at the edge of the misty valley. Both moons shone from high overhead, casting an eerie radiance over the landscape, shrouding any detail.

"We don't even know if they still know we're following them. How insane are we to rush so deep into the Deadvale, just the two of us?" Eleanor glanced up from the glass lenses and etching rod she'd been fruitlessly toiling over the last half hour. "I can't do this, Valoria. We have to stop. It's the middle of the night. I'm exhausted. I can't finish these modifications without a steady work surface."

"There is no point to that. We will catch up to the marquess and force him to return."

Eleanor squeezed her eyes tight. They burned from so many hours of focus beyond her usual bedtime. "There's something more to Lady Marwol, some strange magic at play here."

"As I said, learning about her will be a waste of time." Ravell continued forward, but Eleanor moved to lean against a boulder. The commander circled back. "We are not stopping yet."

"You go right ahead. I'm not navigating a swamp at night when I can barely stay upright." Eleanor looked at the lens, trying to focus, gave up, and tucked it into the pouch at her hip. The modifications would have to wait for the morning.

"This is unacceptable, Miss Lane. I demand—"

"I don't care."

"You don't ca... You clearly do not understand the importance of my position, Miss Lane, and the respect owed to me. Duke Highgate gave clear orders, and I will see those through."

Eleanor waved at the misty valley beyond Ravell. "Don't let me stop you."

Ravell squeezed a fist with an audible cracking of her leather gloves. "You know your importance in this mission. Would you have me beg?"

"Beg? No. A bit of respect and common sense would go a long way, though. I heard you were a grand military strategist, yet here we are, wandering a swamp on foot in the middle of the night."

"They would have gotten away had we gone after the horses."

"They got away, anyway, and they'll continue getting away. We need rest and an actual plan."

Ravell tapped a finger on her plate tassets. "Six hours, that's how long we have until first light. We can rest for six hours."

"Well, that's something, at least." Eleanor found a patch of ground and started to spread out her tools. She quickly decided against it to instead curl up on her side with her back to the commander. The damp ground immediately leeched into her clothes, slowly soaking her while tiny rocks found all her joints.

It would be a long night.

Despite it all, her eyes refused to stay open.

Infuriating woman. I should be taking my time to record every detail about the magic here, not racing after a man who doesn't want to be caught.

A boot scraped on the loose rocks behind her, and she sensed Ravell sitting nearby.

"It would be better if we worked together," Commander Ravell whispered.

Eleanor pulled her cloak a little tighter, curling into a smaller ball.

"I want to blame you, Miss Lane... Eleanor. My life has been dedicated to the military since I joined almost twenty years ago. I am not accustomed to traveling with civilians, and you are not accustomed to taking orders."

Eleanor couldn't stop herself from laughing. "That's what you get from this? That I'm bad at taking orders?" She rolled back just enough to see Ravell sitting behind her, outlined by the moonlight.

"Were you a soldier, we would have given immediate chase from the cemetery—"

Eleanor rolled back, tossing her cloak over her head. "Wake me up in six hours. Then I'll need another hour to work."

She imagined hearing the commander's teeth grinding, but that only made her grin.

Eleanor extended her senses to the surrounding magic as she lay there but couldn't determine much without her instruments. She lamented the loss of most of them with the fleeing of their horses but wondered how effective they would be in the Deadvale, anyway. At least not without heavy modifications, which Ravell seemed hellbent against allowing time for.

Between the day's physical and mental excitement, it felt like only minutes later a hand shook Eleanor's shoulder.

"Miss Lane, the sun is rising soon."

Eleanor rolled from the same position she'd laid down in, stretching and staring up at a dark sky with only the faintest hint of some distant dawn. She sat up, unbuckling the pouch from her hip to carefully lay the contents before her. Eleanor noticed her companion's distant stare even in the dim early light.

"Did you sleep at all, Valoria?"

"How could anyone rest in the Deadvale, where not even the dead sleep?"

"So dramatic." Eleanor turned her attention back to her goggles, array of lenses, and compass in front of her. There was also the commander's pistol. She carefully turned the ammunition wheel, counting three more shots. Eleanor itched to admire the thing's craftsmanship, but reason told her there was a better use for her time. One final item, her father's puzzle box. She clearly remembered leaving it in Treasure's saddlebag, yet there it was beside the rest of her possessions.

Ravell shifted to face her. "What do you intend to do with all of that?"

161

Not spend time explaining magic to you, for one.

"Brynmor's companion had some queer magic about her. The better I can see and understand that, the better our chances of countering her."

"May I help?"

Eleanor paused with an etching rod in hand. "Help me with my work? No. You can by getting some rest. Leave me to this."

"The puzzle box. I thought that lost when the horses fled in the Gardens."

"Me too, but I'm glad it's here." She traced a finger along a steel cog on the box's edge.

"I saw you working to solve it for hours before we reached Crystalwood Gardens. It must be well-constructed."

Eleanor hummed an affirmative. "My father sends me one every year on the same day, always trying to outdo himself."

Ravell said nothing for a long breath before asking in an uncharacteristically small voice. "May I attempt it?"

"Attempt the puzzle? It can only be solved once. When it's opened, that's it. I eat the chocolate inside and send the wrapper and parts home as proof."

"Then could I look it over? Perhaps I might notice something you have overlooked."

"No, thank you. I'll solve it alone."

"You insulted my ability as a military strategist last night, Eleanor. I readily admit we are in a dire situation, but you must understand that I am not a field commander. During the Ironcliff Campaigns, my maneuvers saved untold lives."

"You're good with board games but not thinking on your feet. Got it."

"That is a gross oversimplification."

"And you thought you could show that off by solving the puzzle box, thus forcing me to admit your superior intellectual prowess."

The commander's back stiffened. "Do not put words into my mouth, Eleanor. We might have bonded over it, but you will not even allow me to look at the thing."

Eleanor snatched up the little cube, held it toward Ravell for a breath, then dropped it back into her pouch. "Maybe I don't want to bond with the person that dragged me into the damned Deadvale."

Ravell shifted away, her eyes traveling over the items before Eleanor. "Is this why you were... excused from the academy? This tinkering?"

Eleanor held back a sigh. She didn't want to waste time explaining her life but wondered if some context would garner her owed respect from the commander.

"The long story short is I found some shortcuts to magic. Well, that's not right. It isn't as though I discovered anything new, I just tried out something that seemed the logical next step, and, what do you know, it worked." Eleanor idly rearranged the colored lenses before her without any order in mind. "Turns out, the church gets really upset when you don't follow the lessons exactly, but I've always been one to learn more from understanding why something is done the way it is, not just copy the examples from the textbook."

"A heretic."

"A free thinker. That you go straight to 'heretic' says a lot about your indoctrination, Valoria."

"Magic is a gift from the Elysara, a tool to serve Her will."

Eleanor picked up and waved her goggles at the commander. "These let me see the flow of magic through the ground and air. Three years at the academy never came close to mentioning what I can easily see with these, yet I learned a dozen ways to pray to the goddess for minor spells to create light or turn sand into food. Tell me, why learn an unnecessary ceremony when I can access magic without the goddess's express consent? With these, I can see the eddies of magic and pull on them directly to light a candle. I can do that without a single phrase uttered to the goddess."

"You are defining heresy."

"Am I? How is magic the goddess's gift if I don't *need* to pray to use it? That means I, an insignificant mortal, can circumvent Her will."

"I have more than once heard you utter a prayer."

"Habit. They still serve a purpose to focus the mind in a way needed to use magic, even if the words go unheard."

"Elysara hears all."

"I'm sure She does. You wanted to know why I left the academy. I submitted my theories on the ebb and flow of magic. My professors threw up an alarm. The deans voted to expel me, but I was already set on leaving. They said they wouldn't pursue any charges against me so long as I didn't teach my methods."

Ravell traced a finger along her lips. "That is far less fiery than I thought."

"Well, that's it. I wanted to explore the nature of magic. They asked me to go. I said I already had my stuff packed. It's not that interesting."

"Then, even knowing all this, Duke Highgate brought you into his employ almost immediately after."

"He needed someone to watch his nephew from afar but had no problem trying to blame me for letting Brynmor get himself killed."

"Thank you for sharing this with me."

Eleanor waved her off with a grunt. "Now, stop talking to me and rest for an hour. My compass readings imply they've been stopped for a while. Maybe we can catch up, but only if you've rested."

CHAPTER 22

THE HAT MAKES THE DIFFERENCE

"Wakey, wakey, Princess!"

Lord Sebastian's urgency, more than his words, cut through her slumber. She stirred, stretching on a bed that barely reached her knees, kicking the far wall.

"Is it morning already?" she asked, wiping a forearm across her eyes.

"Past, yes." Lord Sebastian fluttered the single thin blanket from her, folding it in one smooth motion. "Far too past. We must be off."

Gabriela rolled from the bed, pulled on her boots, and exited the hut to a world of deep mist. The fog choked any vision beyond a few dozen feet, bathing the world in a quiet shroud. The sun hovered a few inches over the horizon as Lord Sebastian rushed past her to stand beside Carmel. Brynmor stood in front of his own horse, looking to be still attempting communication.

"Where's Executor Smithies?" Gabriela asked.

"They received some communiqué in the night and rushed away. They left their condolences for not seeing us off but didn't want to wake you. Up on Carmel, let's be off."

"Will they be back soon?"

"I couldn't say."

"You have the sword? Will that work for the ritual?"

"Yes, I secured it to the viscount's horse. Brilliant job on that last night, Princess." Lord Sebastian shooed her forward. "Come, come."

"Why the rush? Can't I have something to eat first?"

"No time," Lord Sebastian patted Carmel's saddle. "Aura just saw the viscount's lady friends in the fog. They'll be here any moment."

"What?" Gabriela rushed to clamber onto her pony, and Lord Sebastian mounted Harvey. "Why didn't you say that immediately?"

"Please don't yell at me. I'm not used to being on the run."

"The scary lady is close! So close!" Aura's words came from the air itself without making herself visible.

"I thought they didn't have their horses," said Gabriela. "How did they catch up so quickly?"

Lord Sebastian trumpeted, like clearing his throat. "I may have lost track of the time after Executor Smithies left in the night. We've likely been stopped for over ten hours, and..."

"What is it?"

"And I don't think we took the most direct route through the Mire last night. Or really at all since your mother wasn't the one leading us. You know how I tend to weave and wander when the road is unclear."

"Unclear? We should be going directly to Mama's tower by the straightest path." She glanced back at Brynmor silently trudging behind them. "What's wrong with him?"

"His condition is starting to set in. He tried to talk with his horse all night, and that went as well as you would expect."

"Well, yes, what would he expect? Horses can sort of sense ghosts, but horses can't talk."

"This coming from the person who regularly talks with skeletons."

"That's different. They have human body language they can communicate with."

"And no ears with which to hear."

"What are you implying, Lord Sebastian?"

"Nothing, Princess, not a single thing."

"You hear me just fine without ears."

"And I'm sure the skeletons can, as well."

Looking back at Brynmor again, Gabriela caught movement in the mist that burned with the early day's light. They couldn't be more than a hundred paces away, jogging through the fog, the woman in big armor and the other wearing a leather hat and coat three sizes too big.

"Aura!" she hissed. "Aura! Do something about them!"

The green ghost faded into sight, hovering a few inches from Gabriela's nose. She was upside-down, though the hair that draped around her shoulders must not have known that.

"What'll I get?"

"I can't barter every time I ask something of you, Aura. Whatever you want, just help us get away from them."

"Anything?" Aura swirled around Gabriela's head twice before settling right-side-up, floating in front of Carmel. "Will you do for me what you're doing for him?" She pointed past Gabriela to Brynmor trailing behind.

"Don't be silly, Aura. That's impossible."

"But you're trying for him. Try it for me."

"Since when do you even want— We can't debate it right now. Just help me!"

Aura screwed up her face with genuine anger. She drifted backward, creating space between her and Gabriela, moving closer to Lord Sebastian atop Harvey.

"You won't? You won't even try?" she asked, pouting.

"No. Mama says you need a body, and I've no idea where yours is."

The ambient temperature dropped suddenly. Aura's glow flashed a blinding brilliance, and she screamed, a single prolonged wail that bored into Gabriela's skull, forcing her to clap her hands over her ears. Lord Sebastian turned in his saddle just as Aura blasted backward, impacting Harvey's rump. The noble steed screamed, leaping into a buck that tossed his rider, and was bounding away before Lord Sebastian hit the marshy ground. Gabriela reached for the fleeing mount, as useless as the motion was.

"Dammit, Aura!"

Lord Sebastian rose, seeming to favor his right leg as he did. "Well, that was less than optimal. I think the good sir's leg might have taken a beating on..." He paused, looking down at the small, but very jagged, rock he'd landed on. "I think it's broken."

"Can you walk?" Gabriela glanced back again. The mist had thickened, and she saw nothing of the two women. "Or run?"

"His broken leg means nothing to me, but I worry about the— No, I can't spend all my effort worrying over him. There is nothing to be done about it. Take Carmel on a gallop. Get to your mother. I will hold off the women." Lord Sebastian limped to stand with his fists on his hips behind her.

"No, you won't. We can't outrun them, these women with unending stamina. Let me talk to them this time." Gabriela dismounted. She took Brynmor's hand as she approached him. As she did, he looked up, his eyes focused for the first time all day.

"Brynmor, I need you to focus. I need you to help me talk with your girl-friends."

"They aren't my—"

She waved him to be quiet as the first pursuer resolved from the mist. Her polished armor's white and darker blues gleamed in the diffuse morning light, contrasted by the dark metal of the massive blade she held resting on her right shoulder.

"Viscount Highgate," she said, "come with me immediately."

Gabriela blew out a quick breath and stepped forward. "Commander Ravell, we weren't properly introduced before. I am Gabriela Marwol and this..." She bit her lip, gesturing at the knight in soft leather at her side. "This is my knight protector, Lord Sebastian Rafferty."

Commander Ravell's eyes flicked between the two, but there was no other hint of body language. No shift of the hips, squint of the eye, or tilt of the head. Completely unreadable.

"That was the name on the crypt you entered," said the commander. "I do not know what game is at play here, but I suspect all denizens of the Deadvale are up to odd and nefarious things. Very well." She hefted the blade from her shoulder to rest the squared end against the ground with both hands on the pommel. Her icy gaze shifted to Lord Sebastian. "Remove your helmet. Deepen my confusion about the events and dialog yesterday, but prove this one thing for me. I will leave you to whatever trivialities fill your time."

Gabriela glanced up at the knight at her side. "Where is your partner? Miss Eleanor Lane, with all her tracking magic?"

"I feel woefully ill-prepared." Ravell's lip twitched with what might have been the beginnings of a smirk. "You know so much about us, but we so little about you. Were you not introduced as a lady yesterday?" There was the smirk again.

"You're enjoying this. Where is Miss Lane? Are you planning some ambush? I read all about those in my mother's library."

"Your mother? Was she the woman across the bridge? The one that summoned the dead against us?"

"I summoned—" She bit her lips to stop the flood of words. "Leave us be."

"I cannot do that. My duty is to return the marquess to his uncle. Miss Lane's devices point to that suit of armor being him, though I do not understand how. Take off your helmet. Prove you are not the viscount, ensorcelled."

Brynmor wandered forward, halving the distance to the commander. "Tell her my uncle isn't worth her loyalty. Tell her it won't make up for her loss."

Gabriela took a deep breath. "The duke isn't worth your loyalty, Commander. He's a selfish man, ruled by blind grief. Nothing you do for him will make up for your losses."

Ravell's stone countenance shuttered just slightly. "Do not pretend to know me."

"She blames herself for a friend's death," Brynmor continued. "Honestly, I never paid that close attention to the details. I suppose I should have."

"Your friend," said Gabriela, invoking the softer voice her mother sometimes used. "They're gone, but you cannot dedicate your life to that guilt."

Ravell grasped her sword, swinging it forward to an aggressive stance. "What foul profane magics have you wormed into my mind? Release them, or I will part you from your head."

The woman in too-large clothes ran in from the left, yelling and waving her arms. She stopped between Ravell and Brynmor. "Stop, Valoria, stop! I can see him!"

"What are you prattling on about?" Ravell growled.

Eleanor turned to face Gabriela, but it was Brynmor she looked at. She adjusted the lens of her huge goggles, covering only her right eye. "It's the marquess," she said, leaning nearer.

"Then remove your helmet and prove it," said Ravell.

"Not there, here," Eleanor waved at Brynmor's ghost.

"You can see me?" he gaped.

"Illusory tricks and profane magic," Ravell scoffed. "There is nothing there, Eleanor."

"Not that you can see, but—" she turned to Gabriela, her eyebrows high with excitement. "What am I seeing here?" She whipped back to the confused marquess. "My Lord, can you hear me?"

Brynmor winced away, sticking a finger in his ear. "There's no reason to shout."

"She can't hear you," said Gabriela. "I don't know why she can see you. Miss L... Eleanor, how can you see him?" She knew it must be the work of those intricate goggles, not that she could guess beyond that.

Commander Ravell bristled behind her companion. "Eleanor, step aside. We do not know the threat here."

"You two are the threat!" Brynmor waved his arms wildly. "You two are not to interfere. We are on a mission beyond your ken."

"What's he saying?" Eleanor asked.

Gabriela grunted, seeing what would be her role for the moment. "He wants you two to leave."

"See for yourself." Eleanor pulled off the goggles, offering them to Ravell.

After a long moment of drawn-out hesitancy, the commander accepted them and shifted her sword to set the flat end against the ground again. She squinted through the glass, her face vacillating between confusion and incredulity. She handed them back within a few tense breaths. "I will not ask again. Remove your helmet."

"I think you must, Lord Sebastian," said Brynmor. "We can't outrun them and can't fight them. I doubt we can sway the commander's insistence on her goal, but maybe you can explain it in terms that Eleanor will be sympathetic to."

"Doubtful," grumbled Lord Sebastian.

"What was that?" Ravell snapped.

"We are on a mission for the queen of the Deadvale," the knight boomed. "Viscount Brynmor is in no danger of injury." He limped forward one step. "Further injury."

Gabriela hissed and waved Lord Sebastian back.

"I shot you," Ravell growled. "How are you—"

"The queen of the Deadvale?" Eleanor said, suddenly with a notebook and pen in hand.

"My mother." Gabriela stepped in front of Lord Sebastian, urging him back. "I am Princess Gabriela Marwol of the Deadvale. I rescued Viscount Byrnmor Highgate after he was injured in Mytara and am taking him to my mother for healing."

"Your mother, the queen? What is her name?" Eleanor scratched in her notebook while Ravell fumed behind her.

"Queen Venica Marwol."

"Queen?" Ravell said, her expression shying back just half an inch. She shook her head, taking a deep breath. "Then she is in charge of the Deadvale's armies. Eleanor, step away."

"Armies?" Gabriela raised a hand to cover her laugh.

Ravell raised her blade again. "Why are you laughing?"

"We don't have an army."

"Should I do it?" Lord Sebastian asked, bringing both hands to his helmet.

"What? No!" Gabriela gasped when she saw what he threatened to do.

"Do it," said Ravell, her mouth barely parting with her demand. "Remove your helm, or I will end this here and now."

"Threats! Threats!" Aura flew between Brynmor and Eleanor, who fell back a step, her mouth wide as she adjusted the goggles.

"What in all the hells was that?" Eleanor gasped.

"This will never work," said Brynmor. "Unless they can both see and hear me, they will assume you're up to some trick."

Ravell had rushed forward, taking Eleanor by the shoulder and pushing her to the side. "Final warning."

"I have to do it, Princess!" Lord Sebastian said, but she could hear the humor in his tone. There was no way to stop him when he set his mind to a task. Except with another, shinier task, and Gabriela had no others in mind. This would at least advance the conversation, if nothing else.

Lord Sebastian pulled his helmet up, and Brynmor's head flopped to the side. Eleanor gasped and fell back another step, but Commander Ravell surged forward, blade held in a high stance that Gabriela didn't recognize from all her books.

"What have you done to the viscount?" she screamed.

"That's what I've been trying to tell you," said Gabriela, unsure if that was true. The conversation had rather gotten away from her. "He's been injured, and we're taking him to my mother."

"No more foul, profane magics of the Deadvale will touch the viscount's body or soul," Ravell glanced sidelong to where she'd seen Brynmor's ghost. "Villains!" She flourished her blade and settled into yet another stance.

"Oh, just do it if you're doing it," said Lord Sebastian. "Why do you keep hesitating, commander? Unsure of your orders as they apply here? I was a knight before I was an earl. I outranked the one that gives you orders today. So I say you must return to the duke and... I don't care what. Just go away." He shooed her.

Eleanor stepped up behind Ravell, pushing her aside to hold up a leather glove. "This is his, isn't it?"

"My glove!" Brynmor exclaimed, raising and flexing his naked ghost hand.

Eleanor noticed his attention. "How injured is the marquess? Some sort of out-of-body experience? Is this aetherial projection?"

"You could say that," said Gabriela.

"If you," Eleanor said to Brynmor's ghost, "are the real marquess, prove it somehow. If Princess Marwol—"

"You can just call me Gab."

Eleanor frowned but nodded. "If Gab can hear your words, prove she isn't altering them. Tell us something only Viscount Brynmor Highgate would know."

"Didn't I already do that in the cemetery?" Brynmor asked, putting his fists on his hips.

Eleanor glanced at Gabriela expectantly.

"He did that in front of the Rafferty tomb, feeding words to Lord Sebastian."

"Something else, then," said Eleanor.

Brynmor sighed, rolling his eyes and neck. He tapped his gloved hand to his forehead before silently snapping his fingers. "My uncle is allergic to mushrooms. He says he doesn't like them and that he passionately hates their taste and texture. He forbids any in the kitchens of Montker Abbey. He even fired an aide, sending them from the duchy last year because they brought some in from town."

Gabriela frowned. She'd hoped Brynmor would reveal some juicy secret about himself, not his uncle. "That's all? Mushrooms?" she said. "The duke's allergic to them."

"Tell them about the aide," Brynmore pressed.

"No. This conversation is exhausting."

Eleanor looked back at Ravell, who relaxed her stance. Not that that meant anything. It might have just been exhausting to hold still for so long.

"They won't just let us walk off," said Brynmor. "They think I'm asleep inside Lord Sebastian and just took some terrible fright."

"What do you suggest then, good sir?" asked the knight.

"Same as the cemetery, but without the tricks."

"To what end? Will we take two mortal women to Mum's tower and... what? Let them watch the... procedure? I suppose they could put in a good word and escort you back home to your loving uncle."

Eleanor glanced between Brynmor and Lord Sebastian, only hearing half the conversation, but eyes squinting, either trying to read ghost lips or guess at the missing lines. "You speak without anger," she said. "My Lord, you are either a clever illusion only visible to my enchanted lenses or the marquess. Do you control this suit of armor remotely? Why, if it can talk, do you not have it speak your words directly? I have so many questions!" Eleanor's suspicion gently morphed into excited curiosity.

"There's more to it than that," said Gabriela.

"Brynmor is dead," said Lord Sebastian. Everyone shifted to him with faces of stunned awe. "What? She's talking about me as though I wasn't standing right here and this is taking too long."

"Fiends!" Commander Ravell dodged around Eleanor, swinging her blade high overhead to bring it down on Gabriela. The woman's white armor filled her vision, and the contrasting dark blade was a blur. Soft leather replaced the white. Lord Sebastian raised a forearm to block or deflect the strike, the commander's sword biting deep into his gauntlet. His other hand rested on her chest plate, his fingers spread.

Neither moved for an agonizing moment.

Gabriela skipped to the side as Lord Sebastian collapsed before her, but Ravell remained frozen. A look of horror plastered her face.

"What foul sorcery is this?" she bellowed, shifting slightly but maintaining the stance with her blade where it hit the knight. "What have you done to my armor?"

Gabriela stepped around the frozen commander, barely noticing Eleanor drop beside Lord Sebastian, putting her fingers to Brynmor's neck.

"I wasn't sure I could do that. How fun," came Lord Sebastian's voice from Commander Ravell.

"What have you..." Ravell gritted her teeth with her effort to move.

"He's dead," said Eleanor, sitting back on her heels.

"That's what I told you," said Lord Sebastian.

"What did you do?" asked Gabriela.

"I shifted to the commander's armor. I can do that, apparently."

"And what if you couldn't?"

"I suppose she would have cut off mine and the viscount's arm, then moved on to cutting off other things." Ravell's arms shifted a few inches. "Goodness, you are frightfully strong."

"Release me!"

"Not yet."

Eleanor stood, brushing her hands over her leather jacket, looking as casual as if she'd just overturned a rock to look for beetles. "The magic at play here is so far advanced beyond anything I imagined. Is that... Is that Brynmor's ghost, then?"

Gabriela nodded. "Everything was an accident. A completely innocent accident."

Brynmor scoffed.

"Eleanor!" Ravell yelled. Sweat poured down her face.

Eleanor looked between each person, ghost, and corpse around her, considering each in turn before settling back on Gabriela. "Your mother, this queen, you intend for her to resurrect Brynmor? Is that even possible?"

"Mama seems to think so, but not for much longer. Her magic is getting thin, as is what's tethering Brynmor to me."

Eleanor stared for a long moment, her eyes sinking into Gabriela's. "Explain in detail how this was done and how it will be remedied." She had her notebook out again.

"Eleanor! We have no time for this!" Ravell grunted. "Release me, abomination, and I will grant you a swift release from this world."

"That is exactly the sort of talk that makes me not want to," said Lord Sebastian.

"Do you have her secure?" Gabriela asked.

"I think?" His voice lilted upwards with uncertainty. "She's strong, but all I have to do is hold still."

Ravell again screamed with rage as her fingers twitched and her sword clattered to the ground.

"Well, look at that," mused Lord Sebastian.

Eleanor stepped between Gabriela and the struggling commander. "You speak of resurrection. No magic is more profane, more blasphemous to the church. Nothing so directly subverts the will of the goddess."

Gabriela shrugged. "If you say so."

"But you think it can be done?"

"That's what Mama thinks. Or thought, unless she... Well, she still thinks it, I'm sure."

Eleanor's brow pinched, but she shook it off. "The duke would see the Deadvale wiped clean, your home destroyed. I could spare you his wrath if you share this magic with me."

"Mama didn't seem too worried about the duke's armies."

"Not the duke's armies," said Ravell. "The king's. His paladins once harried the Deadvale, but at the combined command of the king and church, they will call the divine word of the goddess to cleanse this land of your kind." She let out

175

a long breath, pausing her struggle within her armor. "You will swing for this, Eleanor, for even considering partnering with denizens of the Deadvale."

"No! Think of it, Valoria. If death could be reversed, imagine what good could be done."

"At what cost?"

"We can find out."

"You're mad. You would stand idly by and allow profane magic against your superior?"

"I've made my thoughts about my position relative to nobility clear. We will witness the cost and process, then report that to the duke or king. I will bear full responsibility; you can say I forced you, should it come to that."

"You... force me? You would trust them? Known agents of the Deadvale, when you wouldn't trust me with a puzzle box?"

"That was different. That was my father's and the only one he made."

"Your life and freedom are less unique and valuable than a puzzle box?"

"Yes. I would give my life for such knowledge as what Prin— Gab may offer."

"You are a fool."

"I don't like where this is going," said Brynmor. "What about my body?"

Gabriela frowned at Lord Sebastian's crumpled form with Brynmor's head where the helmet should be. "We need that, but Lord Sebastian was carrying him. I don't suppose you could both move him and restrain the commander? Or have her carry, erm, you?"

Lord Sebastian's laugh echoed strangely from Ravell's plate armor. "Goodness, no. She's wickedly strong. It would take only the slightest distraction for her to do something dramatic."

"And we know how you are with distractions," Brynmor murmured.

"You would be wise not to release me," warned Ravell.

"Fish eyes!" Gabriela shouted. "The blood! Harvey had the sword."

"That's it then." Brynmor threw up his hands. "We fail because my horse ran off with a rusty sword, and no one will knock the commander over the head with a rock."

"That does give me an idea," Gabriela said.

"What did he say?" Eleanor asked.

Gabriela ignored the question. "Commander, we are on a mission, and you are the only thing stopping it right now. I was kind at Crystalwood to raise the dead only to stand in your way. I could call them now for violence. You would be helpless as they..." The books in Mama's library never went into detail about small combat. "Hit you."

Ravell raised her face to look down her nose at Gabriela. "Then I will die knowing I have not given in to heathens and heretics."

"What a waste," said Lord Sebastian.

"That helps no one," said Gabriela. "What good are personal morality codes when you're dead?" Gabriela asked.

"Those codes define me."

"What is your idea, Princess?" asked Lord Sebastian. "I'd rather not stand here all day."

"Brynmor suggested we bash the commander over her head, but we're not violent people, and I think it's important that we show that to our guests." Eleanor and Ravell looked aghast at Gabriela's casual tone. "You wait here, Lord Sebastian, until she falls asleep, swap back to yourself, and run after us." She beamed. It was a clever plan.

Brynmor groaned.

"I will not abandon you here, Princess."

"I won't be alone. Eleanor, you'll come, right?"

Eleanor sputtered a response in the affirmative.

"You can't be serious!" Brynmor shouted. "You can't trust her."

Eleanor's face was a mask of shock but no malice.

Gabriela shrugged. "She wants to learn about magic. So do I."

"Far be it for me to deny you a new companion," said Lord Sebastian. "But you can't leave Brynmor's corpse lying out in a puddle. Don't forget it's a key component in returning him. You could strip me and toss him over Carmel's back."

Gabriela looked back at her pony, and the sharp rock Lord Sebastian fell on. He had a point. If the commander fought him too long, it might be too late for Brynmor once Lord Sebastian caught up with the body.

177

She knelt to start pulling the soft leather armor from the body, stacking it in a neat pile to the side, knowing that once he inhabited it again, Lord Sebastian could reassemble the pieces far easier than she could without a mannequin. To her surprise, Eleanor helped wrangle the embossed chest piece around Brynmor's bulk and took one arm to haul the body over her pony's saddle.

All while Commander Ravell continued a litany of dark curses and threats, Brynmor fretted for them to take care of him.

"Princess, if you beat me to the tower, promise me you will find your mother immediately. Eldrisil bristles with untold dangers beyond mere physical threats that wouldn't spare the time to differentiate you from a foe."

"I will."

"Why?" Eleanor asked when the body seemed secure. "Why are you trusting me?"

Gabriela could have described the profound sense of kinship she felt for the woman or the soft glow of her soul. She could even cite the shape of Eleanor's orbital bone as a proven indicator of trustworthiness.

Instead, she said, "I like your hat."

CHAPTER 23

SWARMING DEAD

*S*tubbornness and stupidity, that's what this is, and that's what will be my death. No, not stupidity, not when I know and vaguely understand what I'm doing. This is a special kind of madness, to follow this girl alone into the very heart of hell.

Eleanor glanced back once more at the commander, her gleaming armor stark against the ever-present mist before the fog took the last sight of her.

She had a point. I wouldn't trust her with my father's puzzle box for fear she would damage it, yet look at me now.

"How did you find us, Eleanor? Brynmor thinks you have something on him that you can track with magic."

"Yes, his necklace with the Highgate family crest." *Also, his boots, coat, gloves, breeches, and pocket watch.* "It was necessary for my job that I follow the marquess at a distance and keep my interference minimal."

"Look where that's gotten you," said Brynmor.

"I wish I could hear what you're saying, My Lord."

"Maybe if you're here long enough, you can pick that up." Gabriela led her pony but with a distinct lack of confidence. "We have to rush," she said. "Once the commander is free, she'll be hot on our trail. Our only hope is to lose her and get to the tower well in advance."

Eleanor noted Gabriela's shifting glances and the slow weave to their path that had nothing to do with avoiding the terrain. "Then I would suggest a direct path," she said. "I assume you know the way?"

Gabriela's silence stretched.

"Princess?"

Gabriela turned a slow circle, eyes flicking across the mist.

"Gab, you know the way to this tower?"

"Not exactly, but how hard could it be to find? It sounds like a huge tower. I'm surprised we can't see it from everywhere in the Deadvale."

Eleanor's pace slowed as she saw her new companion in a different light. They hadn't been outmaneuvered in the cemetery by some magical mastermind. This young woman and the enchanted armor, whatever he was, were idiots.

"How can you lead us to the tower if you don't know the way?" Eleanor asked.

Gabriela shrugged. "Again, I expect we'll be able to see it eventually."

"Hold up a moment. I may be able to see the way." Eleanor removed her goggles to swap the lens for the red one. Magic swirled just below the ground, drifting in lazy circles. She watched it through the mist, noting that while the tiny eddies spun, they favored a direction only a few degrees off their current heading. If that wasn't the tower, it was something interesting in that direction, and that was good enough for Eleanor.

"That way," she pointed, swapping in the green lens to see Brynmor again.

Gabriela intently watched the change of colored lenses. "Is that how you tracked us down so quickly?"

"I have other devices at my disposal."

"Did you lose much when your horses ran off? I'm a little sorry about that. Aura isn't the most predictable, as you can guess, since she made Brynmor's horse run off and broke his leg in doing it."

They started in the direction Eleanor indicated. Though she'd rested some insufficient hours last night, her exhaustion was more than that. The Deadvale seemed to sap her strength faster than usual, as though it took her body more energy than it should just to stay alive. Which, by the name of the place, made sense.

"I lost most of my things, but nothing too critical. Aura is the other ghost? The green one?"

Gabriela nodded.

"Who was she? When she was alive."

Gabriela shrugged again. "Mama never told me, as many times as I've asked. Aura's tethered to me like Brynmor is, but her leash is much longer."

"Have you asked Aura?"

Gabriela blinked at her, tilting her head as though she'd spoken a profound riddle.

"Nevermind," said Eleanor.

"I hope Lord Sebastian can hold your friend long enough for us to get to the tower."

Valoria relied wholly on me to guide us here. She'll never catch us once we get onto the hard-packed ground. Where does that leave me, though? I'm leading a death mage to her mother, the queen of death mages.

Ravell's horror stories of the front line rushed back to Eleanor, of death mages raining oblivion, slaying entire battalions with an uttered phrase. How much was a fantasy constructed to keep the soldiers terrified of their supposed enemy? Gabriela claimed the Deadvale had no army, yet any news source would assure their readers otherwise.

Eleanor swapped the lenses again, adjusting their heading. The land sloped gently upward, bringing them out of the soft ground of the misty marsh, into the warm, early summer afternoon sun. She half expected to see a tower hazy between the streaks of white cloud against the blue. But then she did see it. The black needle didn't stretch to the sky, but it must have been a dozen times the height of any structure on the other side of the Crack. She stumbled a step, not at seeing the tower, but at what surrounded the base of it.

A dark mass slowly undulated, visible even at their distance. She swapped in the red lens again to confirm what she expected; the magic underground flowed to the tower.

"Why don't you wear both lenses?" Gabriela asked.

Eleanor expected any discussion to be about the sight before them, so the question took a moment to register. "It would be overwhelming to wear both. Too many types of magic input. What is the marquess saying?"

"Pulled in what way?" Gabriela asked the viscount. His ghost lips moved in response. "You haven't been feeling it before? Aura mentioned it, but... Oh, true, you haven't been dead long enough to know the difference."

Is the marquess being pulled to the tower? Does that mean some entity there is drawing in ghosts, or whatever energy the marquess consists of now?

"Aura?" Gabriela called to the air, but there was no response.

"What is that mass around the base?" Eleanor asked. "It almost looks like... bodies."

"I think it's the dead milling around. Maybe they do that here in preparation for the solstice and full moon. The dead at home return to their crypts, but maybe these can't do that." Gabriela urged them to continue. Her pony followed obediently, unconcerned about walking toward a throng of risen dead.

Eleanor stayed a few paces back, splitting her focus between the tower and the two in front of her. Despite Gabriela's tendency to repeat half of the question in her answer, Eleanor could only infer what the marquess said. *I am mad? Completely bonkers to be following still? I could, I should, return to Valoria, rescue her from that cursed armor, and return to the duke. This is madness. What came over me? Will authoring a few groundbreaking research papers be worth my soul?* She focused on Brynmor, smirking at the irony of it. *Which apparently really do exist.* Each step brought them closer, very literally, to death, but Gabriela's total lack of concern seemed infectious. She appeared to be completely innocent and naive, but not suicidal. If she had no reason to worry, maybe it wouldn't be as bad as Eleanor assumed.

Yet, how could it be anything short of as bad as she assumed? Ahead writhed a horde of risen dead. Ten minutes closer only brought the figures into focus across the flat terrain of scattered rocks. Not just the shambling, slowly shifting skeletons and others with bits of flesh or scraps of clothing, but above, wisps of spectral energy soared, leaving streaks of azure or chartreuse in their wake.

Ghosts.

Brynmor waved his arms in some grand expression. Gabriela covered her mouth to suppress her giggle, but the way she looked up at him was unmistakable. The three were approaching the queen of the death mage's tower, and two were flirting.

"Gabriela!" Eleanor called ahead.

She looked back, still grinning from Brynmor's words, her eyebrows high on her otherwise calm countenance.

Eleanor jogged to catch up. "What is our plan?"

"Plan?"

"Yes, plan. That's a legion of dead. We can't just walk through them to the tower?"

Gabriela glanced forward, then back to Eleanor. "Why not?"

The simple question struck her silent for a moment. "Because they'll attack us."

Gabriela's brow creased. "Why would they do that?"

"Why?" Eleanor never knew a motive for why the dead attacked, but everyone knew they did. Why was this even being asked? "Just trust me. They will."

"Oh, I don't think so." Gabriela flashed a grin and turned forward again.

Eleanor grabbed her by the elbow, spinning Gabriela to a stop. Brynmor leaned back with his arms crossed, apparently enjoying the show. "We have to find another way, Gab."

Gabriela stared down at the hand on her elbow until Eleanor released her. "We're going through. My mother came through this way without trouble, and so will we."

"Oh? Where is his horse?" Eleanor waved at Brynmor. First at his ghost, then the corpse slung over the pony's rump. "Your ally scared him off, so I don't think you're in a position to judge how others will respond right now."

Gabriela's hazel eyes widened as her lip curled downward. "You don't have to say such hurtful things. Aura's always been a free spirit. Pun unintentionally intended." Her lip twitched with a smirk. "But really, I think we'll be fine."

"You *think*? I won't walk through *that* based on what you think."

Gabriela shrugged. "Suit yourself." She turned, clicking her tongue to call her pony along as she continued toward the tower.

Brynmor said something, winked, and turned to follow. Eleanor stared at her back, again at a loss for words. She considered leaving. She never stopped considering leaving. She even turned and took a few steps toward the misty valley. But what lay back that way? Valoria promised all manners of violence for Eleanor's betrayal, and if she returned now, there would be nothing to show for her act of defiance. With her notebook in hand, Eleanor turned back to the tower and the terrifying mass of dead swarming the base.

This is the farthest anyone's gone into the Deadvale in decades that we know of. Other than the incident in the plague village, it hasn't been too bad.

Eleanor snorted. If she told herself a week ago that being waylaid by a town of risen dead wouldn't be "too bad," she'd call herself a nutter. She barely recognized that past self as she followed a stranger, a known death mage. She, who wouldn't trust a companion with her father's puzzle box.

With a groan, Eleanor continued toward the tower.

CHAPTER 24

TALLOW CANDLES

"There is no way my uncle pays that woman enough." Brynmor's eyes kept flitting to his body over Carmel's back as he walked backward.

"What's it like, Brynmor? Do you see the same way now as before?"

"What?"

"I notice you keep looking at your corpse, and I'm wondering if the world looks the same to you as a ghost as through living eyeballs."

Brynmor blinked hard, turning to walk forward. "I hadn't thought of it. I suppose things look like they have a harsher outline, almost like a pencil drawing. Will the dead really leave Eleanor alone? I don't like the woman, but I don't want to see her torn to bits."

"Now that you word it like that, I might be slightly concerned. The dead wouldn't normally do anything, but I see a few that aren't naturally risen." She squinted into the roving pack milling around the tower's base. The vast majority radiated a gentle, utterly harmless green magic, but a few glowed a darker hue, implying they were infused and bidden to stand by someone, rather than by the ambient magics of the Deadvale. Someone, by the number of them, with power on par with her mother.

"I didn't realize there was a difference," said Brynmor. "Though I guess some look a little pinker than the rest if that's what you mean."

Gabriela had never noticed the color pink when seeing the colors of magic associated with the power of necromancy, but agreed with him that must be it. "Some wake up on their own, others are woken up."

"Naturally, those that are woken are angrier. I know I would be."

The slowly pacing dead were under a hundred feet away when their heads pivoted to consider the approaching group. Two alive, one ghost, and another resting like they wished they were across the back of a pony. Their stares through dark, empty sockets gave Gabriela the first hesitation. They let her mother pass, but of course, they would. She was their queen; she commanded endless fonts of magic. Gabriela was none of that. Her feet slowed, seeing none of the benevolence like the skeletons from back home. These were feral dead, if there was such a thing. Set to wander a circle around a tower as their final existence. Why would they have any reason to be friendly?

"No," she said out loud. "I am my mother's daughter, the princess of the Deadvale. They will know and respect my position."

"I appreciate the optimism, Gab," said Brynmor. He moved a little nearer to her, perhaps for protection, but it wasn't clear who was protecting whom.

They paused at the outer edge of circling bodies and yet another hurdle struck her. How could they pass the fifty or so feet to the tower without getting swept in their movement and slowly trampled by a thousand bony feet?

"Valoria would just hack her way through," Eleanor said at her shoulder, making Gabriela jump. She was quickly alternating between the red and green lenses, rarely blinking.

Gabriela took a deep breath and took one more step forward, close enough to touch the nearest dead as it passed, staring at her.

With much jostling and bumping, the rotating mass stopped its pace and turned to face her. She imagined even those on the tower's far side bore into her with those blank sockets.

They were mad, angry. They would step forward to hit her and Eleanor, just as Eleanor was so worried about.

But the dead didn't step forward; they only kept staring.

She cleared her throat.

Sometimes, asking directly is the simplest way to get what you want. She read that in a book.

"Make a path, please. I want to get through."

One by one, their heads cocked to the side as if confused by her request. Brynmor made a small, uneasy sound while Eleanor scribbled furiously in her notebook.

Though she shouldn't have been surprised, because it was exactly what she asked for, the skeletons and fleshier bodies nearest her shuffled back, jostling against those behind. They continued slowly through their tight press, creating a narrow alley just wide enough for her to pass.

"Gods and saints," whispered Brynmor.

Without a glance at her companions, Gabriela raised her head high to step forward, pulling docile Carmel on his rope lead. She only knew Eleanor was following by the feverish, mumbled prayers behind her.

The dead brushed her sleeves as she strode by them, and she worried they might bump Brynmor's body from Carmel's back, but surely Eleanor would say something if that happened. The last bodies shifted away to reveal an arched door made of some dark metal inscribed with the outline of a skeletal oak tree. Gabriela touched the cool stone in the amulet around her neck bearing the same symbol.

The doors split with a crack, swinging inward just before Gabriela could reach to run a finger along the fine design. Beyond, a narrow staircase stretched into the pitch darkness, lit by thick tallow candles.

"Can't stop here," she said. A chill breeze flowed from the depths, bringing the familiar scent of an old tomb, charged with the electric buzz of magic. She breathed that slightly sweet aroma, closing her eyes and thinking of home. She'd never been away this long and had to force out the encroaching worries for her friends.

"Are we standing in the door, or are we going in?" Brynmor asked from behind.

Only the first dozen steps were lit, so Gabriela bent to pry the first tallow candle from the floor, but it was firmly melted in place. The next was the same. She would need a tool to scrape them loose. That was fine; darkness never bothered her.

As she passed the last candle, more ignited with their small flares, pushing away the darkness to reveal more and more stairs continuing in a straight line.

"That's a nice trick." The darkness devoured her words, and she kept unsaid the rest of her thoughts about how much it saved on replenishing candles.

They climbed the stairs dotted with candles until her calves burned, and she wondered how they were still within the tower. Surely such a long, straight staircase would be longer than the tower was wide by now. Ahead, five candles lit themselves at the ceiling of a round room, and the stairs finally ended. A single door to one side leaked daylight through the shutters on its top half, and on the other side was an iron banded door with a brass plate tacked to it. Gabriela ignored the second door, petted Carmel's nose because he was a good boy, and crossed the wood planks to the shuttered door. A simple latch held it closed. She opened it and stepped onto a narrow stone balcony, barely an arm span wide and half that deep. Gabriela put a hand on the railing at hip height, marveling at the view. It must have been over a hundred feet to the ground, but the Deadvale opened below her. It looked so vast, yet she'd crossed so much in the last few days. The swarm of dead ringing the tower was again circling, and she imagined the low cloud in the distance was the Misty Mire.

Which direction was Soulhaven? Were all her friends safely back in their tombs?

She stepped back inside, closing and latching the door after her. Eleanor looked up from where she leaned against the wall, fiddling with her colored lenses. The red and green ones let her see either the flows of magic or Brynmor's ghost, but now she had a blue lens in hand that Gabriela hadn't seen before.

"The view is beautiful. You could probably see all the way to the Crystalwood Gardens on a clear day if you got up a bit higher."

Eleanor's gaze flicked up, but she focused back on her blue lens with a grunt.

"I didn't expect Mama's tower to open to those stairs and then... this." She waved a hand around the unadorned space. The rooms in the Guardian Arms were better furnished.

Eleanor looked up again; her face pinched with thought.

Gabriela moved to the iron banded door, running a finger along the rivets of the hinges. "I guess we only have one way—"

188

"Quiet," whispered Eleanor. "Do you smell that?"

Gabriela breathed deeply but didn't notice anything besides what she smelled when first entering the tower.

Eleanor put on her goggles with the red lens in place, carefully storing the others in the pouch at her hip. She joined Gabriela at the door, running a hand along the smooth wood grain.

"There's holy magic beyond here," Eleanor said so quietly, the words might have been meant for her alone.

"That must have been some side entrance we came through," Brynmor said at full volume, making Gabriela jump, which made Eleanor jump. "There's no way this is the main entrance to the queen's sanctum. The Queen of Death Mages."

"Mama isn't a death mage," said Gabriela, drawing Eleanor's wide gaze. "At least, I don't think so. I'm not sure what that is."

"She's one," said Brynmor.

"They focus on heavily destructive magics," said Eleanor, overlapping Brynmor. "The term is more about their ability to cause death rather than mastery over it."

"Doesn't mean she isn't one," said Brynmor.

"This is annoying," said Gabriela. "Can't you enchant a piece of cotton to stick in your ear so you can hear Brynmor?"

Eleanor snorted, shaking her head. "Artifice doesn't work that way."

"If you say. Time to see what's behind this door."

Gabriela grasped the iron ring and pulled. Murmured conversations flooded from the crack, and she stood at the top of an auditorium. People in dark robes bustled by, hurrying to find a seat, arraying notebooks and quills on the tables before them.

"How..." Gabriela glanced back, but the door and room with the balcony were gone, replaced with a solid wall painted beige. Carmel stood to her left, looking bored, and the other two to her right.

"The academy," said Eleanor with her jaw hanging open.

At the bottom of the half-bowl-shaped room, a rail-thin man in a similar dark robe adorned with yellow and blue tassels entered. The crowd redoubled their

189

efforts to settle as the man stopped at a podium centered in the front, hefting a folio of papers.

Silence fell over the room so complete one could hear a tombstone sigh. The man cleared his throat.

"The vast majority of your recent research papers were uninspired. You retold known truths in manners so tedious and droll, they bring shame to this great institution." He raised a stack of papers, shook them, and tossed them to scatter on the floor beside him. "I wonder what great offense I made against Elysara in this life to justify the torture that was reading your work. A few, very few, failed in a way that leaves the barest glimmer of hope that your young and soft minds might yet be molded into something resembling an academic, or at least the assistant to the assistant to an academic. I have marked those papers, but do not get your hopes up." He waved at the mess beside him.

"I do not consider your papers a failure because I expected nothing greater from this group," he continued. "I said 'vast majority' because not every paper bored me in the same manner. One stood out, and I would like its author to step forward now." He raised a sheet of parchment with two fingers, holding it at arm's length as though it might bite or explode. "Come forward, Miss Eleanor Lane."

Like the circling dead, the students turned as one to face them. Five hundred pairs of eyes drilled into Eleanor. She took a step back, bumping into the beige wall.

"Miss Lane," the professor repeated. "Come down here."

CHAPTER 25

ELEANOR'S PAPER

This was too much for an illusion spell, which implied the image from Aetheria was being inserted directly into Eleanor's mind. The beige wall pressing against her back felt real enough, though. It couldn't be real. Why would everyone be staring at her but ignoring the girl wearing strange clothes and holding the lead of a pony draped with a corpse? They were the ones out of place here.

She stared down at Professor Senin, looking exactly as he had when last she saw him. That had been a private meeting in his office, attended by the Dean of History, the Dean of Divine Lineage, a secretary from admissions, and two priestesses from the Divine Grace Cathedral.

The room had been very crowded.

She had been asked to come for a "discussion regarding the inappropriate topic of her recent submission," which lay on the professor's desk when she entered. Chairs were carefully arranged so all would face her, but no one raised their voice. It might have been better if they had. An hour later, she left the room, no longer a student.

Even at a distance across the packed auditorium, Eleanor could clearly read her paper's title, 'Transcending Belief: An Inquiry into the Intrinsic Nature of Magic, Independent of Religion.'

A thousand eyes bore into her, waiting for her to either move or shrivel away. The beige wall was too solid to pass through, and the room's only exit was the one Professor Senin entered through.

"I think you should go," said Gabriela.

"Thanks, Gab," Eleanor grumbled. Whatever complex magic was at work here wanted to be played out. The simulacrum of Professor Senin would scold and demean her just like the live one had. Like some live nightmare, it would force her to relive that moment that both broke and redefined her life's trajectory.

The words that she left unsaid, unshouted, bubbled forward in her mind. Maybe this construct of cruel magic would allow her to vent what she wished she had years ago.

Eleanor descended the stairs slowly, with purpose, breathing in that odd blend of aromas that were the same as the room with the balcony rather than the parchment, ink, and nervous sweat of five hundred young adults that would usually permeate this auditorium. The heads pivoted as she descended. Professor Senin's tenuous grip on her paper never wavered until she stepped onto the stage beside him, standing on the discarded work of her classmates, and he peered down at her, more than a full head taller.

"So good of you to finally come when called, Miss Lane." He held her paper just a little higher and addressed the room. "I would request the majority of you take your futures into serious consideration. Aetheria Academy has no intention of producing graduates lacking a modicum of original thought. The same can be said for the opposite."

Here it comes. Eleanor rolled back her shoulders, licked her lips, and prepared for the onslaught.

"Miss Lane has produced..." He twitched the paper again for the gathered students to see before slamming it down on the podium. "...the bravest piece of academic work I have ever, in my fifty-three years at this noble institution, had the opportunity—nay, the honor—to read."

Thunderous applause erupted. Robed students jumped to their feet to clap and whoop. Professor Senin, now joined by the other deans, the secretary from admissions, and flanked by a score of priestesses, offered her a framed glass case containing a gleaming platinum medal. "Dean of Magical Research: Miss Eleanor Lane" was carved into it, the letters catching and shining back at her from the gas lamps around the room.

"The only greater honor," Professor Senin continued, "would be for you to accept the position as head researcher, Professor Lane. Only you can lead this next generation of acolytes out of the darkness caused by our religious miasma." The other deans, the secretary, and the priestesses echoed his pleas.

This isn't real. This is a dream, an illusion, a fantasy plucked from my mind. But... why? Why would a force so deep into the Deadvale contrive a scene fitting what I once wanted most in life?

"Come on, Eleanor, we can't stay in here." She heard Gabriela's words, but it didn't make sense. Her name and that title glistened, almost wetly, in the light. All she needed was to reach out and take it. Maybe this wasn't a cruel construct. If agents of the Deadvale had power over death, why shouldn't they be able to create an alternate reality?

If my parents walked in, loving and accepting of my chosen work and research, that would be it. I would be convinced.

The professor, deans, secretary, and priestesses stepped aside so Eleanor could see the door leading from the lecture hall. It opened. Two figures framed the doorway.

I would be convinced this is an illusion set to play to my every whim.

The door slammed shut before the figures could step forward and reveal themselves.

That was just as telling. Eleanor called out for Gabriela, spinning to search for her, but the professor and deans crowded around, shoving the medal forward, reminding her it was what she wanted.

She pressed her eyes closed. Pulling off her goggles, she pressed the heels of her palms into her eyes until pinpoints of light overtook her vision.

Still, they begged her to stay, begged her to lead them. She screamed, pounding her fists against her thighs.

Something sharp stung across her left cheek. Eleanor snapped her eyes open, and she was no longer in the auditorium but a moldy circular room no larger than the last with the balcony.

Gabriela stood in front of her, rubbing her palm. "Sorry, I had to stop your screaming."

"What happened?" Eleanor took in the other details of the room lit by more tallow candles set into alcoves in the wall. Below them, a dozen suits of embellished gold and silver armor lay strewn around the room's edges. She knelt to inspect one with an emblem of a stylized woman with a delicate yet complex headpiece. These were Elysara's warriors. "Paladins," she said, backing away a step.

"Brynmor says a battalion's worth was sent to the tower over the decades, but none returned. I don't know how many are in a battalion, but I'm guessing a lot."

"They were probably given their own visions to make them stay, something that gave them a purpose greater than their reason for coming to Eldrisil. Who could resist that?"

"Lord Sebastian said the tower has dangers beyond physical threats."

"It showed you the same room, the academy lecture hall."

Gabriela nodded.

"Perhaps that means there is a limitation to the magic. All these paladins would have had similar life experiences and goals, meaning one vision could ensnare them all. You and I, however, could hardly be more different. We together may be able to defeat the magic of this tower, Gab."

"Maybe if all the traps are just like this one. But I think you're wrong. Look, their armor isn't all the same."

Now that Gabriela said it, Eleanor noticed the slow evolution of paladin armor. Bulky, lean, plain, embellished. It changed with each new head of their orders. She'd seen it in the museum's armor display outside the Divine Grace Cathedral when her mother took her as a child, lined up behind glass plates.

"If there's enough skeleton left, Mama could raise them to leave and tidy the place up," Gabriela was saying, likely in response to some comment by Brynmor. "Oh, that's a good idea. I think it takes an intact ghost, though." She paused, listened, and laughed. "That would be silly. Could you imagine Aura stomping around in armor? It makes me wonder why Mama didn't give you some armor back in Soulhaven. That would have made everything so much simpler."

Eleanor jumped to her feet to stand between Gabriela and the nearest paladin. "You can't be thinking of defiling the memory of these brave men and women by raising them with profane magics."

Gabriela looked at her like she'd forgotten Eleanor was in the room. "Oh, not entirely. I mean, a little. Brynmor said giving them a proper burial would be nice, but we'd need someone much stronger than us to move their armor. Paladins like to be buried in their armor, he says." She paused, listening, and Eleanor scrabbled in her pouch to find the green lens to see the marquess again. Gabriela chuckled. "I don't know about that. You have a lovely face, but your arms and shoulders are for show, Brynmor."

Was he joking about being able to carry the paladins in their armor himself? He's making jokes while standing before noble soldiers who gave their lives in the goddess's name?

"If we survive," said Eleanor, "I will report this directly to the king. He will send the appropriate agents to recover the dead."

"You don't think he already knows they're stacked up here? It sounds like the church was sending them for decades."

The room only had one door, and even if it led to the room with the balcony and stairs, it was better than staying with the armored corpses. Eleanor opened it to a well-lit room, again circular. On the far side, three figures in soft leather armor exactly like Lord Sebastian's held poleaxes at their side, standing before another iron-banded door. Eleanor turned and, not surprisingly, the door behind was gone. So too were Gabriela, Carmel, and all of the marquesses. She stood alone before the armored three.

Maybe they're just hidden from my vision.

The first tapped its weapon on the floor with a sharp ring that cut the silence.

"Miss Eleanor Lane," it said in a voice far gentler than she expected. "You pass through Eldrisil on the tails of another's mission. You seek knowledge, though not for purely innocent reasons. You wish to be known, to be respected."

"There is nothing wrong with that," said Eleanor, licking her lips and taking a step forward. "Doesn't everyone want to be remembered?"

"Perhaps not. You are ruled by logic, Miss Eleanor Lane, so we three have a challenge for you. I can be cracked, made, told, or played. What am I that you fear becoming?"

Riddles. Shit.

Eleanor's mind went to throwing pottery, to instruments made of delicate porcelain. Music couldn't be cracked, nor did she worry about becoming it. It was the same for a story. A puzzle? She didn't want to be that. She may hold her private life close, but she would want others to know her as precise and succinct.

No, that was it. What did she expect the scene in the auditorium to devolve into?

"A joke."

The first armored figure stepped away from the door, leaned their poleaxe against the wall, and collapsed into a heap of armor.

"You do not disappoint, Miss Eleanor Lane," said the next suit of armor in the same voice. "I can be shared but never divided or given away. My value grows as I age. What am I that you will never have enough of?"

Eleanor's mind again spun to material goods. Gems, wealth, and possessions, but those didn't fit. She started to guess at the more psychological answers the tower seemed to wish to draw from her, to force her to face. 'Love' may be an answer for most, but not for one so deep in her mind.

"Time."

The armor stepped aside, placed its weapon, and collapsed.

"I can be earned in an instant, but I take a lifetime to build. Once broken, I am difficult to heal. What am I that you lack more than anything?"

Eleanor ground her teeth. The audacity of the tower's magic to pry into her every thought, to seek to force her into voicing her darkest truths. At least the others were not in the room. They were probably shunted to their own questioning trio. Or standing beside her, shrouded by magic.

Eleanor swallowed the dry lump in her throat. "Friendship."

"Wrong," said the armor. "I am deeper."

It tapped its weapon on the ground as the first had, except the ringing echo never stopped. It reverberated across the room, doubling and multiplying with each bounce until it overwhelmed her. Eleanor clutched her palms over her ears, but the sound only grew louder, piercing her brain. She dropped to her knees, and the world squeezed to a point of light.

Somehow, a single word cut through the cacophony, clear as a bell.

"Trust."

She fell into oblivion.

Chapter 26

Three Keys

A veil of shadows swallowed Eleanor the moment she opened the door. Gabriela shouted after her, and Brynmor even jumped forward with an arm outstretched for as much good as that did.

"That was dramatic," he said.

"I'm starting to see what Lord Sebastian meant." Gabriela stepped near enough to the door to touch the black curtain across the doorframe. "Do we follow? I suppose we should, right? She seems to need help getting through here."

"What choice do I have? I go where you go." Brynmor softened his words with a wink.

She hesitated but couldn't voice why. The darkness or unknown never gave her pause before, so why now? She shook it away. If Eleanor were in danger, then she would help her. Even though they'd only just met, and that too was as enemies, it was no reason to refuse aid to another.

Gabriela clicked her tongue, tugging Carmel after her, and stepped through the veil.

The blaring sun blinded her after so long in the dim of the tower. Gabriela raised a hand to her brow and squinted, slowly recognizing the colorful stalls of the Mytara marketplace. There was even the fountain where she'd first seen Brynmor atop his majestic palomino.

Unlike that day last week, the market was now empty of the bustling crowd. A comforting silence pressed into Gabriela's ears as she spun a slow circle, taking in the details she missed when the mass of shoppers overwhelmed her. The flaking paint, the sunbleached tiles, the water stains around the ice vendor. When she returned to the direction she'd started, three figures in oversized leather coats, just like Eleanor's, stood behind a booth. Their faces were smooth white, glistening in the sun from where they stood, shaded behind a stall.

"What fresh hell is this?" Brynmor gasped.

Gabriela tucked Carmel's lead across his neck and approached.

"Good afternoon, Princess," said one, though she couldn't guess which.

"Good afternoon," she said, waving at the three white cups laid upside down on the counter before them. "What's going on here?"

"We debated if it was necessary to put you through the trials based on your parentage. We decided we must."

"Because this was my mother's tower?"

"Your mother is half your parentage."

Gabriela's mother never spoke of her father, changing the subject whenever the conversation went in that direction. It instilled a healthy lack of interest in Gabriela.

"Was Eleanor through here? She has a coat like yours."

The three shook their plain heads. "She is elsewhere. Do not worry about her well-being at the moment. To continue, you must find three keys hidden in this market." The middle figure waved at the cups.

"Queen's Cups," Brynmor said at her side. "It's a hustle they try at all the sleazy inns. You have to watch closely."

The three stared at Brynmor for a moment, even without eyes. "That is not the game." The figure in the center touched the cups with white porcelain hands, sliding them across the counter, exchanging their positions. Gabriela followed the center one but quickly lost track of which started on the left.

It pulled its hands away. Flourishing them across the three cups. "Where is the first key?"

"You're supposed to show where it started," said Brynmor.

"This is not your challenge, Marquess."

"He's right, though. I— Wait..." Gabriela couldn't stop the grin that slid across her lips. "Oh, you're sneaky. You already told me where the keys are."

"What?" asked Brynmor.

"In this market," Gabriela said.

The middle figure held out a golden skeleton key. "Clever."

Gabriela accepted it. As her fingers touched it, the figure compressed and disappeared as if sucked into the key with a puff of wind.

"Gods and saints, I'm looking forward to seeing that happen twice more," Brynmor groaned.

The two figures shuffled to close the gap between them. The one on the left flicked away the middle cup.

"Well done, Princess, well done," one said. "You may ask us a single question and lift only one cup. Only one chance to find the second key, which is under one of these. Be wary. One of us will always lie, while the other speaks only the truth."

"That's an old one," said Brynmor. "A child's riddle. Ask one what the other would say. That way, you know the lie is included in the answer, then do the opposite."

"Everyone knows that. Let me do this, Brynmor." She studied the two cups, then the two blank places where the faces should be behind them. Her grin twisted to something feral, and she slapped a hand on the left cup.

"You have to ask them something!" yelled Brynmor.

"Are you sure?" asked the figure.

Gabriela nodded, pulling her hand back to rest the palm on the wooden counter.

"Ask them a question, Gab!"

"There's no need, or no use," she said. "The tower wants us to fail unless we think differently."

"So you leave our fate to a flip of the coin?"

"Fine," she said. "What happens if I'm wrong and don't find all three keys?"

"You will remain here forever."

Gabriela nodded.

201

A white hand pulled away the cup, revealing the bronze skeleton key under it. Slender fingers grasped it, offering it to Gabriela. She took it, and the figure was again sucked into the key.

"How..."

"The one giving the rules lied," said Gabriela. "I had all the questions I wanted and could lift both cups if I chose."

"But... no. How could you have known that?"

Gabriela shrugged. "I didn't know for sure, but it makes sense."

"You didn't know, but you were confident. Gods and saints, Gab, you are difficult to understand."

"Are you ready for the third key?" asked the sole remaining figure.

"Sure," said Gabriela.

"A favorite of the tower, a riddle. In moonlit nights, when spirits awake, I emerge from the shadows, a mischief I make. With ghostly whispers and spectral grace, I haunt old halls and abandoned space. What am I?"

"Hello." Brynmor waved a ghostly hand in front of Gabriela.

She waved him off. "That's too obvious. Dreams, maybe?"

"Is that your answer?" asked the figure.

"No, just talking out loud."

"If the other two were about subverting an expectation, then so would this," said Brynmor. "Don't overthink it."

"Fine. You're a ghost."

"I am, Gabs, I am that," it said in a voice Gabriela knew too well. It pressed a silver key against her palm, and the figure and the rest of the market pulled into it. She, Brynmor, and Carmel stood in a void lit only by the wide beam of light shining over them.

A small, frail girl with rags for clothes and dark hair that clung close to her tan face stepped in from the darkness. She looked nothing like how Gabriela had ever seen her but instantly recognized her.

"Aura."

Brynmor gasped.

"They made me, Gabs. They made me do it."

202

Gabriela rushed forward, taking Aura by the shoulders. She felt cold and clammy, not the usual gentle resistance a ghost should have, like pushing on a bladder. Aura's body was solid. Real.

"Who? What did they make you do?"

Brynmor circled the pair, eying Aura with confusion and clear awe. "It can work."

"This isn't resurrection, Brynmor. At least, I don't think it is. Aura, what happened?"

Aura stared at the floor, only flicking her gaze to meet Gabriela's for an instant. "You don't even know him, but here we are, Gabs. You never would have done all this for me."

"We had to leave Lord Sebastian behind because of you," said Brynmor. "Gab doesn't owe you anything."

Gabriela bit her lip, fingers fiddling with the amulet at her throat. "It's different with him, Aura. We have his body to put him back into."

"You never tried for me, Gabs. Never tried."

"You always seemed so content as a ghost. I never thought you wanted more."

"She tied me to you, kept me from moving on. Forced me to stay, driving me mad."

"Mama..." Gabriela knew her mother bound Aura to her but never considered the motive. There was a lot about those closest to her she didn't know.

"What did you mean when you first stepped in?" asked Gabriela. "Who made you do what?"

"Choose," said Aura. "The voices offered me back my mind, but I had to leave you."

Brynmor scoffed but thankfully said nothing.

"I don't understand," said Gabriela.

"Fifteen years, Gabs. That's how long ago I was a girl like you. Then I fell into the water and never came out. Mama... The Dread Lady Venica snatched me before I moved on. She ripped, stretched, and patched, fraying my mind to the edge of sanity before wrapping me around her favored child. You."

"No, that can't be right, Aura. That's torture, and Mama wouldn't have done that."

"Open your eyes, Gabs. This was her tower, full of traps to ensnare her enemies like ants in sap. She reigned here for decades, maybe centuries. How many paladins did the church dispatch to bring her to justice? Their armor lays scattered around moldering rooms."

Gabriela brushed the hair back around Aura's ear. "Maybe that's all true. If she did all that to you, I'm sure it was with good reason. But I know my mother, and she's no monster. She's loving, in her way, and cares deeply for those around her."

"You must not know the truth of what she did to Lord Sebastian," said Aura. "How she murdered him and forced him into servitude."

"Is that true?" Brynmor asked.

"Of course, it's not true! Lord Sebastian loves and respects my mother. Why are you saying these things, Aura?"

"It's all true. You know it's true." Aura finally looked up, her dark eyes piercing with a ferocity that made Gabriela shy back a step. "Admit that you know it. Admit that Venica is the monster you know her to be."

"No. No, you're not Aura. This is another test. The Aura I know is mischievous but not malicious like this."

"The Aura you knew was shackled by the madness Venica gave her. The tower has given back what was taken from me years ago. Your beliefs and willful ignorance have no bearing on the truth."

Gabriela watched those dark eyes, seeing an expression of deep resentment she'd never witnessed in Aura before, but she couldn't deny she still recognized the girl. She had a point that Gabriela's personal feelings for her mother would make no difference in whether this was real or another illusion. "Was your name always Aura? When you were alive before?"

"It... yes, it was my grandmother's name. My father's mother."

"Why ask that?" asked Brynmor.

She ignored him. "Do you remember when the Sunara twins first emerged from their crypt? Poor things were so confused at being out in the sun." Gabriela covered her laugh with a hand.

"You made them hats out of woven reeds," said Aura. "They never took them off, picking them up if they fell."

"They were so easy to tell apart from the rest after that." Gabriela smiled and squeezed Aura's arm. "I'm sorry for your past, for what you lost. You and I have a unique relationship, but I love you, Aura. I can't remember a day of my life without you at my side. I also love my mother. I won't condemn her without hearing her side." Her hand slid down Aura's arm to take her hand. "Let's keep going. We'll find her together."

Aura snapped her hand away. "I tell you of her lies and what misery she enacted, yet you won't denounce her?"

"I won't."

"Have you no respect for me?"

Gabriela pulled away to fiddle with her necklace. "It's not between us, Aura. You say my mother did you wrong. I want to hear it from her. You can't call it disrespect to not turn against my mother without first talking to her. I wouldn't do the same to you. We've been through so much together, so let's keep going." Gabriela extended her hand.

"Your ability to forgive is to a fault, Gab," said Brynmor.

Aura stared at the proffered hand for a long moment before slowly raising her own, pressing her clammy palm against Gabriela's. "I'm sorry," she whispered.

A chill breeze flowed from above as if from the shaft of light. It washed over them, stripping away Aura's finer details, burning away her living form until she was again a specter of translucent green.

"They made me do it," she said.

Gabriela didn't understand but wrapped her arms around Aura, holding her as tightly as she could a ghost.

CHAPTER 27

UP OR DOWN?

The cold woke her. A cold that no amount of shivering could cease. A cold that was known more than felt. She woke in darkness, and her memory struggled to catch up.

I am Eleanor Lane, age twenty-six, daughter of Dylan and Rebeca Lane. I work for Duke Rhys Highgate, keeping his nephew Brynmor out of trouble. Brynmor is...

The image of Brynmor as a smudge of green mist floating beside his body slung over a pony came to mind. The rest slotted into place. She had seen proof of life after death, or at least of existence after it, so she couldn't rule out that she wasn't having these thoughts posthumously. That ringing, that awful ringing. Maybe this was how things started as a ghost; cold and dark.

No, I don't want to be dead. I need to write all that I've learned into a paper first.

A light approached. Two candles bobbed in the distance, along with something that might pass as humming. The lights were straight in front of her, and Eleanor realized her position: sitting up, perhaps on the floor, and leaning against the wall.

As the light drew nearer, she could make out the source. Short, its two legs ending in hooves, a red vest stretched over a pot belly, eyes like black pits, and twisting horns ending in two tiny flames, what she thought were candles.

A week ago, Eleanor might have thought they were a terrifying creature of nightmare, but after what she'd seen since, she couldn't help but think they were... cute.

"Oh, hello there," they said, coming close enough to touch. They adjusted the leather satchel strung across their shoulder. "You look fresh. That's odd."

"Am I dead?" Eleanor's mouth felt like it was full of glue, but she managed to get the question out.

The creature hopped back. "A live one! Oh no, you're not dead. At least not as far as I can tell. I'm no expert. Could I, uh..." They glanced down the hall, to the way they were headed. "Can I help you in some way? I was running right on time, so the quicker, the better."

Questions flooded Eleanor's mind. *Who are you? What are you? Where am I? How do I find my...* Even to herself, she hesitated to call Gabriela a 'friend,' but the girl seemed genuinely kind-hearted, without deep-seated motives.

"Water?" she asked.

The creature fumbled for a flask at their hip, holding it out for her. "Good day to you then." They turned to hurry away the moment Eleanor accepted the flask.

She drank a mouthful of the water that tasted like iron but smelled like sulfur and shouted after the thing. "Wait! Who are you?"

They stopped, shoulders slumping, and turned back to her. "Executor Smithies is my name. I hope you can appreciate that I am now behind schedule."

"Where am I?"

"In Eldrisil," said Executor Smithies impatiently.

"Where in the tower? I was... I was being asked riddles and got one wrong, and... I don't know."

"The tower doesn't have rooms and levels, as you might understand. Just go up to reach the top and down to go elsewhere." They glanced back toward their destination. "I think a balcony nearby will help you see how far you are from where you're going. Now, if you don't mind...?"

Eleanor nodded, and Executor Smithies whisked away, leaving her in the dark again.

But not completely dark.

Light shone in strips, like through the slats of shutters, just like in the room at the top of the stairs, where Gabriela stepped out on a balcony before they entered the lecture hall. A quick horror flashed by of this being the same room and her progress in the tower being reset. Surely the tower would be better now at keeping her in the auditorium. Without Gabriela to slap her out of it, she would be trapped, believing she was performing worldview-altering magical research while she was actually lying down between decades-dead paladins.

Stop. Stop. This place will feed on that sort of thought.

A week ago, the thought of a tower with intelligence or sentience would have been a thing of fantasy.

It tasted terrible, but she finished the rest of the water and used the wall to help her to her feet. Pulling open the door to the balcony, it took a moment of blinking away the late afternoon glare before she could see any detail. The dead still circled over a hundred feet below and... no. They weren't circling. They were all facing left. Eleanor pushed at the railing, testing its strength before putting much weight against it to lean out farther and see around the tower's slow curve.

There, in the distance, an army in gold and white. Paladins bearing the church's sigil flapping high on their banners, at least a hundred of them. At the head of their ranks was a figure in dark armor, a smudge against the otherwise pristine shine.

She knew that armor and knew it was no paladin that wore it.

Duke Rhys Highgate was marching the king's paladins against the tower.

How does he already have an army here? I left him only two nights ago.

Another figure stood out beside him, in regal armor that was still different enough from a paladin's. White and dark blue...

Valoria? How? What happened to Lord Sebastian?

Eleanor looked up but couldn't see the tower's top.

They can't come here. Even if they make short work of the dead below, the traps of this tower will defeat their minds. They're marching to their deaths. Besides...

She cut herself off from the thought, but the more she tried not to believe her mindset, the more it wanted to be said, even as a thought only to her.

Memories of Gabriela's constant babble about all her 'friends' at home, which Eleanor assumed were nothing more than shambling skeletons. There was an innocence, a friendliness to the girl.

"The dead are harmless. They just want to be left alone," she whispered to the army.

She slipped back into the room and, with the added light from the open door, could make out two stairways, one twisting up, the other down. There was no sign of the path Executor Smithies had come or gone on.

Eleanor stared at the stairs down but knew her presence before the duke, Valoria, and paladins would amount to nothing. They were here because she stood before the duke and told him the dead killed his nephew. This was all put in motion on her word, but her word alone could not end it. She needed solid and physical proof to prove the dead were not the enemy.

Maybe if she went out on the balcony and returned, the room would shift again, leading to different options, but her destination was clear.

Eleanor rushed up the stairs.

CHAPTER 28

BEFORE THE THRONE

One by one, torches flared to life behind Aura, revealing an arched hallway of mottled stone.

Gabriela couldn't hold Aura's hand too tightly, but they turned to face the hall. Carmel followed without being bidden. The passage ended in a larger room, and as they neared, she heard snippets of a distant conversation interrupted by the clang of steel and the hiss of magic. The first voice was a baritone that vibrated Gabriela's chest, but she immediately knew the second, soft and breathy, even if the words were lost to the acoustics.

"Mama!"

Gabriela ran down the hall, dragging Aura until their fingers slipped free of each other. Brynmor hissed something after her, but she paid him no mind.

The room was huge, larger than the auditorium from Eleanor's memory. Crystal chandeliers cast fractal light across the stone walls and floor from the myriad tallow candles. A figure in massive black and deep blue armor and visored helmet stood to her right, with their back toward her. From the partial stories by Lord Sebastian, this must have been the fallen paladin, Ser Mourningsword, though his armor was nothing like the gleaming gold and silvers of the other paladins she'd seen. He held a winged sword that looked like it weighed as much as she, pointed at the only other person in the room. Queen Venica Marwol stood before gigantic arched doors, her hands clasped before her, looking as calm and regal as ever.

"Your power is faded, Venica," boomed Mourningsword. "When last I saw you, you would have ended this fight with the flick of a finger."

He rushed forward in a black blur, arcing his massive sword parallel to the ground at waist height. Venica grasped at the air, pulling shadows in the space directly in front of her. Mourningsword's blade struck hard, but he jumped back with a grunt. "Coward, fight me!"

"I have not come to fight, Oswin."

"You lost the right to call me that."

"Get back!" Brynmor hissed, and Gabriela slid close to the wall.

"Was it so terrible?" asked her mother. "I gave you Eldrisil."

Mourningsword's scoff echoed in his armor. "Eldrisil is a tomb." He swung his blade, casting a shockwave of deep purple iridescence. Venica batted it away with a hand shrouded in shadow and immediately raised the other to block the paladin's downward strike. He pressed his attack, pushing Venica to a knee before she twisted away and back to her feet to keep her distance.

"You're stronger. Your power has acclimated to that of Eldrisil," said the queen.

"You cursed me to remain, surrounded by your concentration of profane magic, forgotten. Only when the last bit of what was holy within me burned away did I no longer live in agony. I will never forget the torture I endured at your hand."

"Agony? Perhaps when you first arrived."

Gabriela frowned. This is what Aura accused her mother of doing, yet it couldn't be true. *Why doesn't she deny it? What was Mama's history with this paladin to call him by his given name?*

"Of course, you misunderstand me," said Mourningsword with a wry chuckle. "Any shred of what was human in you dried up two hundred years ago. I do not speak of the pain you inflicted as my jailor but that you could leave me so suddenly. It never occurred to you that I might also suffer from our shared loss."

"No apology would be sufficient for what harm I have caused."

"Perhaps not, yet you never tried. Though I must thank you," Mourningsword continued. "Each day, as Elysara's holy grace burned away, I realized the truth. Simple and pure, something I could never have come to alone. The goddess is a lie. The church holds Her over us as the only path to salvation and Her gift of magic. Yet I can command the dead now, thanks to the vile magics glutting this tower. Thanks to you. This has nothing to do with the goddess."

"Nothing was 'burned away' in your time in Eldrisil. You only realized the simple truth that the goddess is a fabrication. It was your faith you lost."

Venica's gaze flicked quickly, but deliberately, toward Gabriela and the others. Mourningsword spun to face her, leaving Gabriela feeling naked and vulnerable for just a breath. Venica used the distraction to pull the shadows, ripping the sword from the paladin's grip. She was on him instantly, tying a band of shadow around his neck and kicking out his knee. He dropped with a choked cry, and she ripped his helmet away, tossing it to clatter into a dark corner. Mourningsword's fingers clutched fruitlessly at the shadow tightening around his throat.

"Gabriela, I told you not to come here," she said, still as calm as ever.

"Gabriela." Mourningsword's hazel eyes widened, and he stopped his struggle. "This is her, then." He twitched a long lock of pale blonde hair from his eyes to stare up at her.

Venica watched Gabriela for a long moment, seeming to weigh what to say next, if anything at all. "Yes," she breathed, looking away. Gabriela barely recognized the emotion, especially not in her mother: shame. What could Queen Venica Marwol of the Deadvale possibly have to feel shame about? Mourningsword looked up at Gabriela and saw a familiarity in them, like looking into a mirror.

"You will answer my questions," Venica said, tightening her grip around the paladin's neck.

"You hoped parading her out would loosen my tongue?" Mourningsword choked. "You are despicable."

"Why have you called the dead to Eldrisil?"

Gabriela stepped fully into the room. "What's going on, Mama?"

"Will you tell her, or shall I?" Mourningsword grinned despite his face turning purple. He wasn't risen dead or some devil of malice. Mourningsword was just a person like her.

"Not another word from you, Oswin." Venica shoved the man forward, releasing her hold on his neck. He fell forward to his hands, gasping for air, but still managed to look up at Gabriela as he did. Unlike her mother's gaze, his spoke of something very different: pride.

"You will disband your armies; release the ghosts," said Venica to his back. "The living pose no threat here, behind the Crack."

The paladin's expression soured as he rose to his feet. With a deep breath, he tore his gaze from Gabriela. "The church will attack, as I was once sent, and dozens before me. They will come in force, but I will meet them first. They will see the futility of what protection the goddess offers as their sons and daughters fall and rise to march in my cleansing army. That was your goal once, Venica. A goal you failed."

Venica glanced past the paladin to Gabriela, then took a few steps to circle Mourningsword. Either so that neither had their back to Gabriela or so that Venica could no longer see her directly.

"You're wrong, Oswin," she said. "I never wished to extend beyond this tower. My research was unrivaled, unfettered by the arbitrary ethics of others, but I was content to remain in these walls."

"You would have, in time, sought to extend your reach when you ran out of things to torture here."

"The citizens of the Deadvale are not your army to command. Release them."

"Such hypocrisy. Shall I enumerate the dead abominations and devilspawn I fought to reach you all those years ago? The next generation of holy warriors will restart their crusade against this tower, but I will not wait for them."

A door in the hall opened toward Gabriela with a riotous creak. In the space behind, in her overly large leather coat and hat, Eleanor stood panting. She lumbered forward, grabbing Gabriela by the forearms, sweat pouring down her brow. "Paladins coming... Duke and... Valoria..." She gasped to catch her breath. Then she noticed the two others in the room, letting out a small shriek and falling back.

"Valoria? What happened to Lord Sebastian?" Gabriela asked.

Eleanor shook her head.

"See, Venica?" said Mourningsword. "Paladins are at my gate, says the girl. They prove me correct the moment the words come from my mouth."

"Oswin, it is this tower," said the queen. "I feel it again, even after being back for such a short time. The overwhelming magic calling to deep within me. You must get away from here."

"You cursed me to remain! For decades, I could barely step onto a balcony. How can you blame this place after what you did to me here?"

"Please..." Venica glided forward, extending a hand toward the paladin, her rings flashing in the candlelight.

His hazel eyes...

Gabriela stepped forward, almost between the two. "Mother, who is this man?"

"She never told you?" Mourningsword asked. He laughed, deep and rich. "I apologize, but again, the hypocrisy. Queen Venica, who sought a divine truth without the presence of the divine, never told her daughter the truth of herself."

"What...?" Gabriela looked between them but knew what truth he alluded to. She saw it in his eyes that were the same as hers. "You're my father."

A grin flicked the edge of the paladin's lips while Venica couldn't meet her gaze.

"Did he..." Gabriela wasn't sure of the rest of her question. Did he love you? Did he force himself upon you? Did he want to be in my life? Did he know I existed?

Venica waved off the question, pacing to the enormous arched doors. "You heard the girl. Paladins ride on the tower. They will attack at the solstice when the defenses are at their lowest."

Mourningsword glanced at Eleanor and the others by the hall as if seeing them for the first time. "Who are all these?"

"Oh, yes," said Gabriela, pointing to each. "Miss Eleanor Lane, Viscount Brynmor Highgate, his body, and Carmel. Aura is... around here somewhere."

"Aura," said the paladin, turning to speak to Venica's back. "How?"

The queen remained silent.

"She's tethered to me," said Gabriela.

"Monsterous," growled the paladin. "You inflicted enough torment on our daughter trying to bring her back, then to bind her—"

"Enough!" Venica slammed a fist against the door; the deep reverberation echoed across the high chamber.

"She drowned," Gabriela said. Her mother, still facing away, raised a hand to cover her face. "You stopped her from moving on, tried and failed to resurrect her, so bound her to me, her baby sister. But you were sloppy, emotional, and so much of her was lost, shattering her mind." Gabriela's legs felt wobbly, and she sat on the stone floor. "Aura's my sister. How did I never guess that? Why didn't you ever tell me? You fled immediately after, leaving him here."

Venica shook her head slowly. Her words came slower and softer when she spoke, with a faint quiver. "There are no words to describe the depths of my failure, my tiny."

"I'm sorry, but there isn't time for this," Eleanor said gently. "The paladins are just outside. Shouldn't we see to them and deal with this later?"

Mourningsword rolled his shoulders back with a deep thudding clink of his heavy armor. "Who's side are you on, Miss Lane? What is your stake in this?"

"Stake? I'm on the side where I can help the fewest people die."

"What would you suggest, Miss Lane? The paladins will dash themselves upon the forces of this tower, as have generations before them. No defenders will remain as I lead my armies across the Crack. We can sit back and let this play out."

"I don't know about that," said Eleanor. "The number of paladins I saw will make short work of the undead around the tower's base, decimating your army. You would be better to call the dead into the tower and ride out to parlay."

All the recent revelations left Gabriela stunned, but Eleanor's words cut through to her. She put a hand on Eleanor's arm. "You want to protect the dead now? This is wonderful."

"It's not that. I'm just thinking of avoiding a conflict."

"No," said Mourningsword. "Call the dead into the tower, and the paladins expect a siege. Let them plow through, thinking they're winning, and Eldrisil will confound them with its mental games. I can raise more dead on the way to the king's throne."

"Not with the full moon and solstice tomorrow," said Gabriela. "If the paladins hold off a little bit, the tower will be defenseless. The power is strong here, but noticeably less than when I arrived."

Venica scoffed, finally turning to face them. "That would require the church to know of the cycles of magic. They focus solely on the gifts of their goddess."

Eleanor's expression fell as she staggered back a step.

"It doesn't matter. There is only one course," said Mourningsword. "Let the paladins smash the dead and allow the tower to defeat them."

"No!" Gabriela shouted, grabbing his gauntlet to keep him in place. She could understand some of the man's pain, losing a daughter, then the other, but what could justify killing all those he called brothers? Why march from this tower to attack the king? Was it any different than Brynmor's uncle's story? "Don't sacrifice the dead; call them into the tower. Let the paladins enter, but don't harm them. We need just a little more time."

"Time for what?"

"To finish what we came here to do. Maybe the marquess can do something."

All eyes turned to Brynmor.

"No," Venica said flatly. "Resurrection is a fool's hope, Gabriela. I placated your fantasies before, but now, with the king's forces at our feet, it would be a waste of magic and resources."

Mourningsword moved to her side, threading his fingers through hers. Venica looked down at the gesture, and though she didn't return his squeeze, neither did she flinch away. "Ah, then you are back in my court," he said. "We will make quick work of my misled brothers and march across the Crack after the solstice."

Venica pulled away, taking a small step back and folding her hands across her stomach. "I cannot deny my desire to join you, Oswin, but that is a voice I have learned I must needs shut out. Reckless research fueled my every moment and nearly brought this world to heel, for the living and not and all who are between or neither."

"You were always so dramatic, so passionate, Venica. That quality may have been what first broke through our differences and began my attraction to you." He pulled off his right gauntlet, letting it drop to the floor, and raised his hand to brush the knuckles along Venica's sullen cheek.

Gabriela glanced at Brynmor and saw he was already looking at her.

Venica pushed his hand away and turned to Gabriela. "There is a vault deep under the tower. We will weather the solstice there." She glided forward, taking Gabriela by the arm as she passed.

"No!" Gabriela shook from the hold.

Venica wheeled on her, eyes streaming blue mist and brow pinched. "You will obey me."

"I've come this far because you said we could help Brynmor, so I intend to see it done."

"I have spoiled you, girl, to spout such insolence. I know what is best for you."

"You do? Did you know what was best for Aura as you twisted her spirit, dealing unknown agonies to her? It wasn't just her time forced to exist as an incomplete ghost that ruined her mind, Mama. It was what you did to her when you failed to save her."

The accusations flooded from her, but the genuine hurt on her mother's face verified their accuracy.

"Why are you so sure I'll fail?"

Venica scoffed. "How could you not? I was at the height of my power and did not succeed. You have the barest grasp on your magic, spending your time reading works of fiction and talking to skeletons rather than practicing your fundamentals."

"Maybe that's why I could do it, because I'm different."

"Let her try," said the paladin. "If you hold her back now, she will never forgive you. The world might end if she fails, but what would your world be without her?"

Venica breathed in sharply, focusing her misty gaze on Gabriela. "He is right. Your... father is right. You are the only thing in this world that means anything to me, Gabriela, my tiny. If you feel so strongly that this must be attempted, then I will aid you. I will not fail you as I did Aura."

CHAPTER 29

THE WORLD IN HER HANDS

S er Mourningsword pushed wide the massive arched doors. Beyond, another room as large as the one they stood in lay lit by the early evening sun streaming through the stained glass windows that reached the distant ceiling. He stepped in, crossing the barren room with heavy footfalls, to stop in the center. Turning, he clicked his tongue once. "Carmel, come."

Gabriela watched in awe as her old pony started forward, carrying Brynmor's body into the next room. "He never comes to strangers."

"He has a long memory. Carmel was my squire's mount. I brought him to Eldrisil almost thirty years ago when I came to slay your mother. I'm shocked to see him again after so long but glad to know he's had a good life." He rubbed the pony between the ears before shifting to pull Brynmor from his back.

Venica entered, her eyes sliding over the empty space. "You have remodeled."

"Your throne was better on the eyes than on my back," said Mourningsword.

The queen let out a deep, loud breath before stepping forward. "I do this for you, my tiny, my love. It is all for you."

Gabriela fell in beside her. "How can I help?"

"Help? No, my love, you must perform the magic. The viscount is bound to you, so it must be you that restores him to his proper place."

"How do I do it, Mama?"

"Like any magic, believe that you can. See the result. Do not allow a shred of doubt to distract you."

"Yes, but what about words? Or gestures?" Gabriela looked down at her hands.

"None of that matters."

"And the other reagents? We lost the divine blood."

Venica started, staring down at Gabriela. "You had it? How?"

"From a demon prince. I raised the paladins under the Devil's Pit and then he threw a sword at me and... I'll have to tell you the whole story later." Gabriela took Lord Sebastian's hand from her bag.

Venica glared at her for a long breath. "Those were your quest, my tiny. Only the viscount's body and ghost were necessary for the magic."

"Wait, we didn't need to go to Crystalwood Gardens or the Devil's Pit? You made that up?"

"I did not expect events to unfold as they did. We were to travel on this adventure, culminating in failure at the fae ring. The viscount's pursuers and Oswin's machinations spoiled those plans."

Gabriela's pulse thudded in her temples. She spoke through gritted teeth, "You never intended for the resurrection to work? This was all a grift?"

"Resurrection is not an act to take lightly. I wished to instill that in you while not squelching your adventurous nature."

"You knew we'd fail, yet you're inviting me to try it, still?"

"I would like to watch your attempt."

"Um, I'd like to discuss this, please?" called Eleanor from the doorway, wearing the red lens in her goggles. "The magic twisting into this tower spreads to every corner of the world. I can see it like tiny strands. Will it be safe to cast some big spell here?"

"No magic can ever be used without some risk, Miss Lane," said Venica. "Even a minor glamor has the potential to rip apart the fabric of magic. Especially here."

Eleanor looked up from her notebook, pen mid-scratch. "What now?"

"How do I start, Mama?"

Venica took Gabriela's hand; her cold fingers pressed into her palm to lead her toward Brynmor's body lying in the center of the room. "When you open yourself to the tower's magic, it will seek to overwhelm you. Do not let it. The confluence of energies here is far beyond what you have experienced elsewhere."

Gabriela nodded along with the sage advice. "What else?"

"What more can I say for an act that has yet to be performed successfully?" asked Venica.

Gabriela looked down at Brynmor's body. "I thought you researched how this is done?"

"I can only speak to the failures," said her mother. "My failures."

Gabriela circled Brynmor's body once. The one missing glove, the deep cut in his other forearm from Lord Sebastian blocking Commander Ravell's sword strike, the odd bend in his shin. But also his dark, wavy hair, the tailored cut of his waistcoat, and his soft lashes. After their few days together, she barely knew the man, but she liked him more now than when he first touched her cheek. How much more could she like him in another week? Possibly quite a lot less, of course, but her feelings were swelling.

"Focus, my tiny. Feel the convergence of magic coursing under our feet. The entire world is accessible from here. Do you feel it?"

Gabriela felt nothing beyond the pressure she'd noticed since entering the tower. She closed her eyes, sealing off one sense to heighten the others. She never spoke to another in length about her ability to sense the flow of magic, but from Eleanor's myriad devices, she gathered it was something not everyone could innately do. She began to feel it like her eyes adjusting to a dark room after the day in the sun. Her mother appeared as an inky slash in the air. Mourningsword was just as dark but with a distant and dim core of pure gold. He spoke as though that no longer existed; perhaps he didn't think it did. Eleanor was speckled with points of white and gray, but Brynmor, the ghost, was barely discernible from the background magic drifting through the room.

Then she turned her focus downward.

The interweaving levels of the tower swirled and undulated below her, making her sway, but firm hands took her shoulders. Farther down, delicate tendrils collected at the tower's base, looping and soaring off in mostly straight lines across the land. The paladin army shone bright with the barest blemish at its forefront.

"Lord Sebastian," she grinned. She recognized him as a smudge as easily as she recognized one skeleton from the others in town. "I can see him." The smudge broke from the mass of gold to approach the tower. "I think he's coming here."

"I should like to know why he did not oversee your care to this point," said Venica.

Gabriela focused on the threads of magic twisting around the tower, looking not unlike a bird's nest of loose twigs. She tugged at one, feeling an electric bite, but didn't let go. Gabriela pulled it to her and reached for another. How many would she need? She snared another, until she felt like she had a fistful of magical threads. This was nothing like how she always used magic, grabbing at loose motes as they floated by. Here she stood at the convergence of all magic.

"More," Venica coached. "You need far more than that."

Gabriela wanted to disagree. This was more magic than she'd ever touched at once, more than she thought existed in the world. It felt like enough to do anything she wished. This was too easy. No wonder so many wizards in her books turned to evil plans of world domination. With an endless supply of magic, she could do anything. Gabriela gathered another handful of magical threads, unwinding them from the tower's base. She saw them like streamers hanging in the air, connecting her to the farthest reaches of a world she'd only read about.

"That is enough," said Venica.

Now that she held so much, Gabriela doubted her mother's confidence. Sure, this might be enough, but wouldn't more only enhance the likelihood of the spell succeeding? Gabriela no longer felt the shock as she snatched up more threads, gathering them into her. Her mother had only ever failed at this, so what did she know about how much it would take?

"That is enough, Gabriela," her mother repeated. She sounded so far away. The magic buzzed in her mind like a swarm of wasps, making anything else difficult to perceive.

Just a few more threads. She almost had all the easiest ones. Though... just as she thought she had all those not tightly twisted and snagged on the tower, she found more. It was a fun challenge to gather them all.

"Gabriela! Stop! Cast the spell!" The scream cut through her haze, clear and direct.

The voice was oddly shrill, but it must have been her mother, and maybe she was right. Gabriela twisted the threads into a single tight bundle, straightening and twisting the lengths until they became as fine as any single filament. From that thread, she saw the world's magic spread from her like she was the center pole of a circus tent.

Magic licked from the end of that thread, eager for her touch. She solidified the image of Brynmor on his horse across the market, then him smirking at the top of the steps. She imagined as he might be once he was alive again. His arm was bandaged, and his leg splinted, sitting overlooking the Misty Mire at sunrise. She was there too, sipping tea and laughing at something he'd said.

Gabriela touched the magic coursing from the end of the thread, invited it to pass through her, and enact her will.

Restore his body to how it was at the top of the stairs, like I see him rocking beside me on a wooden porch. Put his ghost back where it belongs.

Her thoughts came as a plea to a third party.

"Tie it off. Now."

Gabriela didn't know what her mother meant. She saw the magic as a single, thin wire. There was nothing to tie off. Now that she was touching it, the magic coursed through her, electrifying her every organ and fiber. It surged, but as hard as she focused on the image of Brynmor, the magic vibrated too harshly, blurring and making it impossible to focus.

"This is how she tried it with me." It wasn't her mother's voice. This was the other that screamed for her to cast the spell. Aura?

A single black filament lashed out like a sword, severing the bundle in Gabriela's grasp. Magic tendrils exploded away, some coiling around the tower's base again, but most lay abandoned in the surrounding fields. Some intersected the shining paladins, who scattered and brightened.

The magic drained from her faster than it had entered, feeling like it took something else in its passing, like she was an old pot rinsed of a decade's dust. She opened her eyes, staring up at her mother. Venica blinked it away quickly, but Gabriela caught a hint of concern.

"I knew it was more than you could handle," Venica said, brushing a lock of hair behind Gabriela's ear. "This was too much for you. You can now appreciate the truth of my words. Even with all that power, the marquess is no less dead.

"Maybe I could have done it with a bit more."

"No, Gabriela. You nearly lost control."

Gabriela frowned. "I don't think I did." She looked over the others in the room. Eleanor frantically scratched away in her notebook, and Brynmor squatted beside his body, hands covering his face. Mourningsword leaned close to the stained glass, one arm braced above his head as he bent nearer.

She didn't feel as though she was so close to losing control over the magic. Maybe it was slipping a little, but not so much that she couldn't pull it back with enough focus. Focus her mother interrupted. Gabriela might very well have succeeded if not for her mother.

"The paladins are advancing," said her father. "They might have seen that as an attack. I know I would have."

"Where's Aura? I heard her," said Gabriela.

Venica frowned, fingers tracing the locket at her throat. "She must be nearby. Come, we have wasted enough time here. We must get to the vault."

"She said that was the same way you tried it." Gabriela took a step forward, but her legs buckled. Mourningsword caught her with an iron grip around her shoulders.

"Go with your mother," he said. "I will stay behind to fight off these paladins." A wicked grin played at the corner of his lips.

"No, Oswin," said Venica. "Join us in the vault. We can all leave this tower in peace when the solstice passes."

Mourningsword's grip on Gabriela lessened, but she couldn't see his expression.

"Leave," he chuckled, "together. What would happen to Eldrisil without a steward?"

"That is not our concern. Why should the world's magic be placed in the stewardship of mortals? That is Elysara's role."

224

Mourningsword's fingers dug into Gabriela's shoulders. "When you left, my only solace was knowing my place as the steward of Eldrisil would hold meaning. That my presence would maintain some balance in the world's magic."

"Do you feel accomplished?" Condescension ran thick in Venica's tone.

Mourningsword's grip tightened more, and Gabriela shrugged out of it as it became painful. She sidled to the side, as much to see his expression as to get out from between them. His lips were a harsh slash as he looked down at her with a deep exhale.

"We would leave? The three of us together?" He touched her shoulder again, gently this time. His jaw unclenched, and Gabriela could imagine what he might look like with a true, joyful smile sparkling in those eyes just like her own.

"Please... father." The word felt thick on Gabriela's tongue. She never gave him, or the concept he might represent, much thought in twenty years. Yet, now her father stood here, touching her shoulder. How might her life change with the addition of him once he was free of the madness granted by this tower? "Come with us."

He took a deep breath, nodded, and clicked his tongue once. "Come, Carmel."

CHAPTER 30

SUIT YOURSELF

Eleanor gaped at Gabriela's casual control over such a flood of magic. Where before she had scooped at the pools of magic to fuel her works, Gabriela had just diverted rivers to flood an ocean into herself. Eleanor looked down at her notebook, a crazed mess of shorthand filling the page in uneven, cramped lines. Her writing devolved into a shortened version of her shorthand in parts. Unraveling her thoughts on what she'd just witnessed would take a while.

"What did it feel like?" she asked Gabriela as her mother led her from the room.

"How did what feel like?"

"Holding that much magic?"

"Like I was full of wasps."

Venica pushed her daughter through the door and the stairs Eleanor had rushed up so recently. Brynmor passed next, his shoulders slumped.

What does one say to a person who just witnessed the failure of their resurrection? "I'm sorry," she said, but he didn't look up.

The fallen paladin came last with Brynmor's body over his shoulder and the pony close at his heels.

"Is that it? We've failed?" she asked. "Um, sir?"

"Failure is relative, Miss Lane, was it? We often learn more in defeat, so long as we allow ourselves to. Have you learned something here?"

Eleanor could have filled another notebook with observations she didn't have time to put down. "So much, yes. I expected the denizens of the Deadvale to be closer to how they are in the stories, for one. Gab harnessed so much magic, but in the end, she focused it like any spell I've witnessed. I expected it to be different somehow."

"How can you watch the flow of magic so closely? I thought that a trait of the strongest paladins or those like Venica."

They started the long walk down the stairs. At least Eleanor felt it should be a long walk, but the tower seemed to shift as needed.

Eleanor tapped the red lens of her goggles. "I made these to help with my research. I never would have guessed how useful they'd be here."

"Fascinating. I assume Venica means to allow you into the vault. If you're friendly with us, those outside will not treat you the same."

Eleanor gulped with a nervous laugh. "Thank you."

The paladin froze in mid-step.

"They've breached the main doors," he growled, showing a flash of white teeth.

"They went through the dead outside?"

Mourningsword shook his head. "I ordered most of them inside while Gabriela attempted her spell. Venica!" he called ahead, rushing to the others and leaving the pony behind. "Take the narrow path under the tower. They will find you before you can seal the vault if no one stays to slow their progress."

"Let the workings of Eldrisil slow them, Oswin. There is more than sufficient time to lock the way behind us," said Venica.

"No, there is not. I feel the tightening of magics from the coming solstice. The tower's defenses will barely give them pause them at this rate."

"I do not wish to lose you again." Venica's words were tender, entirely unlike anything Eleanor could conceive coming from the woman. Yet, the arm around her shoulder was gentle.

A room opened to their left. Mourningsword grumbled and stepped into it. Carmel approached without being called to accept the burden of Brynmor's corpse again. "Sorry about this, old boy."

"Why have you stopped here?" Venica asked from the stairs.

"You've been away too long." Mourningsword nodded his chin to the darkened hallway on the far side of the room. "Someone approaches. Not a paladin, but one with their determination."

"That's Valoria," said Eleanor. "As much as I'd rather see this out within the safety of a vault, I don't know what kind of a life I'd have after all this is done if I don't stand up now."

"Be strong, Eleanor," said Gabriela. "Do what you must."

Venica's gaze drifted from the corpse and to the paladin. "Where is your sword?"

"I won't need it here." He stepped to kiss Venica on the cheek. "Go. Keep her safe." He looked down at Gabriela.

Venica squeezed his hand as they parted. Gabriela followed with a lingering stare at her father, the pony a few steps behind.

"Venica seems to wish we resolve matters without violence," said Mourningsword.

"I'm surprised you would follow her orders after what she did to you."

"I came to accept the foreign nature of Queen Venica Marwol's mind long ago. She does what she believes is in the best interest of all parties and is rarely wrong."

"It was best that she hid Gabriela from you and never mentioned you to her?"

"I may not agree with her decisions, but she makes them with the best intentions." He nodded down the hall again. "You know these people. How would you recommend we first engage them?"

"Valoria is absolute in her dedication to what she considers honor. She follows orders as exactly as she can and stands superior to others she feels have a lower ethic, even if that means they just have some modicum of awareness or self-thought. Let me talk to her."

The paladin nodded.

The clink of plate armor pulled their attention to the hall. The white in her armor glowed with an internal, ghostly light. She stepped into the chamber a moment later, one hand touching the sword hilt on her back.

"Valoria, I'm glad to see you," said Eleanor.

"You left me a prisoner in the marsh. How glad can you be?"

Eleanor watched the blade across the commander's back closely, wondering why she had yet to draw it. "What happened to Lord Sebastian?"

"So you have fallen to the enemy to immediately voice your concern for one of them."

"I haven't fallen to any side, Valoria. I've seen something in these people that was never taught in any school or sermon. You can't believe the lengths Gab has gone through trying to help Brynmor. I—"

"Enough." Ravell silenced her with a raised palm. "We have only a moment until the duke catches up. I disagree with your actions, but I have heard one voice that gives me pause."

"Lord Sebastian? You came to an understanding?"

"A ceasefire," said Ravell. "He had every opportunity to remove me as a threat, yet did not. Instead, he sang to me."

"Sang? That must have been miserable for you."

Ravell chuckled. "Quite the contrary. Lord Sebastian has the most unique singing voice, melodious and... haunting. He sang a song I hadn't heard since childhood, one my grandnan sang to me."

"That's it?" Eleanor waved her hands, expecting more to the story. "He sang to you, and now you're friends?"

"No, we have the beginnings of an understanding. Lord Sebastian showed me a gentleness in the Deadvale I never thought possible."

The door behind her opened, and Duke Highgate spilled out. His flawless dark armor shone with blues and deep reds. "This blasted tower is a maze. Excellent, Commander. You found the traitor. And..." His eyes ran over Ser Mourningsword. "I don't recognize your armor. Where is your helmet?"

"I am Ser Oswin Mourningsword, former First Brother of the Order of Six and Eight, Steward of Eldrisil."

"Order of Six and Eight?" The duke scoffed. "That order dissolved thirty years ago, old timer. What are you doing here? That doesn't look like standard paladin armor. Are you some vigilante?"

Mourningsword stretched his neck with the barest twitch of his lip.

"What is this goddess-betrayed room we're in now?"

Eleanor didn't notice them until the duke spoke. The hexagon-shaped room was lit by a torch on every other wall, and a paladin's armor lay slumped against each of the others. This tower was a tomb.

"Stand aside, Miss Lane," the duke continued. "We are here to entreat with the master of this tower and accept his full surrender."

The fallen paladin's lips parted in a feral smile. The restraint he showed beside Queen Venica was starting to fade outside her presence. He raised one hand to reach out, fingers splayed against the duke's breastplate. "I will gladly hear your surrender."

Duke Highgate's eyes flashed wide, and he jumped back, hand on the pommel of the short sword on his hip. Eleanor doubted the weapon could do much against Mourningsword's armor. "My terms are non-negotiable," said the duke. "I ride at the head of King Lysander Blackthorn's paladins on a mission sanctified by the church. You are to lay down all arms and allow this place to be cleansed with the goddess's holy fire."

When would he have had time to go to the king and return with an army? They would have had to be riding by Monkter Abbey twenty minutes after Valoria and I left to be here now.

Eleanor tried to catch Ravell's gaze, hoping to learn something by an unspoken eye-roll or brow twitch. The commander did look at her, but her expression never shifted.

"By the power invested unto me, in the name of Eldrisil, I decline," said Mourningsword.

"Fool," Duke Highgate tsked. "The paladins at my back are more than enough to wipe this tower from its dark place in history." His eyes lingered on the armor of the long-dead surrounding him.

"Tell him, Eleanor," said Ravell. "Tell the duke the lengths they are going through to save his nephew."

Eleanor blinked at the commander. "It's... yes. I have witnessed firsthand how the forces of Eldrisil, the so-called agents of the Deadvale, have risked their existence to save your nephew, Duke Highgate."

"Is that so? Where is he now? Where is my darling nephew?"

Eleanor bit her lip, sensing the question was rhetorical.

"Save him how?" the duke asked.

"Resurrect him, My Lord," said Ravell. The duke turned to her, but not with the urgency Eleanor might have expected. "Viscount Brynmor died in an accident days ago, and Lady Marwol has been working to bring him back to us."

"To fill my nephew with vile, profane magics. To go basely against the goddess's will." Highgate spat.

"If it were against Elysara's will, She would stop it." Eleanor licked her lips. "If she succeeds, Brynmor will—"

"Let's hope she doesn't," said the duke. "Commander, I gave you specific instructions to return Brynmor to me, yet you have failed."

Ravell stood a little taller, rolling her shoulders back.

"Duke Highgate," Eleanor tried to pull his attention back. "I... I think Gabriela, Lady Marwol, has a real chance of succeeding. There's something about her. She doesn't give up. She has a unique way of seeing the world."

The duke stepped close enough for Eleanor to smell the rank of his breath. "A dead nephew will do far more for me now than a living one. And call me 'My Lord'" He stepped back, sliding the sword from its sheathe. Ser Mourningsword to her side didn't move, but she couldn't believe he was frozen by fear. "Finish them quickly, Commander. We will find my nephew and show his head to the king. The whole of the Deadvale will..." The clink of heavy metal echoed across the room. "...burn."

The three suits around the room rose, circling the duke.

"Gods and saints, what in all the hells is this devilry?"

"I am the steward of this tower," said Mourningsword. "With the power granted to me when I was cursed to remain here, I will expel those that would harm Eldrisil."

The duke stepped back again, bumping against one of the paladins with a wide frame and helmet patterned with feathery wings. Eleanor tried to focus on the swirls of magic throughout the room, to understand if Mourningsword controlled the armor or what remained within it, but the chaos was too much.

"You wouldn't dare harm me," said the duke, his darting eyes betraying his bravado. "Commander, attend me."

Ravell shifted but remained frozen in place. "Ser Mourningsword," she said. "You are the steward of this tower, but I wish to speak to its master. Take me to her. The duke will remain here, unharmed, as collateral for my good intentions."

The fallen paladin ran a hand through his lanky hair. "I do not need a hostage, but I will humor you."

"You cannot leave me here," the duke screamed. "This will be the end of your career."

"No matter what he is now," said Ravell, "this man was a paladin of the highest order, My Lord. No matter what curse has befallen him, I would believe his word when freely given." She stared at the paladin, one eyebrow raised.

"I give it," said Mourningsword. "I accept this, but only to reunite my dearest with her most trusted advisor. Good day, Sebastian."

"Oswin, funny to run into you here," Lord Sebastian's voice echoed from Ravell's armor.

The duke jumped. "All your miserable, vile magics will amount to nothing against the might of the king's paladins," he growled.

"You never took the oaths, so I would never expect you to understand," said Mourningsword. "A paladin of Elysara will not raise arms against their brothers and sisters. It was my downfall, and so will it be theirs."

"You command this tower, yet the forces assault those paladins, your brothers."

"My vows became null when I accepted Elysara is a fiction," Mourningsword growled.

"Blasphemy."

Mourningsword shrugged. "Sebastian, wouldn't you rather take one of these armors?" he gestured at the three plate suits surrounding the duke.

"No thanks, Oswin. I think I better stay where I am."

"Suit yourself," said Mourningsword, shifting to wave an arm down the hallway they'd entered the chamber through. "Ladies first, Miss Lane."

Stairs lit by flickering tallow candles twisted downward. Ravell joined her on the steps a moment later.

Lord Sebastian was quietly giggling. "Suit yourself," he said as they descended. "Get it, with the armor?"

Ravell stepped beside her. "I would never have expected to say this, Eleanor, but I am happy to see you. Trapped for a day with this idiot, I felt myself going mad."

"I thought you loved my singing voice, Val," said Lord Sebastian.

Eleanor ignored the knight. "How did the duke call the paladins so quickly? He's been pleading with the king for years to let him bring war to the Deadvale."

"You are the reason the paladins are here now, Eleanor. Your papers at the magic academy went through the ranks, and those that decide these things agreed that now would be the best and only time to attack the heart of the Deadvale."

"My papers? No, that can't be right. They dismissed everything I submitted. That's what got me kicked out."

"I can only repeat what I heard. Something you wrote was persuasive enough that your superiors ignored your heresy."

While she felt traitorous to be supplying the damning details, she also beamed with pride, knowing her work had made such an impact. A major military offensive was launched based on her research.

"The duke had nothing to do with the army of paladins, then? They were already dispatched before we left Montker Abbey?"

"Yes. The paladins were mobilized almost two weeks ago. By chance, they passed through the marsh shortly after we left, where the duke joined them, then through the valley to find me."

"Why are you doing this, Valoria? Why do you want to see Queen Venica? I'm sure Lord Sebastian would stop you if you had some assassination plot."

"Oh, I definitely would," he agreed.

"Then why?"

"You don't see what you have," said Ravell.

"What do I have?"

"I accused you of treason in that valley, yet you did not flinch. Your desire to learn something new about magic made you dismiss my threats or other repercussions."

Eleanor scratched her nose. "I might recall something about that."

"What is that like? To do something completely for yourself?"

"I... I don't know. I've always done everything for myself. I don't rely on others if I can help it in any way."

"Is that from a need for self-reliance or a lack of trust?"

"Either? Both?" Eleanor shrugged, tossing up her hands.

"Thus, you would not allow me to attempt the puzzle box."

"Oh, for the love of all the saints, Valoria, that again. If we make it through this alive and out of prison, I'll have my father make you a dozen."

"Thank you, Eleanor."

"That was sarcasm."

The stairs ended abruptly with a sharp turn to the left. A torch flared on the right wall. More came to life until they cast light across the heavy-looking door at the end of the fifty-pace stone hallway.

"What is this place?" Eleanor asked.

"The vault," said Mourningsword. "But no one has been here in ages."

"Then where are Gabriela and the others?"

"I bet I know," said Lord Sebastian.

"As do I," said the paladin with a sigh. "Follow me."

CHAPTER 31

FOUR FIGURES

"Let me try again, Mama. I almost had enough. I would have done it if you hadn't stopped me."

"No, Gabriela. You would have lost control. You know I am right."

Gabriela followed her mother for a few more steps in silence, interrupted only by Carmel's cilomping hoofs.

"How could I know?" she finally asked. "I didn't feel like I was losing control. You couldn't know, either."

"So much, Gabs, all for him." Aura faded through the stone wall to float beside her. "All for him."

"Aura! Where have you been?"

"Around. I hear, but stay small."

"Aura..." Venica paused, turning to face her daughters. "Did you hear everything above?"

Aura nodded slowly. "I heard, but I already knew. Always knew."

"Do you remember anything of your life before?" Gabriela asked.

Aura shook her head, lanky hair spilling over her shoulders.

"Oh, my pet, I did everything for you. I nearly tore down the world to bring you back."

"But you didn't."

"No, I failed. Come, girls, we must get below."

Down and down they went. The stairs curved left, then right. The walls were tight-fitting masonry, then mudded stone, then looked to be carved from the world's bedrock. The air grew stale and damp, smelling both like an ancient cave and moldering library.

"How much farther is it?" Gabriela asked, worried more for Eleanor and Lord Sebastian above than what she may find at the tower's base. Her mind had been blissfully devoid of thoughts of her father.

No sooner had she asked than the stairs spilled into a cave. The rocks glowed steady blues and greens, illuminating an impossibly colossal space. From the center, a single stalactite dangled a hundred feet from the ceiling, its tip a few inches from the cave floor. Dripping water echoed, and somewhere, a stream slipped over rocks.

No, not a stalactite. It was a tree. Huge and triangular, growing downward to almost touch the cavern floor.

"What is this?" Gabriela asked.

"The anti-tower," said Venica. "All things have a duality, and Eldrisil is no exception. Magic flows around the tower, twisting and spiraling off to all corners of the world. It also casts through the anti-tower to absorb back into the world's bedrock, maintaining a balance."

"Making sure there isn't too much magic in the world?" asked Brynmor. "Where is the goddess's role in all of this?"

"She is a tool for focusing and controlling weak minds. If Her followers see magic as a gift, they are less likely to abuse it."

"Where is the vault?" Gabriela asked.

Venica raised a thin finger to the tip of the tree. "There, directly below the point."

She started forward again, but Gabriela didn't move.

"I don't like this, Mama. Can't we talk to these paladins? Can't we work out whatever's between us? Why do we have to hide?" She tugged at her fingers.

"There is no time to debate. I know best."

"How could you? You weren't worried about an invasion when we were back home. Now you want to cower until they're gone."

"Enough." Venica's single word, though not shouted, echoed through the chamber, silencing everything for a heartbeat. "This does not stem from fear for my well-being but from fear for yours. I will not allow any harm to come to you, Gabriela."

"Shouldn't I have some say in that?"

"Absolutely not. You will obey me."

"Eleanor obeys no one but herself. I think it's quite brave how she stayed behind to confront Valoria and the others."

"Brave or foolish, the two are often confused." Venica reached for Gabriela's arm, but she snatched it away.

"Ser Mourningsword was right, Mama. If you hold me back here, I'll always wonder and regret what I could have done differently. Let me try the resurrection once more. I have an idea about what to do differently."

"This is not a spell for trial and error. We have no time for this idle banter." Venica crossed her arms and raised a hand to trace the edges of the amulet at her throat.

Just under the tip of the tree, a laughably simple wooden trap door lay inlaid in the stone ground. With the flick of Venica's finger, a tendril of darkness tossed it open. Below, yet more stairs circled into the gloom.

Gabriela groaned. Her calves would feel this tomorrow. She would owe Carmel an orchard's worth of apples. "Fine."

"It is only one level down," said Venica, taking the lead.

The single, small chamber at the bottom, lit by more of the glowing rocks, had no other doors or hallways.

"How can this be a secure vault, Mama? There's a wood hatch, and that's it."

"I had to be sure of your commitment."

"What?"

"Gab, over here," Brynmor called to her. He stood close to one wall, his ghost light reflecting and enhancing the mossy glow. Crude pictures were carved into the wall, not much more advanced than stick figures. They showed a story in panels, starting with four figures, one lying prone and three standing over them, one with a large hat. After much hand waving, the prone figure stood between the one with the big hat and the other.

"What is this?"

"The story of the first resurrection," said Venica. "Or how it was intended to be. Bishop Aurelius Lightbringer, one of the founding members of the modern church, lost his only son. The details no longer matter. He brought him to this tiny chamber at the center of the world's magic to bring him back to life."

"Who are the others?" Gabriela pointed to the figure standing to the left of the one with the big hat.

Venica stepped nearer. "That is me."

Gabriela gawked. "This has to be almost two hundred years ago."

"The church's early days were more lenient on those that harnessed magic as I am able. I was an advisor to Aurelius and brought him here when his son died."

Gabriela scrunched her nose. "You attempted the first resurrection. What happened?"

"The Deadvale," said the queen. "The uncontrolled magic pulled all life from the land. When it reached the limits of my spell, the world split, rebounding the power inward."

"Creating the Crack."

Venica nodded.

"Then your resurrection did work," said Gabriela.

The queen raised an eyebrow.

"You didn't resurrect the bishop's son but raised the dead and seeded the land to continue doing it for centuries."

"Clever. The magic fractured my mind, driving me to near madness. I became obsessed with how magic and life intertwined. The church's holy warriors saw it a great honor to dash themselves against the tower's defenses, and I toyed with them. Until one made it through my haze of lunacy."

"Mourningsword. My father."

"An infuriating man, but honorable and loyal. I am sorry I never told you of him."

"Why did you bring us here, Queen Venica?" asked Brynmor.

"This room was once called the heart chamber. I once knew who called it that and why, but my memories from that time are imperfect. This is the true center of power in Eldrisil. I had to see your level of commitment, my tiny. How determined are you to bring this man back? You say you would try again, but what foolishness is it to attempt something so dangerous, with such vast repercussions, without some plan of a vastly different approach? I might have ended the world attempting to raise the bishop's boy."

"I thought about that," Gabriela said while tracing a finger along one of the figures beside the bishop. "You said you pleaded to have Aura returned to you."

Venica's silence was her confirmation.

"And I'm sure the bishop begged the goddess to do the same for his son. You've always told me that magic is an expression of your will. See what you want with confidence, and it will happen. Were you always that way, Mama?"

The queen's eyes narrowed. "No. I was once faithful to the goddess, asking boons of Her."

"Instead of having confidence, you asked someone else to do it for you. What did you do differently with Aura?"

Venica raised long fingers to brush the necklace at her throat, her misty gaze not quite meeting Gabriela's. "I was distraught. I called to the goddess I had so long ago discarded."

Aura faded into sight beside her, reaching ghostly fingers to touch their mother's hair.

"That's what I'd do differently, Mama. I wouldn't ask for the magic to work. I would just... make it work."

"Would it be that simple?" Venica raised her gaze to Aura, brushing her knuckles down the ghost's cheek. "Could I have brought you back to me?"

Aura leaned into the tender touch. Gabriela had never seen such a show of intimacy from her mother, not toward her.

"Maybe if this works with Brynmor, we could try again for Aura after the solstice. Where is her body?"

"Gone. I would not stand for the magic of the Deadvale to raise her mindlessly. I spread her ashes across Crystalwood Gardens and kept a bit with me always." Venica again touched the amulet at her throat.

"Does this mean you'll let me try again with Brynmor?"

"I will not stop you," Venica said without looking at Gabriela. "You may very well destroy the world with your spell, but that no longer matters to me. You are all I care about, Gabriela. I would rather the world end than you resent me for standing in your way."

"I know she intends for that to sound loving..." said Brynmor.

Gabriela stared up at her mother. Brynmor was right. "Thank you, Mama."

She closed her eyes again, focusing on the delicate magic tendrils around the tower. She saw those she dropped earlier. The paladins still glowed, but their numbers were scattered, fractured into groups, likely by the machinations of the tower. Gabriela gathered the magic, stopping at a single handful that buzzed in her grip. It urged her to reach for more, but she ignored the call. Like all magic, this wasn't a matter of brute force but intention and finesse.

Gabriela again thought of Brynmor as he was when they first met. Virile and handsome. She willed his body to return to that state. Feeling his heart beat and chest swell with breath. She saw it calmly, never entreating a third party to get involved, only willing him to be as he was.

But a body without a soul was incomplete.

She looked at his ghost, looking just as she willed his body, seeing the fine thread tethering him to herself. Aura was tied to that same place somewhere deep in her chest. Perhaps even to her own ghost, as it existed within her. Gabriela knew that to complete this, she would have to unravel that thread. Only then could she put him back into his body. She started to work at the knots but felt Aura's coming undone with it.

"Do it, Gabs. I'm ready."

"Ready for what?" She wasn't sure if she said the words out loud.

"This is no existence. Let me go."

Gabriela ignored Aura, continuing to work at the lines fettering the two ghosts to herself. The lines burned the more she touched them, becoming more confusing and intertwined. Brynmor's felt brittle, ready to snap with the punishment. The point of attachment within herself became red and angry, like an insect bite. She could rip them both out and shove Brynmor where he belonged, but that would leave Aura drifting in her grip.

"Please, Gabs."

The tendrils of magic shook violently, and she lost her tenuous hold on them both.

CHAPTER 32

A FATHER BREAKS

The paladin guided them through tight warrens so narrow he had to turn sideways in places to get by in his armor. Eleanor had no reason to think he led them in circles, but she knew nothing about the man or his intentions, so why not?

"Where are you leading us?" asked Valoria from behind, the irritation thick in her tone.

The floor shuddered, tossing Eleanor against the rough stone wall, dust filtering down to catch in her eyes and throat.

"The anti-tower," said Lord Sebastian. "The tower focuses magic upward, refining it as it goes, but down there, it's raw, elemental, far more powerful. At least I assume the resurrection did not go as planned in the throne room?" The words spilled from him, unwinded as he was from their sprint through the claustrophobic hallways.

"No," Eleanor shook her head. "Queen Venica stepped in to stop the ritual. Why would they be going somewhere else with power? They can't mean to attempt it a second time?"

"That's exactly right," said Mourningsword.

"Val doesn't want the resurrection to go through," said Lord Sebastian.

"I asked you not to call me that," Ravell bristled.

"Why are you two here?" asked Eleanor. "What ceasefire did you come to if Valoria is still so against this plan? I assume you still want to do what the duke demanded?"

The commander was quiet for a moment before responding. "No. I have heard Duke Highgate's motives quite clearly. He wishes for war to play out his vengeance. I never doubted the villainy of the Deadvale, but when I was left to its mercy, the only thoughts of violence came from those on our side of the Crack."

"Brynmor suggested bashing her over the head with a rock," Lord Sebastian added helpfully. "You probably didn't hear that part, since he's a ghost. Val wasn't happy when I told her."

"And you believed him?" Eleanor asked the commander.

"I do." Ravell's voice was small. "Lord Sebastian is brutally mischievous but not malicious."

"Masterfully manipulating minds with misdirection and mirth, mysteriously mischievous, I'm a mischief-making maven," said Lord Sebastian.

"Did you just make that up?" asked Eleanor.

"Does it sound like I did?"

Eleanor shrugged.

"I've been working on it. I've had some free time while hiding amongst the paladins, and before that, Val here isn't much of a conversationalist. Valoria, sorry."

"Why do you object to the resurrection? The living marquess could take the wind from his uncle's sails. He could start a dialog between the king and Queen Venica."

Mourningsword snorted. "There are few things she would hate more than that, but she'd do it if it meant no more paladins coming to die here."

"Are you sure you aren't taking us in circles?" Eleanor asked.

"I am, but on purpose. The paladins—"

The floor shook again. Dirt and stones bounced on their heads.

"Back, back, back!" Mourningsword ran at them, forcing the women to retreat. The ceiling collapsed at his heels. He shook his head at the mess, his hands on his hips. "The paladins are assaulting the tower, throwing off the magic within. I hoped to avoid a direct confrontation with any, creating paths to the anti-tower, but they disrupt my every attempt."

"You shape the tower with your mind?" Eleanor asked.

Mourningsword nodded.

"Then what if that door takes us right to where we're going?" Eleanor pointed at the blank wall of stone beside her.

"I think the dust has clogged her brain," said Lord Sebastian.

"What do you assume I have been doing, Miss Lane? I have been trying to create a tunnel to the anti-tower chamber."

"Well, stop *trying* and just do it. Magic is ninety-five percent confidence."

Mourningsword narrowed his eyes, tightening his gauntleted fist. "You would assume to teach me about magic? I have been in this tower longer than you have been alive."

"If not teach, then remind."

He stepped closer, towering over even her oversized hat. He shot out his fist, missing her nose by a hair, smashing it into the wall. The stone splintered, cracked, and fell away in chunks. Light poured through the gap, wildly flicking between pale green and blinding white. The air ripped past as the light came in as if sucked through the hole to fill a vacuum. Though it didn't look large enough to fit his armor, Mourningsword stepped through the hole with Ravell close behind.

Eleanor couldn't see through the dizzying strobe but sensed she should follow, and quickly. She put one foot on the collapsed wall.

"Wait, wait, wait!" cried a voice from down the hall. The little horned creature from before was sprinting toward her, waving what looked like a rolled piece of parchment in their clawed hand. They stopped just short of Eleanor, breathing heavily.

"Miss... Water, please give this to Queen Marwol, as you are about to see her."

Eleanor accepted the scroll. "I will." Her voice lilted up as a question. The creature turned to leave, moving slower than before. She watched them for a moment before giving up on knowing anything more and stepped through the wall.

Glass cracked, and something bit into her right cheek.

Clapping a hand over her eye, Eleanor felt the sting of shards of glass from her shattered goggle lens. She tore them off, cringing as she pulled out a piece that missed her eye by a measurement she didn't want to consider.

The dazzle faded, and she took in the room.

The pony looked unamused by a set of stairs with Queen Venica beside him, fingers clasping the amulet at her throat. Brynmor's body lay sprawled in the center of the room, with Gabriela floating with her toes a few inches from his chest, pale hair whipping in an unfelt gale. Mourningsword and Ravell stood on either side of Eleanor, looking equally unsure of what to do.

"She looks so much like her mother," said Mourningsword with a tear running down his cheek.

Eleanor focused back on Gabriela. The young woman was crying, too.

Chapter 33

Sugar in Water

G abriela grabbed at the tethers floating away like weeds on a raging river.

"I can't do it, Aura. Please don't make me do it. It'll kill you."

"I died a long time ago. You didn't even know I was your sister."

"Why didn't you tell me?"

"I forget. I forget a lot."

"It doesn't matter. I still loved you as one. There's still time. I can stop this, and Mama can do it. She'll know how to untether Brynmor without harming you."

"She can't, or she would have days ago. Or she would have bound me to something else years ago like she did Lord Sebastian. Mama knew Brynmor would fade with the solstice. She knew there was no untangling us."

"Maybe she can by using all the magic in the tower. She can at least try."

"She'll fail again. She knows she'll fail, so she will. That's how magic works. It will destroy her. Gabs, I want this. Your chance is fading. You can't hold onto all that magic much longer."

Until Aura put doubt into her, Gabriela thought she might hold the world's magic indefinitely. Or at least until her mother devised a solution to save both

Brynmor and her sister. But, if Aura was right, their mother knew from first seeing Brynmor's tether while standing in her library that the whole mission was doomed. It had all been to placate her, to amuse her and make her feel like she was heard and her desire cared for.

Gabriela wanted to rage at her mother, but what choice was there? She would have gone through her mother's books, slowly simmering that the most powerful magic user she knew stood in the next room, flatly refusing to help.

No, she couldn't be upset with her mother about this. Her mother never thought the resurrection would succeed, yet she wanted to instill hope in Gabriela. The fae ring, the material reagents. A pointless quest to make her feel heard.

Not until her mother allowed her to attempt the resurrection, knowing it would be Aura's end. Queen Venica quietly put that decision into Gabriela's hands without warning. Though, she never expected it to come to this point.

"Gabs..."

Gabriela parted her lips to speak but could only manage a quaking breath. She breathed in slowly, squeezing her eyes tight. "I'll never forget you, Aura."

"I wish we could have grown up together."

"We did."

If she didn't act now, she never would. Gabriela ripped the ghostly tethers from her chest, feeling a spreading chill where they connected. Once free, they came apart easily. Brynmor's felt like a brittle, rusted chain, but Aura's... Hers faded, dissolving like sugar in water, slipping through Gabriela's fingers.

Just like that. There was no chance for a last word or to wave as her ghostly frame dimmed.

Gabriela knew it would happen, but that knowledge did nothing to lessen the sting. She stared at the space her annoying, ever-present companion had occupied. The sister she loved.

Something tugged hard in her hand. Brynmor's tether. It longed to follow Aura, to follow the natural order of things denied it days ago, even as his ghost stared at her with eyes wide, terror naked on his face. Gabriela took that rusty chain and drove it deep into Brynmor's physical chest, tying it to him as best she could guess. There was no one to ask—not that anyone had done this successfully before—so there was no point in second-guessing what to do.

Satisfied, she pulled out her arm, or what amounted to her arm in this dream-like state. Or at least she tried to pull out her arm. Brynmor's body grasped at her like some suckered sea creature. Gabriela drilled her power into him, demanding he live and let go of her.

Intense cold prickled over her body, cold enough to stiffen her joints and freeze her muscles.

Then, pain as she'd never imagined. A thousand stubbed toes focused into her leg. Bones ground together, sliding into place. Only when the cold was replaced with heat even greater than what she felt in Malphas' lair did a single thought pierce through the agony. This sensation wasn't hers, but Brynmor's, as her power knitted his body together, restoring it to as it was when they'd first met at the top of the steps. Fire burned deep within the leg, binding the bones before moving to his arm, searing away the deep wound from Valoria's blade. Finally, his neck. Though she felt every tiny movement as its own private torment, it was more the sound of every snap and click that drove Gabriela near to cutting off her power and ending the process.

This will work. For you, Aura.

The inferno reduced to a comfortable warmth, like sitting by her hearth to read a book. It spread over Brynmor's body, settling deep into his flesh and through his bones. His chest ached with a single, shy heartbeat. His lungs burned with their first breath in days. The grip holding her to him lessened, allowing her to free herself.

Something wasn't right. Separated from Brynmor, she sensed a much larger mind, ancient and slow, and she felt dozens of tiny attacks against her. Not her, the tower. Eldrisil. It followed a command to ensnare the paladins in deadly traps, but its power waned rapidly.

Do not kill them, she commanded the tower. *Confound them in impossible geometries. Put them to sleep in fields of poppies.*

Gabriela didn't know if the tower heard or would listen to her as the last tendril of magic slipped from her unnoticed and her vision returned to the heart chamber. She looked down at Brynmor with Eleanor kneeling over him, recognizable by her oversized hat. When had Eleanor arrived?

Her body tingled with the magic leaving it.

Aura.

Where was Aura?

Oh...

There was her mother beside Carmel. Valoria beside Mourning... her father.

Brynmor's ghost and Aura were gone.

The thought floated by that perhaps the surge of magic blocked her ability to sense the ghosts; that Aura was doing something annoying right in front of her with Brynmor rolling his eyes as she did. But she knew that wasn't the case. She saw no ghosts because there were none to see. Looking back at her mother, she knew it was true by the vacant stare in her misty eyes. How long did she know this would be the outcome? How long ago did she choose to give her daughter the decision to do what Gabriela had done?

She sucked in a deep breath, determined not to grow angry with her mother. Not yet. She had to know if it had all been worth it. Worth it... trading her sister's existence for a man she barely knew.

Gabriela knelt beside Eleanor.

"You did it," Eleanor said, pulling her fingers from Brynmor's throat. "He's breathing, and his heart is beating, at least." She pulled open his eyelids one at a time, squinting close to each as she did.

Gabriela sat back on her heels, staring at the roughly scratched mural on the wall. Mama failed the first resurrection, creating the Deadvale. She failed the second, casting Aura's sanity away with it. Her gaze slid down to the man lying prone before her, with his soft, wavy hair and strong jaw, looking as vibrant as he did days ago at the top of the stairs. Was he in there, or had she revived him as a mindless, soulless husk, what her mother called a hollow?

It didn't matter right now because nothing could be done to change it.

"What's that?" Gabriela pointed to the rolled scroll in Eleanor's other hand.

She looked down at it as if she'd never seen the thing in her life. "It's from the... I don't know what it was. It's for your mother." She pushed the scroll forward.

Gabriela took it, staring at the tiny orange wax seal. If only she could avoid her mother for another few minutes, but the little slip of parchment drew her forward.

"What is this?" Venica accepted the scroll without looking down at it. Gabriela followed her mother's gaze to the paladin helping Brynmor to stand on wobbly legs.

"You did it, my tiny. You did what I could not."

"Aura..."

Venica inhaled sharply. "I know. Again, you did what I could not."

"You knew this would happen. You knew from when you first saw Brynmor in your library. Saving him would mean sacrificing her. That's why you lead us on a pointless quest."

Venica took a slow breath. "I have wanted a thousand times to do what I knew to be correct. I felt Aura's pain as a constant reminder of my failure. Yet, I could not bring myself to do the right thing."

"So you made me do it instead?"

"You acted as she desired. I could not." Venica choked back a sob, slapping a hand over her mouth to hide it. "You are the stronger of us, my tiny. Stronger in spirit and power."

"The tower's magic is waning," said Mourningsword. "It won't hold off the paladins much longer. It seems to have given up attacking the paladins to merely ensnare them instead. Rally Eldrisil's power and crush Elysara's warriors."

Gabriela turned from her mother, stepping in front of Mourningsword. "The power has corrupted you completely, Father. My mother once loved you and may still. I cannot imagine someone worthy of that honor would so gleefully ask for the destruction of his once-kin."

"I just witnessed the daughter I never knew sacrifice my firstborn to save a man she barely knows. Do not speak to me of a lack of judgment or character." He spat over Gabriela, directing the words at Venica.

She reached up, putting a hand on his cheek, slick with sweat, pulling his gaze down to meet hers. "Father. I don't know you, but I think I want to." She spoke slowly, deliberately. "You must fight this aggression, this violence. We will find a peaceful solution and return home to Soulhaven."

His face again softened as it had in the throne room above.

"Commander," Venica said, turning to Ravell. "Do the paladins still follow the directives of the strongest amongst their ranks?"

Ravell stiffened at the attention. "Essentially. They organize into ranks ordered by their affinity to the goddess's Grace."

Venica turned back to Mourningsword. "Call upon the transformative powers of Eldrisil to guide the strongest paladins and this duke into a single chamber."

Mourningsword sneered, but it twisted to a grin. "Strike the head, and the rest will scatter. Take him." He pushed Brynmor's weight onto Ravell, who accepted it despite her look of disgust. Mourningsword closed his eyes and put a hand on the stone wall.

"I would ask you to remain behind, my tiny, but I have learned the futility in that."

"Please don't hurt these people, Mama," said Gabriela. "There must be some way to get through to them with words."

"Diplomacy is not always possible. Some only understand respect with a show of violence."

Mourningsword slammed his gauntleted fist into the wall with a resounding thud. Stone flaked away, revealing a rickety wooden door behind it with sunlight leaking between the slats.

"Your arena awaits, my queen," he said.

"Wait!" Gabriela called them to stop. "Tell me one more thing first, Mama."

Venica turned.

"Was Lord Sebastian there when you tried to raise the bishop's son?"

"Lord Sebastian Rafferty has been my most trusted protector and adviser." Her mother raised an eyebrow toward Ravell. Or rather, her armor.

"It's true. We go way back," he beamed.

Venica nodded to the crude drawing on the far wall. "You did not ask who the last person was."

Gabriela ran a hair through her hair, tugging at it. "Of course! But if he was here with you two hundred years ago, how could he be the brother of Brynmor's great-something grandfather?"

"Such questions can wait," said Venica.

"It was all a little fib to rile up the good sir," Lord Sebastian whispered with a chuckle.

Gabriela huffed and rolled her eyes. "I suppose someone should tell him. What about Prince Malphas?"

Venica stumbled, slapping a hand against the stone to steady herself. "How do you know that name?"

"We ran into him under the Devil's Pit, Mum," Lord Sebastian's voice echoed from Ravell. "When we went for the blood we thought we needed."

"Of course you did." Venica nodded her chin to the mural. "Malphas Light-bringer, Bishop Aurelius Lightbringer's son. After my failure, the bishop sought assistance from a darker plane. In his haste, the devilkin crafted a contract beyond the bishop's understanding, binding his and his son's souls to the infernal abyss." She squeezed the scroll in her hand.

"His son's ghost had already moved on. So it's possible to get them back? Aura—"

"No." Venica slowly exhaled, softening her tone. "We will speak on this later, my tiny. For now, let us end this." Venica pressed the scroll against Mourn-ingsword's chest plate as she passed and pushed the door open. Gabriela followed her, sparing a glance at her father and his slightly confused look as he scanned the scroll Eleanor had brought.

CHAPTER 34

DUKE HIGHGATE

G abriela blinked away the sun's glare, standing in a gently rolling meadow of knee-high grass. There was no sign of the door leading from the heart chamber, but the others appeared around her. Eleanor, Ravell and Brynmor, then finally, her father and Carmel.

"Who knew it would be such a lovely day inside?" asked Lord Sebastian.

"How is this possible?" asked Ravell. "Are we still within the tower?"

"Fascinating," said Eleanor while scribbling frantically in her notebook.

Fifty feet ahead, three figures in bright gold and silver pushed a fourth in dark blue and red armor into view. They shoved the fourth forward and immediately slumped into the grass, leaving the one in dark colors baffled. Near them, another three paladins appeared, drawing long swords immediately.

"My uncle," said Brynmor.

Gabriela jumped at his hoarse voice beside her. "Brynmor, are you... Did it work?" She grabbed his right hand and flipped it over.

"It seems so."

She looked up at him, but his stormy gray eyes, which had felt ready to pierce through her soul before, now seemed distant and glassy.

The duke scrambled away from the collapsed armors around him, calling to the three paladins with swords drawn. "Ser Theodoric! What is this devilry?" He followed the paladin's stare, finally noticing Gabriela's group. Duke Rhys Highgate fell in beside, and a little behind, the others. "Brynmor!"

"I am alive and well, uncle." Brynmor strained to make his voice loud enough.

Gabriela's mother swept past them. "I am Venica Marwol, self-proclaimed queen of the Deadvale. The church has thrown its greatest warriors against this tower for centuries, but it ends today."

"The paladins will raze this tower and bring justice to all that the dead have slain!" shouted the duke, but he withered when the paladin in the center glanced back at him.

"I am Ser Theodoric the Shield, First of the Order of the Eternal Vigil." His words echoed from his visored helmet. "Do you wish to surrender to Elysara's Grace?"

Venica stepped forward again, now halfway between the groups. "The Deadvale is a direct result of my failure. If it will end in a truce between the sides of the Crack, yes, I offer myself freely."

"No!" Mourningsword rushed forward, grabbing Venica by the wrist and spinning her toward him. "The church believes the Deadvale is at its weakest. Now is the time to strike against them, paving the way for their destruction."

Venica wrenched her arm from his grip. "My daughter—our daughter—wishes for peace, and she shall have it." She strode forward another few paces as the three paladins moved to surround her, swords raised.

"You are the Dread Lord of legend?" asked Ser Theodoric.

"I am."

"Mama, no!"

Brynmor grabbed Gabriela's shoulder, but she shrugged away from him, running to take her mother's hand, hoping to pull her back. "Mama, you can't give yourself up to these people. There must be a compromise."

"By the king and grand matriarch," said Ser Theodoric, "I accept your surrender, Queen Venica." He flourished his sword before snapping it to his back. "I will return you to their company to discuss terms."

Duke Highgate surged forward, brandishing his short sword. "What of the Deadvale and the thousands she has slain? You cannot trust bringing this vile creature to the king's presence."

"The duke speaks true," said another of the paladins, a woman. "No living mage can contend with Queen Venica's power. She cannot be taken across the Crack."

"Then kill her now and return her head to the king," said the duke.

"Uncle, stop this!" Brynmor pushed forward to stand within inches of the duke's outstretched blade. "The dead are not to blame for our tragedies. Queen Venica had no involvement in our family's death."

"You reek, boy," the duke spat. "Reek of profane magics glutting this foul place. Why did it have to be you and not any of my children? You're a disgrace to the Highgate name."

Ser Theodoric flinched.

"A swift death is more than you deserve," the duke continued. "Even Commander Ravell and Miss Lane, now in league with the dead. Do your duty, Ser Theodoric. Strike them down in Elysara's name. Here is the root of evil in this tower. Cleanse it, that we may return victorious."

"We are not executioners, Duke Highgate," said Ser Theodoric.

"Yet you would kill them, were it in battle?"

"Only the commander carries a sword, yet she leaves it undrawn."

"Commander!" Duke Highgate shouted at Ravell. "Do your sworn duty where these holy warriors will not. Strike down these enemies of the goddess."

Ravell raised a hand over her shoulder to her sword hilt but hesitated.

"Treasonous," the duke growled.

"Enough." Mourningsword burst forward, showing that same speed as outside the throne room, driving a gloved fist into the third paladin's gut. In the same motion, he spun, aiming a backfist at Ser Theodoric's face. The other paladin stopped it with a raised forearm, stumbling back with the impact. The one hit in the gut recovered quickly, and the paladins adjusted to surround Mourningsword.

Ser Theodoric did not draw his sword, and his helmet pivoted up and down as if examining Mourningsword for the first time. "Your armor is of a paladin's design, yet the colors are wrong."

"Twenty years imprisoned will change a man."

"Ser Mourningsword..." said Ser Theodoric. "I hardly recognize you. You were the greatest of us. Indeed, I took the vows after seeing you at parade. It speaks to the power of this place to have taken one as high as you."

Mourningsword was on Ser Theodoric with fists and elbows, blows of steel-on-steel ringing across the meadow. Yet Ser Theodoric only blocked and evaded, slipping around the strikes and knocking others away.

"Fight me, damn you!" Mourningsword screamed.

"I will not strike a brother." Ser Theodoric jumped backward. "Very well. If no scrap of Elysara's Grace is left in you, Brother, strike me down." He let his arms drop.

Mourningsword paused for a breath, then raised his gloved fist, rushing forward to drive it through the paladin's skull.

A tendril of shadow snapped around Mourningsword's throat, halting his momentum and jerking him to crash on his back with bone-jarring force.

"Apologies," said Venica, shaking the other end of the tether, dispelling it with a casual gesture. "Oswin's fall was my last great failure. As I held him, studying and toying with him, Elysara's light faded. As his humanity lessened, mine returned after so long left cold in this tower. We met in the middle."

Mourningsword writhed on the ground.

"Sheathe your swords. I give myself freely," said Venica.

Gabriela tore her eyes from her struggling father. "No, Mama! What will giving yourself accomplish?"

Ravell stepped forward, but it was Lord Sebastian who spoke. "The king will want a sacrifice, Princess. Someone his people can blame their fear on."

"We came expecting a fight, not a surrender," said Ser Theodoric. "The... voice from Commander Ravell is correct. It bends my honor to take a prisoner, but as long as the Deadvale defies the goddess's Grace, Her people will need a sign that Her warriors work to undo it."

Venica scoffed. "There is no undoing the Deadvale."

"All things are possible by Elysara's Grace," said Ser Theodoric as though he repeated it often.

"Eldrisil is filled with two centuries of paladins that would say otherwise," said Venica. "Were they able."

Gabriela thought of the cavern filled with paladins under the Devil's Pit. The church once sent whole crusades there to die, forgotten. Now they did the same to the Deadvale. What was life like on the other side of the Crack, where the people seemed defined by their fear of her home? Were the people delighted and emboldened to see their warriors sent off to pointless conflict, never to return? What if they no longer had that?

Ser Theodoric clenched a fist and slowly released it. "No matter your beliefs—"

"What if I could undo the Deadvale?" Gabriela asked.

"Your mother tried for centuries," said Mourningsword, his face flushed and sweaty. "She tirelessly researched the magics until concluding the change was permanent." He closed his eyes with a deep sigh. "I think my back is broken."

Venica dropped to his side, wreathing her hands in shadow. "That is not true," she said while touching the joints of his armor one at a time. "I sought to understand the magic, but not to alter it."

"Would it be possible?" asked Ser Theodoric.

"Absolutely," Eleanor said for the first time, stepping forward and waving her notebook. Eyes and helmets shifted in her direction, and she shrank under the attention. "Magic swirls in tight spirals along lines, like roads."

"Call them 'mana lanes,' Miss Lane," chimed Lord Sebastian.

"Sure," she continued. "I theorized a while ago and recently proved that the direction of the spirals slow and reverse at the Crack. After watching Lady Marwol's feats of magic that restored life to the marquess, I can see those mana lanes clearly, all leading away from Eldrisil. I also note a drastic reduction in the speed of the spirals."

"Because of the coming solstice," said Gabriela. "You think magic spinning the wrong way is what causes the Deadvale to be how it is? Making the dead rise?"

"That's a bit of an oversimplification, but essentially, yes." Eleanor fanned her notebook to a page in the middle, pointing to a complex diagram that meant nothing to anyone but her. "Furthermore, Eldrisil and the solstice would be the only viable place and time to do it."

"Elaborate," said Venica.

Eleanor licked her lips. "This tower is like some grand hub of magic. It would have to be from here if you wanted to affect the world on any scale. This is the center of a wagon wheel. The mana lanes are spokes, and the Crack is the rim."

Gabriela twirled a finger, imagining the motion of magic. "And because the swirling is slowing with the solstice, it'll be easier to change its direction. It's easier to spin a wheel the other way when it's stopped."

Eleanor snapped her gloved fingers with a dull thump. "Yes, you got it. It would have to be done now. Gab, can you do it?"

"What would happen to everyone that relies on magic spinning the way it is? Mister Tanner? Mister and Misses Popkin? All those outside?"

"A bunch of skeletons?" asked Brynmor. "I would have never understood your hesitation a week ago, Gab. Now I see they are nothing less than your dearest friends and family. Even if only you know it."

"The Deadvale has never known peace and never shall." The dark magic faded from Venica's hand. "If Miss Lane is correct, you may have a unique opportunity to correct my mistake of centuries ago. Save the lives of untold witless paladins and the torment of citizens for a hundred miles."

"I can't, Mama. I'm just so tired." It was only half a lie. Even after days of harrowing adventure and loss, the magic still sang in Gabriela's veins, making her feel more awake and alive than she had in memory.

"You are the only one that may do it, my tiny. My magic is too tightly bound to the Deadvale."

"It shouldn't be that hard, I don't think," said Eleanor. "At the current rate, the spirals will be their slowest in twelve to fourteen minutes. If you gather up all the mana lanes as you did for the resurrection, you should be able to draw magic toward you, channeling it upward and away. Do it fast enough, and the spiraling direction from the other side of the Crack will, for lack of a better term, overwrite that in the Deadvale. It won't be an immediate effect, other than for the constructs and animated creatures that rely directly on magic going the wrong way."

Venica's gaze twitched, and Gabriela followed it to Commander Ravell.

Not Ravell, Lord Sebastian.

Magic sustained those closest to her. She just lost Aura. She would not lose the other two.

"Gab?" Eleanor prodded. "Did you hear me? You'll have to start—"

"I'm not doing it."

The corner of Venica's lip curled up as she turned back to resume her magic on Mourningsword. The two paladins with their swords still raised tightened their grips.

Gabriela continued before Eleanor could form her words. "This is my home. This is my family and friends. You say magic spins the wrong way here, but that's the only way I've known it. Why should we surrender our way of life because it goes against someone else's? The Deadvale and its denizens are hurting no one."

"My family—" started the duke.

"—was killed in a fire they started," Brynmor finished.

"The death mages were born on our side of the Crack," said Ravell. "They only learned to harness the magic of the Deadvale."

"The paladins entombed here came of their own will," Mourningsword spoke through gritted teeth between gasps of breath. "They thought they served the goddess, but if She exists, She has no interest in the matter."

"Heresy," said Ser Theodoric without any real venom.

Gabriela stepped beside her parents, rolling back her shoulders to stand a little taller before the paladins and duke. "Leave here. Return to your king or matriarch. Tell them you have subdued the forces of the Deadvale, who have resolved to remain on their side of the Crack, so long as you do so as well."

"They will not accept your terms," said Ser Theodoric.

Grabriela took a deep breath. "My mother created the Deadvale and the Crack by accident. I just succeeded where she failed. Imagine what else I could succeed at doing."

"Is that a threat?" spat the duke.

"As much as a legion of paladins is," said Gabriela.

"What of the traitors?" Duke Highgate jerked his chin at his nephew.

Ser Theodoric waved for the other paladins to sheath their swords. "The Grand Matriarch does not hunt down nonbelievers. It is only punishable to spread those beliefs."

"Worthless! I have suffered for decades with no chance for vengeance. When it is finally within my grasp, the king surrounds me with cowards too trapped in their flawed faith to take action!" The duke rushed Brynmor, short sword gleaming over his head.

It happened too fast for Gabriela's eye. The duke was charging toward her, then he froze and Ravell was on one knee behind him, her enormous dark blade drawn and held horizontally at hip level. She rose, flourishing her blade to flick away the blood as the duke dropped. When she turned to face them, her eyes were wide.

"I've been wanting to use that sword for days now!" Lord Sebastian cooed.

The paladins drew their blades again, but Lord Sebastian—or Commander Ravell—raised their hands in a defensive posture. "If there was ever a clear example of acting in defense, that was it," said Lord Sebastian.

Ser Theodoric lowered his sword to touch the tall grass. "Duke Rhys Highgate acted out of grief and anger, but he died defending his family's honor."

"A lie?" Brynmor raised a single eyebrow.

"The truth will help no one. The church understands the need to sculpt a narrative. Would you not agree... Duke?"

Brynmor chuckled wryly and ran a hand through his hair.

"Then this mission is yet a success." Ser Theodoric slung his blade across his back, turning a slow circle. "How does one leave this place?"

"I was told you go down to leave," said Eleanor. The others turned to her, and she shrugged.

Ser Theodoric's helmet tilted, yet he stomped once in the grass with a distinct sound of metal-on-metal. He dropped to a knee, brushing away the grass to reveal a mesh iron trap door beneath. "Odd." He pulled it open, stepping onto what must have been stairs beneath. "I will await your company, Duke Highgate."

Ser Theodoric descended, and the other paladins followed.

Brynmor waved at his uncle's body, only partly hidden in the grass. "It's funny. I spent my life hating him, but I still expected to feel something at his death. Yet, here we are. Nothing."

"Sometimes we don't feel it right away," said Gabriela. "You should go, right? Go build your world of convenient lies."

"That's what we all do." He raised his ungloved hand to brush her cheek, but hesitated. "I can't thank you enough, Gab. You might have pushed me down the stairs, but I might have deserved it."

"You completely deserved it." Gabriela grabbed his hand and pressed it into her cheek, feeling the warmth and texture, the bone and muscles beneath. "Remember to speak kindly of us agents of the Deadvale."

"Won't you come with me?"

"Why?"

Brynmor faltered at her question. "We may have had a rocky start, and we may be better as friends, but I can show you the world. Wouldn't you want that?"

"I honestly don't know. What's so great about the world?"

"It's..." He shook his head and shrugged. "There's a lot going on out there. Wouldn't you like to see it?"

Gabriela bit her lip, brushing her hair behind her ear. "I suddenly have a father, and I think my mother might respect me now. I think I'll explore that for a while."

"Quite fair. And you have..." He paused, gesturing around the endless field. "Whatever it is that you have going on here? The offer stands, should you change your mind."

"Thank you. I promise to visit." She pushed him toward the trap door but stopped before he was too close to the steps. "Goodbye, Brynmor."

He slid his hand into hers, raising it to kiss her knuckles. She shoved his hand aside and stood up on her toes to kiss his cheek. Brynmor smiled, touching the spot before leaving the meadow.

Mourningsword stood jerkily with Venica's help. "The fall severely damaged his spine," she said. "I partially animated his armor, but the magic requires reinforcement after the solstice."

"I will help." Ravell moved close but paused and crossed to the duke's body. She kneeled and put a hand on his armor's chest plate. A second later, the duke pushed to his feet, head rolling uselessly with the movement.

"Bah, glamor armor," said Lord Sebastian, now in the duke. "It's nowhere near your quality, Val, but it'll do in a pinch. Please go on. I'll help with Oswin."

He called after her as Ravell reached the door. "If you come across any shovels, set one aside for me, please. For reasons."

265

Commander Ravell flashed him a grin, then focused her gaze on Eleanor. "I was furious when the duke assigned me to work with you. Now, I'm amazed by how ashamed I feel of that. There is so much I could learn from you." With long strides, she crossed to Eleanor, slipped a hand behind her neck, and kissed her firmly on the lips. "Thank you."

Ravell turned just as quickly and was gone down the steps.

Eleanor brushed a finger across her lips. "What was..."

"Everyone's getting kisses, it seems!" Lord Sebastian stomped on another door with a clang and flipped it open. "This place is just full of ways out if you're looking for them. Don't be too long, Princess. Wonderful work with everything. I'm crafting all my praise to bestow upon you, but it's a lot and will take me a moment." He took Mourningsword's weight from Venica and moved them to the second door.

"He is right," said Venica, crossing to squeeze Gabriela's arm. "I am so proud of you, my tiny. You have succeeded in so many ways, where I have failed. Both your father and I had succumbed to the madness that comes with the power of Eldrisil. I feel you will fare better. Meet me at the top when you are ready." She leaned to leave a cold kiss on Gabriela's forehead, then was gone.

Only Eleanor Lane remained.

"What now?" she asked.

Gabriela shrugged. "I don't know. I guess go back to Soulhaven. Maybe stop by Crystalwood Gardens to put Lord Sebastian's hand back." She glanced down, noticing the scroll Eleanor had given her earlier for her mother. She picked it up, unrolled it, and read it out loud in a mumbled breath. The legal terms confused her, but she understood enough that it was a contract between the devilkin and Bishop Lightbringer involving her mother, signed by Executor Smithies, and a few others too stylized to be legible.

"This binds your mother to the tower," said Eleanor over her shoulder. "It says she and the bishop killed the guardian present when they arrived. This contract instates your mother as the new guardian in exchange for the bishop's... cognispiritual essence."

"His what?"

"Guessing that's his soul. I wonder how a contract can be binding against your mother without her knowledge or consent."

"He traded his soul to bind my mother here?"

"The bishop must have been really upset with her."

"And why was this just delivered?"

"There's a clause." Eleanor reached out to take the contract from Gabriela. Her eyes ran quickly across it. "Your mother's free if she gets someone to take her place. Maybe she was never consciously aware of this contract but transferred ownership to Mourningsword twenty years ago. Now, it sounds like she wants you to take over."

"I don't think I want to do that. Is that what she wants to discuss up top?"

Eleanor shrugged. "You'll have to ask her. Well..." She picked at her notebook's cover. "With the duke dead, I'm probably out of a job. Brynmor seems changed, but I don't want to work for him if I don't have to. I don't suppose I could join you for a while? Aside from what I could learn about magic, I'd love to meet your friends. Misses Popkins, was it?"

"Popkin, just one," Gabriela corrected her. "Oh, now I'm worrying if she and the others made it back to somewhere safe in time for the solstice. I'd love your company, Eleanor. I got a little used to Brynmor talking back at me with more than just Lord Sebastian's jokes and..."

She wasn't ready to grieve for her sister. Not yet.

"Let's go," Gabriela took Eleanor by the arm. "I'll tell you about the phantasmalos I met last year."

AFTERWORD

G abriela really surprised me. As I said in the introduction, I planned this novel. I knew what would happen in every scene, but she just kept taking over. Something would get her oddball mind working and she'd come up with a great idea, but rarely would let me know what it was in advance. The scene with Brynmor feeding lines to Lord Sebastian in the cemetery? That was fun! I totally didn't have that in my notes. Literally, I typed her saying, "That gives me an idea!" and I had to go take a long walk to think about what that idea was.

I say this is my second stand-alone novel, but it's not really stand-alone. If you'll allow me a brief moment of self-indulgence, the tower Eldrisil was clearly the world tree of this realm, implying this world is in the great chain of Trees. So where was its guardian Mraasil? Is that who Venica and the bishop killed when they came to resurrect Malphas? Eleanor's puzzle box really should have been lost when Aura scared off the horses, yet there it was in her bag. Just like Ranmi the Blackwish lost his bag of mana crystals when the bridge collapsed with the daughter of the Exalted's death, then he found them on his person. As a self-published author, I can and do create easter eggs that are just for me. Whenever an object is lost, and then suddenly reappears, it's the Chronicler's doing. Alishia just steps in to move things around to keep the story going. These are not plot holes, they're by design. It's nice that she's looking out for me.

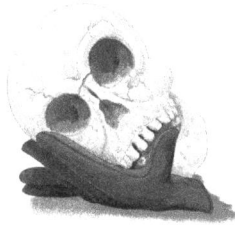

ABOUT THE AUTHOR

Author Jamie M. Samland is a mathematician by training, a web developer by profession, and a martial artist and writer by passion. Math nerd, cat dad, gamer. He always loved to write, but what started in force during the 2020 lockdown has become a driving passion. Jamie lives in Michigan with his husband and their furbabies.

As an indie author, he relies on reviews and word of mouth, so please consider leaving a review on GoodReads and at your point of purchase. Find him on the socials or at jmsamland.com.

ALSO BY

Books by Jamie M. Samland:

Realms of Terswood (2020)
Trials of Throk'tar (2021)
Necromancer of Urbus (2022)
Seeds of Farsil (2022)
Ooo Shiny! Volume 1 (2022)
Arcanym (2023)
The Invisible Castle (2023)
Ooo Shiny! Volume 2, Holiday Edition 1 (2023)
Grave Mistakes: A Necromantic Adventure (2023)

Milton Keynes UK
Ingram Content Group UK Ltd.
UKHW041005271123
433339UK00001B/27